NIGHT OF THE VAMPIRE

DEATHLESS NIGHT-INTO THE DARK #1

L. E. WILSON

ALSO BY L.E. WILSON

Deathless Night Series (The Vampires)

A Vampire Bewitched

A Vampire's Vengeance

A Vampire Possessed

A Vampire Betrayed

A Vampire's Submission

A Vampire's Choice

Deathless Night-Into the Dark Series (The Vampires)

Night of the Vampire

Secret of the Vampire

Forsworn by the Vampire

The Kincaid Werewolves (The Werewolves)

Lone Wolf's Claim

A Wolf's Honor

The Alpha's Redemption

A Wolf's Promise

A Wolf's Treasure

The Alpha's Surrender

Southern Dragons (Dragon Shifters & Vampires)

Dance for the Dragon

Burn for the Dragon

Snow Ridge Shifters (Novellas)

A Second Chance on Snow Ridge

A Fake Fiancé on Snow Ridge

Copyright © 2020 by Everblood Publishing, LLC

All rights reserved. No part of this publication may be reproduced, distributed, or transmitted in any form or by any means, including photocopying, recording, or other electronic or mechanical methods, without the prior written permission of the publisher, except in the case of brief quotations embodied in critical reviews and certain other noncommercial uses permitted by copyright law. For permission requests, email the publisher, addressed "Attention: Permissions Coordinator," at the address below.

All characters and events in this book are fictitious. Any resemblance to actual persons – living or dead – is purely coincidental.

le@lewilsonauthor.com

ISBN:978-1-945499-31-9

Print Edition

Publication Date: October 15, 2020

Developmental Editor: Sara Lunsford @ Book Frosting

Copy Editor: Jinxie Gervasio @ jinxiesworld.com

Cover Design by Coffee and Characters

NOTE FROM THE AUTHOR

If you are new to my books, there are a few things you need to know about this series to avoid any confusion.

The "Deathless Night-Into the Dark" series is an *extension* of the original "Deathless Night" series, picking up the storyline of The Moss Witches that was started in the original series. And, the characters from Deathless Night will be making appearances throughout this series, starting in book 2, Secret of the Vampire.

I'm thrilled to be with these characters again, and I hope you are, too!

Happy reading, and I hope you enjoy Killian and Lizzy's story!

1

KILLIAN

"They'll kill you, Killian. You know that, right?"

My eyes burned. No matter how much I blinked, I couldn't get rid of the grit within them. "They can't kill me. I'm immortal."

Kenya sighed, her chest rising and falling in jerks. Breathing had been a struggle for her the last few nights. I could hear the strain of it on her lungs. Just like I could hear her heart weakening with every laborious beat. It was unusual to see a supernatural creature struggling to survive. Unusual and...terrifying.

A vampire was one of two things at all times. Alive or dead. Never anything in between.

But Kenya's warm, brown skin was ashen from lack of blood because she couldn't hold anything down. Her black hair was plastered to her head instead of sticking out in a riot of curls around her pretty face. It was unnatural for an immortal to look this way. We'd tried everything to get her to feed—animals, reptiles, even some bagged stuff stolen from the hospital.

Well, everything except dragging an unwilling human off of Bourbon Street to supply her with blood. But that was against the rules of the ones who'd done this to her. And it was quite apparent we'd already angered them enough.

"Are you willing to bet your life on that? Or the life of this coven?"

I crossed my arms over my chest in a vain attempt to hold in my own pain as I searched her weary face for the tiniest sign of improvement. "No," I told her honestly. "I'm not. But I don't know what else to do." I felt helpless, and it didn't sit well with me. "This is my fault, Kenya. I have to fix it."

She held out her hand to me, her arm shaking with the effort. Quickly, I clasped it within my own and let her draw me to the bed. "It's not your fault."

I knew well from experience that arguing with her wouldn't help anything, so I didn't bother.

But she wasn't fooled by my silence. "Tell me a story." Her pale lips curved into a smile, trying to distract me.

"A story, you say?"

"Yeah. A bedtime story."

"It's barely past midnight."

She raised one eyebrow. "And? I'm tired." Giving my hand a tug, she tried to pull me down to the bed.

Giving up, I sat beside her on the sweat-soaked sheets. The smell wasn't pleasant, but I resisted the urge to wrinkle my nose. Or to breathe, for that matter. For it was no fault of her own. "What would you like to hear, then?"

"I don't care. I just like to hear you talk. You have such a musical accent."

"It's an Irish accent."

She rolled her eyes. "Yes, I know. I love your accent. Or what's left of it. I don't know why you hate it so much."

"I don't hate it." My heart clenched tight as a fist, making me catch my breath. I tried to rub away the ache with my free hand, to no use. "Kenya..." My voice broke, the rest of what I'd been about to say caught in my throat.

"Stop it, Killian. Just stop it. You couldn't have done anything to keep this from happening."

"You're wrong." This I knew down to my very bones. "If I'd only been with you, instead of running off as I did..."

"If you'd been there, it would be you lying here in your own filth instead of me." She leveled her most severe stare at me, and I hitched in a breath, knowing she was right. Our enhanced abilities were nothing when faced with the magic of the witches. "And how would that help our coven?"

I looked around the room, unable to meet her eyes. The hideout Elias had found for us was hidden in the swampland of Lake Pontchartrain just outside of New Orleans. It was suitable, but nowhere near the luxury we were all used to in the Quarter. However, I'd thought it best to bring Kenya out here as she was in no condition to defend herself or even to run if they came after her again.

"Perhaps with me gone they could manage to get themselves out of this bloody swamp and back to our rightful home in the Quarter."

"You know that isn't true. Besides, this is only temporary until we know we won't be beheaded in our sleep. We're already putting ourselves within easy reach just keeping the club going."

"We need to feed. Without the club we'd have to hunt, and with that comes the risk of being hunted ourselves."

"Or we could learn to like gators."

"Not going to happen. Their skin is too tough and their blood is cold." I'd meant it as a joke, but the humor was lost on us both as the reality of my coven lowering ourselves to feeding on reptiles became very real. My head hurt. Gently, I pulled my hand from hers so I could rub my temples. "I need to do something besides hide out in this house."

"Marching into a group of witches demanding they lift this death spell isn't it. We don't even know if they could do anything. Or if they would if they could."

"Why wouldn't they? It was one of their own who cast it."

"Exactly."

I got up to pace the floor, needing to work off all of this pent-up frustration. I felt Kenya's eyes on me as I wore a trail in the wood, but I couldn't look at her. "I don't understand why they came after *you,* Kenya. You, the nicest one of all of us." I gave a derisive laugh. "I thought the high priestess *liked* you, for Christ's sake."

"Killian, if you go to the witches and they don't throw you out into the sun, and you bring one here...they'll know where we are. They could kill me anyway. Take out the entire coven. Kill you."

"They wouldn't do that. We have a pact."

"The pact they already broke?" She started coughing and grabbed a tissue from the table beside the bed. When she pulled it away from her mouth, it was red with blood. "Killian, we would be completely at their mercy."

I tried to meet her eyes, but she wouldn't look at me. "We have a pact," I repeated. "It can't be broken without bloodshed on both sides."

"The 'pact' didn't protect me from this." Kenya pointed at herself.

"This must've been a mistake, Kenya. I just can't fathom it otherwise."

"I wish that were true."

"If I don't try, you will die." My words were cold, giving nothing away. But my chest already ached with loss at the thought of losing her. I couldn't...I would have nothing if I lost her. I would be completely alone. Punishment for my selfish actions, I suppose. But not one I chose to accept. "I can't lose you, Kenya."

She waved one hand in the air, dismissing my words. "You'll be fine. You have Jamal, and Elias...."

"Jamal hates me."

She continued as if I hadn't spoken. "Dae can do the books at the club for you."

"That's not what I'm talking about," I growled.

Her face softened. "I know."

I rubbed the throbbing pain in my thigh. The scar was ancient, the pain all in my head. Just an old injury from my days as a young vampire, but I still felt the invasion of the sword's steel blade slice through my thigh. How odd it had felt, my leg split into separate pieces, much like the icy burn of my heart being torn apart in my chest at this moment.

I'd won that fight despite my injury. I didn't know that I could say the same for this one. Going to the witches was a risk. Kenya was right when she said it was very likely my going to the witches would put our coven in more danger. But if I didn't, I would lose her. My only true friend.

Was that selfish of me?

Aye, it was. But my self-serving nature was the reason she was in this predicament to begin with. It was up to me to fix it.

"Jamal told me he'd heard rumors of a new witch in town. I'll go find her. From what I was told, she just moved down from

New York City a week or two ago." I couldn't help but feel hope. "What are the chances, do you think, she hasn't been jaded by the others yet and won't cast me down on sight?"

Kenya was quiet for so long I stopped pacing and turned to see she was still with me. I found her running her fingers along the edge of the sheet that covered her to the waist. She raised eyes glazed with exhaustion to mine. "What do you know about her?" she finally asked.

"Not much," I admitted. "As I said, she just moved here. And Jamal's source said he'd seen her go over to the High Priestess's home." I thought back to our conversation. "She has a dog."

"And that's an important fact?"

I narrowed my eyes at her, but it did nothing to quell the smirk on her face. "Yes, it is. A dog makes noise."

The smile faded from her face as she caught my meaning. "Killian, what are you planning to do?"

I stared down at her, this female who—other than Jamal—had been the closest thing I'd ever had to a friend in all of my nearly two hundred years. At least Jamal had been, before I'd made him what he was now. So that left me with one. "Whatever I have to."

2

LIZZY

ALL HALLOWS EVE, NEW ORLEANS

"Are you sure, Lizzy?"

I nodded at Mike. "Really, it's okay. Go on home. I'll close up."

"Cool, thanks." He was already grabbing his coat from under the counter.

That was just one of the things I liked about having him for an assistant. He didn't insist on asking more than the necessary amount of questions, he didn't talk my ear off, and he seemed to sense when I just needed a minute.

"Make sure and lock up behind me," he told me as he headed toward the door.

"I will." With a wave, I sent him on his way, eying the dark sky before I pulled the door shut behind him and locked up. There wasn't a star to be seen.

Great.

It was going to rain.

"Perfect." I heard the first drops patter the windows as I made my way back to the counter and prayed the old roof would hang in there until spring. God, I hated hurricane season, which, from what I remembered and what my local customers kept telling me, should have been over by now.

Personally though, I thought Mother Earth had just had enough, and was now trying to get rid of her human parasites.

And, honestly, I can't say that I blamed her.

Rolling my head on my shoulders, I took a deep breath and let the pressures of the day fade away. It had been a busy week. As I walked around straightening the shelves and displays, I wondered if it was always this crazy leading up to Halloween, or if this was just an especially good season. Of course, I did own a business called Ancient Magicks, which was located right smack in the middle of the French Quarter in New Orleans. So, I suppose it was to be expected. Tourists came here for two reasons: to learn about the history of the city during the day—hitting the ghost and cemetery tours—and afterwards, once they had one—or five—Hurricanes diluting their blood stream and their common sense, they liked to dip their toes into the world of voodoo the city was infamous for.

I tilted my head at the human skull replica I'd just set upright on the shelf beside the basket of gris-gris bags. "Spooky, right?" I asked him.

As usual, he didn't respond.

With a shrug, I continued on, dusting the shelves and making sure everything was ready to open tomorrow, reminding my aching back that having an "authentic" voodoo shop in the middle of this madness just made good sense. I myself, however, knew absolutely nothing about voodoo or witchcraft. But what I did know was business, thanks to having the good sense to get a degree in the subject. Just in case my dream life burned down around me.

Which is exactly what had happened two years ago. And four weeks ago, I'd fled my home in New York City with little more than what I could fit in the rental car and my old dog, Sir Wigglebutt.

Or Wiggles, for short.

Finding nineteen-year-old Mike, with his dark and gloomy— yet highly attractive in a weird sort of way—rock star goth look had just been pure luck for me. Tourists wandered into my shop out of curiosity, and a good number of them returned to show off their collection of plastic beads to my assistant, hoping he'd want to see the goods that had earned them those beads. However, for reasons unbeknownst to me, Mike never took anyone up on their offer. At least, not as far as I knew. And I wasn't about to pry into his personal life to ask.

Pretty sure he was grateful for that.

And that reminded me...I had a bag of gaudy beads in the back I wanted to add to the display of oils and incense in the front window. It needed some color.

I was in the back giving Wiggles some love, who'd just woken up from his fifth nap today, when I heard the bell above the door. For a moment, I froze. I was pretty damn certain I'd locked the door. No, I *specifically* remembered locking it after Mike left, and he was the only other person with a key. Maybe he'd forgotten something?

Giving my sweet pup one last scratch on his old head, I assured him we'd be heading home soon. Something I did every night even though he couldn't hear a word I said anymore. Then I grabbed the bag of beads off the shelf and headed back to the front to see what Mike needed.

As I started lifting the curtain that separated the back room from the front of the store, I heard a low growl behind me and glanced back at Wiggles with a frown. He never growled at Mike. He loved Mike. Although his eyesight was going, too, so there was no telling what that had been about. Ducking through the curtain, I called out, "Mike? Hurry up and get out of here. Gotta close up before the dead start rising—"

Grinning at my own joke, I looked up...and stopped dead in my tracks. Whatever else I'd been about to say dying a swift death on my tongue.

A man stood just inside the door, looking around my store with an amused expression on his face. At first glance, he wasn't anything special to look at. About five foot eleven if the ruler on the door frame was correct, of average build, with pale skin, short, sandy brown hair and a classically handsome face that hadn't seen a razor in a day or so. As I ran my eyes over his suspiciously dry clothes, I noticed he had what I would consider a bit of a European look to him. His dark jeans were fitted to his lean, muscular legs, and he wore a hip-length black sweater with a big collar open over a nondescript, dark green shirt. All he needed was a pair of glasses with thick frames to complete the look he seemed to be going for.

However, despite his nerdy-boy attire, the man standing in my shop was most definitely not a boy. And the look in his black eyes, once they made their way back up to my face, was not in the least bit nerdy.

More like predatory.

My lungs began to ache from lack of air, and I sucked in a quick breath through my nose.

Oh, my God. What was that?

The best cologne I'd ever smelled invaded my sinuses, overriding even the spiciness of the incense, and for a brief moment I closed my eyes as desire wound its way through my body, the sudden ache in my womb sharp and heavy.

A discreet cough brought me crashing back to where I was. Heat crept up my chest to fan out across my neck and face as I remembered myself, and I was self-consciously aware I must look as red as the curtain behind me.

The man smiled a secret smile, as though he knew exactly what was going on inside my body. Could see the carnal images running through my head.

Setting the bag on the counter, I pulled myself together and forced a professional tone to my voice. I think I may have even succeeded once I was finally able to get past the first few words. "I'm sorry, but the shop is closed for the night. However, we open tomorrow at ten." I smiled as nonchalantly as I could manage. "I hope you'll be able make it back then."

Really, I secretly hoped he was just one of the many tourists and would be heading back out of town tomorrow. There was something about this guy that was making me distinctly uncomfortable. Potential customer or not.

Then he spoke for the first time, the musical cadence of his voice sliding over me like the soft notes of some cool Jazz. "Are you the owner of this..." He glanced around. "Shop? Did you call it?"

There was a slight lilt to his speech. Irish, maybe? His "are" sounded more like "a-our". "Did you" more like "didja." Yet he spoke so low, his deep voice so soothing, almost like a purr—or maybe a growl—that it was hard to catch if you weren't paying attention.

"Yes. Is there something I can help you with?" Maybe he wasn't a normal customer. Maybe he was here to try to sell me something, and that's why I was getting such a weird vibe. That, and the fact that he'd somehow gotten in through a locked door.

Reading my mind again, he smiled and gestured toward the door. "Forgive me for coming in after hours. The door was unlocked."

I flicked my eyes over to the door and then back to him. *Like hell it was.*

He cocked his head to the side. "Are you a new here? I haven't seen you around before."

"New Orleans is a crowded city."

"That it is, but mostly full of tourists. Us locals usually stick together."

Did they? "I'm the new owner. My name is Lizzy Smith. How can I help you?" I repeated.

"Smith?" He appeared put off by my name.

I dropped all pretenses of being pleasant and frowned instead. "Yes. Smith. It was the best I could do on short notice." I didn't know what made that bit of truth come out. "Is there something I can help you with?" I repeated.

The lines of concern on his forehead disappeared as he strolled a few steps further inside the store, and closer to me. "Actually, I was looking for someone, but that's not the correct name. Is there a better one you can think of, by chance?"

He was smirking at me. The bastard.

As casually as I could, I stepped back until I was standing at the end of the counter, nearer the pepper spray I always kept within easy reach, because I couldn't afford the gun I wanted yet. "And you are?"

Gone.

I'd blinked, and he was suddenly standing directly in front of me, one hand wrapped around my upper arm. He'd moved so fast, it had taken my brain a few seconds to catch up with what my eyes had just seen. Or not seen, as it were. My heart thumped hard, once, and then it began to race, making me lightheaded. He stood so close, his make-me-want-to-rip-off-my-panties scent teasing my nose, it took another moment for me to be able to form a coherent thought. Unlike a normal cologne, whatever he was wearing didn't get stronger with his near proximity, but mellowed to a mere tease of the scent. It drew me in to him without my realizing it, and I had the sudden urge to bury my face in his chest.

Gradually, I realized my hands were pressed flat against said chest. But whether to push him away or draw him closer, I couldn't have said.

"Lizzy."

Drawn by the soothing allure of his voice, I lifted my chin until my eyes met his. Like his scent, his average good looks became devastating up close and personal. Beneath my hands, his chest was warm. So very, very warm. My head swam and my heart continued its erratic beat as I drowned in the dark pools of his eyes.

My entire body ached to be closer to him.

The material of my jeans was all at once rough and irritating against my thighs as my blood raced to the surface, sensitizing my skin. My soft shirt prickly as hell. I had the sudden urge to offer myself to him. Anything he needed. Anything he wanted. If he would just get me out of these irritating clothes.

Black eyes bored into mine, and I'd swear they could see every dirty stain on my soul.

"I need your help."

I struggled against the urge to obey his every wish. "But you just said I had the wrong name." Though I felt my lips and tongue form the words, they came to my own ears as though through a vast void.

"The name doesn't matter. You're the person I'm looking for. You have to be. Because I don't have any other options."

Warning bells clanged loudly in my head, but I couldn't piece anything together enough so that it made sense. "What's your name?" I asked him through a fog.

He touched my cheek with the fingertips of his free hand, his dark eyes roaming across my features as they followed the trail they made. "My name is Killian. And you are not what I expected."

3

KILLIAN

It was the right one. It had to be.

This slight woman had to be the one Jamal had told me about. I could feel the magic within her, hot and dangerous, pulsing to the notes of the slow, sexy, jazz horn playing on the ancient radio in the corner.

My first instinct was to grab her and take her back to the swamp. Drain her nearly dry if I had to until she lifted the spell from Kenya. The impulse was hard to ignore, and not just because of my concern for my friend...

From the moment I'd walked through the door, this woman's scent had knocked me over, overpowering the lingering stink of incense and the alcohol/body odor mix of unwashed customers. She filled my lungs with every breath, my body absorbing her along with the oxygen until my throat burned with thirst and my blood raced through my veins, filling me with need. With hunger. The urge to drink without restraint hadn't been this strong since I was a vampire newly born, and I very nearly pounced on her without thought.

But something stopped me. Perhaps it was the worldly innocence I perceived in her brown eyes. Perhaps it was the way she was staring at me. Not like a vampire, an enemy, as a witch would. But as a man she desired.

Something else that had rarely happened to me since I was reborn. Especially not by one of her kind.

Her eyes blinked rapidly a few times and then she frowned and purposefully pulled her arm from my grasp. I expected her to lunge for the pepper spray she had hidden behind the counter, but instead, she took two steps away from the counter...and away from me. It broke the spell between us and allowed me to breathe again without being overpowered by my animalistic urges. I relaxed slightly, but I kept a wary eye on her. Her little can of defense wouldn't stop me, but the bloody stuff was irritating.

"I'm sorry," she said again in a breathy voice. "But I don't think I can help you."

"How do you know?" I asked.

"I'm sorry," she shook her head, "what?"

"How do you know you can't help me? I haven't told you why I need you." Having met her, and sensing the power of her magic, I didn't know if I should actually tell her the truth or not. If I were the slightest bit intelligent, I would listen to

Kenya and choose my coven over one lost life. It's what a leader would do. They looked to me for guidance. For protection. Saving Kenya would alleviate my own grief and loneliness, but cause more issues for all of us in the end. I should just make up some foolish excuse and leave this witch to her life.

And yet, I couldn't make myself go. "Look, I need you to come with me."

"I'm sorry, but I don't make a habit of running off with strange men."

I took a step back, giving her a little more space, and saw her shoulders relax slightly. Strange, how bringing her any level of comfort brought me a feeling of pleasure. Maybe I needed to broach the subject from a different direction. "As I said, my name is Killian. Killian Rice. And you're new to New Orleans, am I right?"

She hesitated a moment before answering me. "Yeah. Yes," she corrected. "I just moved down here a few weeks ago."

So longer than we had originally thought. I wondered if the witch coven had had time to indoctrinate her. I could sense nothing about it from her thoughts. Mostly, she was just worried I was either going to accost her or try to sell her something. But she had to be one of them. Witches were notoriously territorial. Almost as much as vampires. "Where did you move here from?"

Those intriguing little creases appeared between her brows again, and for a moment I thought she wasn't going to answer me. "New York City," she said, the frown still in place.

I barely resisted the urge to reach out and smooth the lines away. I didn't like to see her distressed, and that bothered me. "What did you do there, if you don't mind me asking?"

A shadow darkened her eyes, and like the predator I am at my core, I honed in on this weakness. "I'm an actor...*was* an actor," she emphasized. "On Broadway."

My surprise made me lose my train of thought, but just for a moment. "Broadway. That's quite the accomplishment." She didn't seem the type. Soft and pretty with brown eyes and long, thick dark hair that curled a bit on the ends, she easily could have just walked off the page of a Jane Austen novel.

"Actually, I hadn't quite made it there, yet. But I was...aspiring." She paused. Glanced up at me. "I did secure a main role for one show, finally, but never made it to the stage."

There. Right there. This was the cause of the shadow I'd seen. "What happened?"

Another pause, and then she narrowed her eyes, her scattered thoughts coming together as she gave herself an internal shake. To my utter disappointment, the shadows dissipated. "You're asking a lot of personal questions."

She was right. I was. I wanted to know, *needed* to know, more about this woman. And I wanted her to tell me freely, not steal it from her mind. But I was coming on too strong. I knew this. I was going to frighten her away.

"I'm just asking for a few moments of your time. We can go somewhere else if you'd like, and you can get to know me in a more"—I looked around the store—"public setting where you'll feel safe."

"Why are you being so insistent?"

I didn't hesitate with my answer, such as it was. "I couldn't really tell you." That was the truth. My response was as much a surprise to me as it had to be to her.

Something shuffled around behind her, drawing my eyes to the bohemian curtain that hid the back of the store from view. I heard the soft, padded steps of paws and glanced around the end of the counter. Shite! She had her dog here at the store with her. If I hadn't been so fucking distracted with the woman I would have noticed.

Well, there was not a thing I could do about it now but wait it out and see what happened.

A black nose poked out from behind the curtain, giving the air a sniff. It was attached to a little black head with pointy ears and a white muzzle, followed by a little chunky black body.

The curtain flapped down behind it as the dog waddled out on stiff hind legs. I saw right away he was no threat. This pup had to be in his last year of life, and yet when it reached its owner it stared up at me through opaque brown eyes and let out a fierce, protective growl.

Sadness filled me as I stared down at her protector. More than anything else in my life, this reaction from animals was the thing that hurt me the most. I missed their companionship. At times they were the only company I had.

But now, like every other warm-blooded creature—or cold-blooded for that matter—in this world, they were nothing but food to me.

"I think you need to go," Lizzy told me. "You're upsetting my dog."

She was right. I needed to leave before I made an ass of myself. I gave her a tight smile, turned, and left the store. But I didn't go far. Ducking into a courtyard about 20 feet away, I waited for her to finish closing up, grateful the rain had stopped as it would bring more revelers out I could blend with.

A few minutes later she came out, locking the door behind her and double-checking it. Her ferocious beast was now leashed, padding along contently beside her. With a look up and down the darkened street, I watched her study a group of four young men who had stumbled a little too close, obviously enjoying their stay in the city for the holiday. Deciding they posed no threat, she turned and walked away, heading toward Canal Street.

Discreetly, I followed behind her. I told myself it was only to find out where she lived for myself. But if I were to be honest, it was more than that.

Much like the dog, I didn't want any harm to come to her.

Disgust filled me, though it wasn't aimed at her, but at myself. What was I doing? Following her like a love-sick schoolboy. Why not just take her? Force her back to the house to help Kenya. If I did it quickly, I could take advantage of her surprise and restrain her before she could start muttering her witch's curses. Her little, old dog would not stop me.

And yet, as I watched the pair of them strolling along, I couldn't bring myself to separate Lizzy from him. Not when he was looking up at her with such an adoring gaze in his cloudy brown eyes. She moved down the street at a slow pace to allow for his stiff back legs, her full hips swaying seductively as she strolled along, smiling at someone here and there, and avoiding others who'd gotten a little too rowdy. Every once in a while she'd stop and let him piss on something, and then they would continue on their way.

When they reached her apartment near the House of Blues on Decatur Street, I stayed in the shadows and watched them go inside. For a long time, I stood out there on the corner listening to the music and gazing up at the windows. I knew which apartment was hers when I saw the lights come on. Soon after, I smelled the spices she cooked in her dinner and heard the sounds of the TV show she watched as she ate. I could even hear her old dog crunching on his own meal, and then later, snoring alongside of her while she watch TV. But I deliberately stayed out of her mind. I couldn't let her emotions sway my decision.

However, it was quite hard. Did she think about me, I wondered? Or had she already put me out of her head?

Eventually, sometime around eleven, the lights went off. And still, I stayed. Watching through her windows like a peeping Tom, and wondering what I was becoming. I was a predator, aye. But unless I planned to make this woman *my* dinner, there was no reason for me to be lurking about.

It wasn't blood I wanted from her at this point in time, though. Nor was it magic. Tearing my eyes away from her windows, I sighed. At least it showed I still had some humanity left.

The scents of my home—seafood, alcohol, smoke, piss, and vomit, all layered over the heavy smell of the primordial swamp the city was built on—seeped through the cracks in the pavement. Pulling my sweater tighter around me, I crossed my arms over my chest, my mind racing. I needed this witch to help me, yet I could not bring myself to forcefully make her do it, for reasons I couldn't quite pin down and did not want to explore too closely. Not yet, at least.

Eventually, I wandered off and went home to check on Kenya. Her condition hadn't improved in the few hours I had been gone, but it hadn't worsened, either. Peeking in through the cracked door, I saw her eyes were closed, and I was loathe to disturb her. What would she think of me, showing up empty-handed?

As if she sensed my guilt, her eyes cracked open. "Did you find your witch?"

I walked closer to the bed. "I believe I did."

She stared up at the ceiling for a moment, then scooted back on the mattress. I helped her as she propped herself up on her pillows. Looking around me pointedly, she asked, "And where is she? Did you leave her in the swamp for the alligators?"

I shook my head.

Both eyebrows joined her forehead as she waited for me to say more, but I didn't know what else to tell her. "Is she going to help?" she finally asked in a quiet voice. "Or not?"

"I told her I had a friend who needed her help and she refused. She said she didn't make a habit of running off with strangers."

"Smart girl," Kenya said with a tight smile. "At least she didn't smite you where you stood."

A small laugh escaped me. "No. She didn't seem to know what I was. Not unless she's somehow figured out how to hide certain thoughts from vampires." An impossible feat as far as I knew, or the witches would have done it by now.

"Killian, you shouldn't invade people's private thoughts."

"But how else was I to know if she was about to 'smite' me?"

"Touché," she said. "But. How did she not know? She's a witch, right?"

"Yes, she's most definitely a witch. I could sense it inside of her the moment I walked into her store. She has great power." Carefully, so as not to cause her any undue pain, I sat on the side of the bed. "I'm just not sure what kind."

"And you didn't just make her come with you so you could force her to fix me?"

I searched Kenya's face, looking for answers she couldn't provide. Finally, I shook my head. "No," I finally said simply.

"Good," she said. "I'm glad of that, at least. It wasn't so long ago that I was a human woman, you know. I remember how it feels. How vulnerable I was."

"She's not human. She's a witch."

"Mmm-hmm. Still human." A shiver ran through her, shaking the bed. I tugged the blankets up around her shoulders. "What are you going to do now?" she asked.

"I'll go see her again," I said. "Tomorrow, I think. I caught nothing about her family in her thoughts or words. She might be the way to save you without bringing hell down on the coven. I can ask her again, and this time I'll stay until she agrees."

"Well, you'd better hurry, before the other witches decide to bring her into the fold." I could almost feel the fever in her eyes as they studied my face. "What?" she asked. "What aren't you telling me?"

I stared down at my hands. "She said her name was 'Smith'."

"Smith?" she asked. "Not Moss?"

"No, Smith."

Kenya struggled to sit up more and I grabbed another pillow and stuck it behind her. Heat radiated from her skin. But it was better than the icy hold of death.

"That makes no sense," she said once she'd caught her breath. "The Moss witches are the only coven in the area. The only one in this country, as far as I know. If she's from a different coven, it would be too dangerous for her to live here. Witches don't like outsiders. Not even another of their kind."

"That's what I thought, too. That she had to be one of them. But if she doesn't know what she is, she wouldn't know of the danger she is in." That fact struck me harder than it should have. I didn't like the idea of this woman in danger. From me or anyone else. "I have reason to think perhaps she just changed her name."

"But," Kenya said with a thoughtful expression, "If she's not one of the Moss witches, perhaps the odds are better that we can convince her to try to lift this spell for me."

I looked at my friend and gave her a smile. "That's exactly what I'm hoping."

A shadow of hope softened her features, but it was fleeting. "Why do I get the feeling you're not as gung ho about this idea as you were earlier? If she isn't one of them, and she doesn't know about us, then there's no danger to the coven. Right?"

"Right." I tried to give her a smile.

"Killian..."

I scrubbed the top of my head, trying to rid myself of my conscience. "It's just...she's innocent in all of this is all," I told her. "And I find myself hesitating to drag her into it."

Kenya laid her hand on mind. "I don't like it, either. But what's our other option?"

A picture of Lizzy flashed through my mind, her hand inching toward the pepper spray to protect herself from me. My body hardened with the challenge, the memory of her sweet scent still as strong as if she were standing right in front of me. "There isn't one."

4

LIZZY

I waited all the next day for the man to come back. Every time the bell above the door chimed, I would jump near out of my skin, my eyes darting to the front of the store to see if it was him. By the end of the day, the muscles in my neck and shoulders hurt from all the tension I'd been holding in all day.

Rolling my head on my shoulders, I waited for the water to heat and strain the coffee through the little cup and into my mug. I'd lugged the machine here from my apartment. My only other option was to walk three blocks every time I needed a refill, which had pretty much been every hour on the hour today. I'd barely slept last night. And when I finally did drift off around two in the morning, I'd dreamed the strangest dreams, all filled with a twisted medley of nude bodies covered in blood, writhing against the music of New Orleans.

I'd woken up feeling extremely uncomfortable, the erotic images resonating in my mind while I showered and threw on some black jeans and a white sweater with fuzzy cuffs. I'd hoped the dream would fade as the day went on, but although the images faded, the feelings they created had only intensified, leaving me restless and yearning. But by the end of the day, I'd managed to fill my head with enough distractions that, eventually, it fizzled to a mild ache. However, it never completely left me.

I was never so grateful to my old dog for scaring that man—Killian Rice—away yesterday. Not that Wiggles would be able to catch him if he'd ran. But my pup's heart was in the right place. And apparently the guy wasn't comfortable around dogs.

So, today, I'd pulled his dog bed out of the storeroom and set Wiggles up right behind the counter, where he'd be sure to see anyone who entered the store. Funny enough, he didn't so much as grumble at one person all day.

"You okay? You look tired." Mike, as always, got straight to the point.

He was wearing black eyeliner today, and his hair was different. Instead of black with purple undertones, it was blond on one side and red on the other. It looked good on him, and I'd told him so when he'd walked in that morning.

I gave him a smile. "I'm fine. But you're right. I didn't sleep very well. I kept having these weird dreams." I shrugged. No need to mention how I had a hard time getting settled enough to sleep in the first place because I couldn't stop thinking about a guy who made me equal parts horny and nervous. I felt like I was thirteen again.

"There's a spell for that, you know." He leaned back against the counter and put his leather clad elbows up on the counter.

I laughed. "You don't really believe in this stuff, do you?" I asked him, waving one hand at the mishmash of trinkets and candles closest to me.

He didn't laugh along with me. "I do. And you should, too, Lizzy. Especially if you're going to be running a store. Voodoo"—he nodded at the shelves closest to us, stuffed full of books on one side and voodoo dolls on the other—"it's nothing to mess around with. And neither is magic."

"Is there a difference?"

"Hell yeah. Absolutely."

"But don't you have to have some sort of inner ability to make it work?"

He cocked his head as he studied me, and I could tell he was trying to decide how much he should say. "You have it, Liz."

I scoffed, rolling my eyes at the very idea, ignoring the tiny seed of doubt that maybe I was wrong and he was right. "Now you're just messing with me."

He *was* messing with me, right?

Giving me a tight smile, he buttoned up his long, black leather coat over his lean torso. As he headed to the door, he pulled up the hood. The temperature had dropped rapidly into the forties as soon as the sun went down. A huge difference from the pleasantly cool nights we'd been having. But at least it wasn't raining.

Mike stopped to straighten a shelf and I'd turned around to add creamer to my coffee when the front door chimed. My heart stopped, then began to race. As casually as I could, which I was pretty positive was not casual at all, I turned to see who it was.

A pretty woman with stick straight red hair—the exact same shade as Mike's—that ended at her sharp jawline, was standing next to him talking. Her skin was as white and smooth as porcelain, her lips the same red as her hair, and she was dressed all in black from her short jacket to her Han Solo boots. She smiled big at something he said, showing off perfect white teeth.

As she waited for him to finish what he was doing, her eyes shifted over my way.

I smiled, offering her a little wave. One she didn't return.

Mike looked up and noticed her staring. "Oh, sorry. Angel, this is Lizzy. My boss." He emphasized the last sentence just a bit. Was it a warning?

"Nice to meet you," she finally said. It was the right thing to say, but the greeting lacked enthusiasm.

"You, too," I told her as I wandered closer.

I noticed her eyes were a pale hazel. An unusual color. The expression on her face didn't get any friendlier as I approached. Quite the opposite, in fact. She eyed me from the top of my head to the tips of my shoes and back again, like I was a tiny gnat she wanted to swat at. It was the second time someone had done that to me in as many days, only with completely different intentions.

Was this wave of hatred I felt coming from her for real? Or was I was just being overly sensitive because I was tired?

Without taking her eyes from mine, she tugged on Mike's sleeve. "Come on," she said. "Let's go."

With an apologetic look, he followed her out. I caught a glimpse of a large black man in a King Tut costume playing a trumpet solo to an enthralled crowd before the door swung shut. It was Halloween night, and the Quarter was alive with celebration.

After they left, I stood there, confused, staring at the closed door, the celebration outside now muted. What the hell had I done to that woman? I knew I'd never met her before. That red hair would be hard to forget.

An unexpected wave of loneliness overtook me. Just because some chick a good ten or fifteen years younger than me had given me attitude. It was stupid. I'd make my own friends here soon enough. It's not like I was some huge socialite, anyway. My idea of a good time was a nice dinner out. Maybe a movie. And if I was feeling really crazy, I'd order a second glass of wine.

Shaking it off, I turned around to go get Wiggles packed up for the cold walk home, belatedly remembering I hadn't locked the door. Turning on my heel, I went to do that before any unwelcome strangers wandered in, and then realized I didn't have my keys. With a frustrated sigh, I headed back to the counter to get the keys from my purse. Wiggles saw me getting my purse and thumped his tail in excitement.

I gave him a smile. "We might as well just go," I told him, getting his leash out from under the counter. I hooked it to this collar and waited while my old boy got up from the floor. It was a slow and painful process for him these days, and my heart hurt to watch him. "Come on, big boy. Let's go home." With one last look around the store, I shut off the lights and set the alarm. Opening the door, I waited for Wiggles to hobble out. "Hang on a minute, buddy," I told him as I pulled the keys out of my purse and locked the door from the outside, double checking it before dropping them back into my bag.

"I see I'm too late to do any trick or treating."

I jumped, my breath catching in my chest, my heart pounding. Even with the noise from the crowd all around me, I knew without looking who it was. And not just from his accent.

I could *feel* him.

Glancing to the side, I saw the man from yesterday. Even though I'd been watching for him all day, I suddenly forgot what he'd said his name was and I stared at him like a fool while I struggled to remember.

Killian. Yeah, that was it.

He was dressed much like the night before, despite the cooler temperature, only this time his shirt was black. As he stepped out from under the awning over the window and strolled over toward me, Wiggles, being the Very Good Dog he was, growled ferociously at him.

"There, there now," he told him. "Look what I brought for you, fella." Pulling something out of his pocket, he offered it to Wiggles.

I watched as my dog's little black nosed sniffed the treat the stranger had brought with suspicion, deciding if it was worth giving up his guard dog duties. Apparently, it was, for he took it gratefully from Killian's fingers, making me wait while he set it down on the sidewalk to savor it some more before he ate it.

"Sweet potatoes wrapped in dried chicken," Killian told me. "It was always a favorite of my own dogs."

So, I'd been wrong about the dog thing. "What are you doing here?" I asked him, even though I knew.

He looked around at the groups of people dancing around us, most in costume. "It's Halloween," he said. "I thought I'd come do a little shopping."

"You're too late. I just closed the store."

"Perhaps you'd let me walk you home, then," he told me. "It's a bit crazy in the Quarter tonight."

"And then what?"

"And then nothing," he said. "I just want to talk, Lizzy."

My heart slowed somewhat, but I didn't completely relax. After living in New York City for eleven years, I'd developed a pretty good instinct about people. And this man was not as innocent as he tried to appear. There was something about him, something that set off multiple alarms inside of me. Danger oozed from his pores, as sexy and delicious as the cologne he wore.

And yet there was something else about him...something that told me I could trust him completely. Or maybe I'd just read too many romance novels. "Thank you for the offer," I told him. "But I can get home on my own. Wiggles here knows the way."

"Is that his name, then?" he asked with a smile.

"Actually, it's Sir Wigglebutt. Wiggles for short."

Killian smiled. A real smile. "It's a perfect name for the old boy."

I barely heard what he'd said, transfixed as I was by the way his smile changed his appearance. Gone was the average looking thirty-ish or forty-ish-year-old man, and in its place was a guy that made my stomach flip and heat infuse my blood.

The dreams I'd had the night before came back to me in a rush.

Definitely too many romance novels.

His eyes travelled over my face, his smile fading away. "Let me walk you home, Lizzy. I promise I won't do you any harm."

I blinked a few times as I brushed my hair out of my eyes and pulled my old, wool coat tighter around me. It was more of a protective act then anything, as I wasn't cold at all, even though I didn't have a large cup of alcohol to keep me warm like the rest of the people around us. "But you're going to harass me until I agree to what you want," I muttered under my breath.

"I just might," he answered, one side of his mouth curving at my look of surprise.

"So, you're not going to do me any *physical* harm. But every other kind is up for grabs?"

He'd been watching Wiggles, but at that he looked up, his black eyes catching mine. "I don't plan to do you any harm at all." There was an intensity to his tone that was a little heavy for the conversation we were having. "But I do sincerely need your help," he told me. "If you'll just let me explain, maybe you'll change your mind."

I glanced around. Though we were a block from Bourbon Street, where most of the celebrating was taking place, the crowd was still pretty rowdy. I looked back over Killian. "I'll let you walk me part of the way," I told him.

"Fair enough," he said. "I truly appreciate your time."

I checked to make sure that Wiggles had finished his treat, and then we all started off in the direction of my apartment. I discovered I wasn't the only one who found my escort fascinating. He attracted plenty of attention, including uneasy looks from the men and hungry stares from the women. I didn't understand what was so threatening about him just walking down the street. And the slutty nurses and cops, among other, more imaginative costumes, just pissed me off for no reason I could put my finger on. "You've got about five minutes," I told him. "So you'd better make it quick."

"Five minutes is all that I need." He waited until we got past a group of kids who looked like they were barely old enough to go to college before he began his story. "I have a friend. A very special friend. And she's sick."

I glanced over at him, confused. "And you think I can help her?"

"I hope so, yes."

"What makes you think I'd be able to help her? I don't know anything about medicine."

"It's not that kind of illness," he explained. He glanced around, then said, "She's been struck down by one of your own."

I frowned up at him. "One of 'my own'? What's that supposed to mean?"

"Your kind," he explained slowly.

Still, I was confused. "My kind of what?" I asked him. "Another woman?"

Shoving his hands in the pockets of his sweater, he cocked his head, studying me as we walked. I swear I could almost feel him poking around in my brain.

"You said you came here from New York?"

"We're not supposed to be talking about me," I reminded him. "You're supposed to be telling me about your friend."

He nodded. Took a deep breath. "Her name is Kenya." We turned the corner and headed toward my street. "Lizzy, I need to ask you something."

"I wish you would," I told him. The sooner we got this conversation over with, the sooner I could be safe in my apartment forgetting it ever happened.

"What kind of power, exactly, do you possess?"

The laugh that erupted from me was short and loud. The kind my mother would frown about for not being "ladylike." "Power?" I asked. "You think I have a power." I didn't bother trying to hide the sarcasm in my voice. "You sound like Mike. My assistant," I explained at his inquiring look.

He made an "ah" expression. "I know you have magic," he insisted. "I just need to know if it can heal my friend."

I stopped in the middle of the sidewalk, stepping in closer to him to avoid anyone overhearing. A shiver crawled up my arm when our hands accidentally touched. It wasn't entirely unpleasant. "Look," I said. "I told you before, I don't know anything about medicine. I'm an actor who needed to get out of the city and start a new life doing something else and this voodoo store shit fell into my lap. I don't have any kind of magical healing powers. I'm not some kind of voodoo queen. I'm just trying to pay my rent and get some semblance of my life back."

"And running a voodoo store in this den of evil is your big dream, is it?" he asked me.

"Not really," I admitted honestly. "But it's all that's left to me. I'm getting too old to start over." I started walking with Wiggles again, not caring if he followed us or not.

"Why did you leave New York, Lizzy?"

Oh, my God. Seriously. What was with this guy? "I told you why."

"Not the true reason."

We were close to my place now. I could hear the music from the House of Blues and smell the po boys. "I sort of had to," I admitted as I glanced over at a threesome of girls as they stumbled by without really seeing them.

He ignored the girls completely, and every other person around us, too. The guy was completely focused on me. It was disconcerting, and if I were to be honest, kind of flattering.

"But why is that?" he wondered after a moment. "New York is a big city. Lots of people. Easy to get lost in."

"Not the world that I came from," I told him. "Besides, I wouldn't be able to do what I loved anymore. And it was too painful for me to stay there."

His eyes searched my face for a moment before they narrowed in on mine. "What did you do, Lizzy?"

Again, that uncomfortable feeling came over me. The one that nearly had me convinced he could read my mind. I hadn't said anything at all to hint at the fact that I wasn't entirely blameless in what had happened, and yet somehow he knew. I felt it all the way to my bones. "I burned down my dreams." I could barely get the words past my throat. "Quite literally, but accidentally. And while trying to escape, I fell and twisted my knee. I had to have surgery, and I couldn't dance anymore even if I wanted to." I shrugged. "My career as a Broadway star was over before it started."

"But I wonder, how someone as athletic as you—a dancer and performer—would be so clumsy."

"There was a fire," I whispered. "It was chaos." My mind wandered back to that day. Back to my hurt and my anger, and the fires that had appeared out of nowhere.

No, not out of nowhere. Out of my own thoughts. Or so it had seemed, because that was impossible, right? I could still feel the heat of the fire as I fought my way out of the building. My legs useless, dragging behind me. It was the most terrifying thing I'd ever lived through.

Confetti raining down on our heads brought me back to the present and I realized we'd stopped in the middle of the sidewalk and were standing there, nearly touching but not quite, staring at each other. I blinked, breaking the spell, and stepped back.

Killian reached out toward my face. I held my breath as he removed confetti from my hair. I looked down, breaking the spell, and we started walking again.

"So, will you come meet her, at least?"

As we walked, Killian waited for my answer. One I couldn't give him. When we got a few buildings away from my apartment, I stopped. "I'm just ahead," I told him, my tone final and careful not to indicate exactly where I lived in any way. "Thank you for walking me home, but I can make it on my own now."

As I turned away, his voice stopped me. "Lizzy."

I looked back over my shoulder but didn't stop walking.

"I'll be back tomorrow," he told me. "I expect your answer will be different then."

It wasn't quite a threat. More like a promise. I didn't know how to respond, so I said nothing, turning away and guiding Wiggles back to our apartment, checking over my shoulder once when we got near the door to make sure Killian wasn't still watching.

He was gone.

And the loneliness was back.

5

KILLIAN

"How is she?"

As I pulled Kenya's door shut behind me, I looked up to see Jamal coming out of the room next door. "Resting," I told him.

"I don't know how she can sleep with all this noise," he said.

I had to agree. The swamp was thriving with life, and it had no problems making itself known. All night, the insects and frogs sang incessantly, their voices interspersed with the occasional hoot of an owl claiming their hunting territory. To humans, this unending chorus was probably calming. To vampires and other immortals with supernatural hearing, it was headache-inducing. "Me, either. I've never been so grateful to be a day sleeper."

I struggled to find something else to say. This was the most he'd talked to me in months.

Jamal turned to leave, and I stopped him with a hand on his arm. "Are you going to the club tonight?" I asked him. It wasn't what I wanted to say to him. But I knew from experience that any attempt at having a heart to heart would only end up in an argument.

"I am," Jamal said.

"You should feed. You're looking tired."

He yanked his arm from my grip, and I ground my teeth together, realizing my mistake too late. "Don't tell me what to do, Killian. Maybe I just want to dance tonight. Or fuck. Maybe I don't feel the need to drain every woman who pays for a private performance."

"It's just a suggestion, mate."

"Yeah, well I'm not your slave."

His words hit me like a punch in the gut. "Of course, you're not. Fuckin' Christ, Jamal. I'm just worried about you."

"Well, don't be. I can handle my own stuff."

"Can you, then?" I didn't know why I was challenging him. I didn't want to argue. But I was so sick and tired of him acting like I was some sort of monster holding him prisoner in my dungeons. He had a good life. He *had* a life because of me.

For once, he didn't take the bait. He just sighed heavily and said, "Yeah, I can."

I watched him turn and walk down the hall. "How long are you going to hate me for? Just out of curiosity, you know. It's been over a hundred years, Jamal."

He stopped, but didn't turn around. "I don't know," he told me. "When are you going to set me free?"

"You're not a prisoner here," I insisted.

"So I can just leave anytime I want."

"Yes, absolutely."

"I can just leave and have free will and do whatever the fuck I want," he mocked with his back toward me. "Live where I want. Hang out with who I want, and never come back to this coven. Or to you."

No. No, he couldn't do that. I met his eyes as he slowly turned around to face me.

His mouth twisted in disgust when he saw the answer on my face. "That's what I thought."

"I did the right thing," I told him. But I wasn't sure who I was trying to convince more—him, or myself.

"How many times are we gonna go over this, Killian?"

I didn't have an answer.

In three steps he was all up in my face. "You saved my life. Twice. I'm damn grateful for the *first* time, which is the only reason I'm still around for the second." He paused, his black eyes searching mine as they pleaded for me to understand.

"You can free me, Killian. One way or the other. Because God knows I don't have the balls to do it myself."

My stomach clenched at the thought. "I can't do that, Jamal. Shite. You know I can't do that."

"Which one?"

"Either." The truth burst from me before I could stop it.

He stared at me a moment more before he laughed, the sound ugly and harsh. "Of course, you can't, because it's all about you. It's always all about you." His eyes were full of disdain as he ran them up and down my body. "I'm going to work," he said. "Somebody's got to bring some money in around here."

I didn't miss the dig, but I refused to react to it. If it wasn't for me, the club wouldn't exist. And neither would the wealth this coven had accrued by various means over the years. Money had nothing to do with it.

His long legs ate up the distance to the front door.

"Jamal."

He stopped walking, sighing dramatically as his head fell back on his shoulders. Like he was a teenager dealing with a strict parent. It really rubbed me raw, this charade, but playing into it would only encourage the behavior. Just like a child.

He stared at the ceiling. "What."

"Tell the guys..." I stopped. Recalibrated. "Tell the guys, I think the woman you found can help Kenya." I didn't know what I was trying to do. Give him some accolades, maybe. Something to feel good about.

Cool as a cucumber, he looked back at me and touched his tongue to the tip of one fang before he asked, "You gonna make her a prisoner, too? Because that's the only way you're gonna be able to convince a witch to help one of us." With one last hard look, he strode out of the house, slamming the door behind him.

"You're not a prisoner, dammit!" I called after him. I swear to all that was holy, my back ached from the weight he laid on me every time we had this conversation.

I stood there in the hallway of that run down house for a long time, staring at the water-stained walls. Was Jamal right? Had I taken him from one form of slavery only to force him into another?

But I immediately shook my head. No. No, it wasn't the same. I didn't beat him. I didn't make him pick cotton or tobacco. I didn't whip him for waking up late. I had helped him escape all of that. Gave him food and water and clothes and shelter. And when he was able to keep going, I guided him north where he would be safe.

And when I'd saved him again years later, after I had been reborn and we'd renewed our friendship, he'd been dying. After everything I'd done for him, all that I had risked for him, he'd gotten into a fight he couldn't win. What was I supposed to have done? Just leave him to die?

I took a deep breath. No. I'd hadn't saved his life just for him to snuff it out like that. Being alive, even as a vampire, was so much better than being dead.

Apparently, however, Jamal disagreed. He'd made that very clear to me from the moment he'd woken up, horrified he craved blood. I thought, over time, he'd accept what he was now. I was wrong.

I heard his car engine rev and then fade as he drove away. I hoped he would take my advice and feed tonight, despite his inherent need to rebel against anything I suggested. It was the entire reason we owned the club. It wasn't for the money. It was so we could feed without drawing attention to ourselves. If we fed anywhere else, it would break our pact with the witches. My vampires danced at the club. And when the ladies wanted a little private action, they paid for it with a little blood and a hell of a good time. They left happy. We got the sustenance we needed. The witches left us alone. And we provided them with a little added protection when asked. It was a win-win situation all around.

Except when one of them—or one of us—got out of line.

I walked down to the little kitchen to make Kenya some tea. As I waited for the water to heat, Jamal's words spun round and round in my head. In the darkest hours of my life, I had to admit he was right about one thing. I'd turned him so I wouldn't be alone. So I would have a friend. An eternity of watching everyone you knew grow old and die was not a future I'd looked forward to. And I hadn't bothered to ask him if he wanted the same thing.

Just like you're not going to ask Lizzy what she wants.

The kettle whistled, pulling me from my thoughts. I poured the water over the tea bag and took it to Kenya. "A little bit of Irish whiskey would work a lot better," I muttered to myself right before I opened her door. It was a lie. It didn't really matter, since alcohol didn't really affect us. But it sure felt good going down.

"Someone else can make that for me, you know," she told me when I brought it in to her.

"Well, as I'm the only one here, you're stuck with me."

I helped her to sit up and found her glasses. Strangely enough, her eyesight hadn't improved when she was turned, and that fact was a thorn constantly digging in her side. "You are the master vampire of this coven," she reminded me. "Aren't there other things that need your attention besides taking care of me?"

"Oh, probably," I admitted. "But I'm happy to do it." Her hands were shaking so badly I had to help her take a sip.

She eyed me over the top of the cup. "I heard you fighting with Jamal again."

"I wasn't fighting. He was fighting."

"You know," she paused to take another sip before indicating I could put the cup on the nightstand. "Maybe you should consider letting him go, Killian. 'If you love it, set it free...' and all that."

With a sharp shake of my head, I cut her off as I set the cup down. "No, I won't be doing that." The burden of that decision weighed on me, but it was the only one I could make.

"Why are you so insistent?" she asked. "He doesn't want to be here with us. So, why make him stay?"

"Because he's mine," I told her. "Just as you are mine."

"And the rest of the coven? Elias. Dae. Brogan. Are they 'yours', too? You created them, and yet you've let *them* come and go as they please."

"It's not the same," I told her. "And Jamal has no issue with you or the others. His grudge is with me."

Her expression, though tired, became thoughtful. "What about me? You wouldn't let me go off to live my own life?"

"You've never wanted to do that."

"This is true," she said after a pause. "I don't know how you'd keep a business going without me."

I grunted in agreement.

"What about your little witch? Is she going to be yours?"

I looked away so she wouldn't see the truth in my eyes. Because the thought had crossed my mind, more than once. "Would that be so bad?" I asked her. "Am I truly so horrible?" I didn't wait for her to answer. "We could have our own personal witch."

It was the first time I'd said the words aloud.

Her weary eyes grew wide. Magnified by her glasses, they overtook her face. "You're not serious."

"Oh, but I am," I told her. "You know, honestly, I've been going on about it in my head. Back and forth, back and forth, trying to decide how to get her to help us. But she's a stubborn one. And I have a good feeling she will never agree of her own accord. Then I thought, maybe I can just bring her here and introduce you. If she knew you as a person, maybe she'd be more inclined to help you. And then the idea came to me...why not? Why not just take her and make her come here. Once I told her what I could offer her, why wouldn't she agree?" I met Kenya's bemused expression. "I could give her immortal life."

"*Why wouldn't she agree?* How the hell can you even ask that, Killian? What woman in her right mind would want to come live with a bunch of vampires? Would choose to become one?"

"A witch," I emphasized. "Who is in danger from the other witches. We could protect her. And in return she could help us when things like this happen." I indicated Kenya lying in her sickbed.

"We don't know that for sure," she said. "Have you ever seen a turned witch?"

"No, but surely her magic would carry over with her. It may even grow stronger. Like Jamal's stubbornness."

"And if she tells you no?"

"I won't give her a choice." The more I thought about it, the more I felt this was right.

"Killian, you can't do that."

"Why not?"

"Because! That's why not. Besides, we don't know for sure she's in danger. Nothing has happened to her up till now. And I don't think an outsider would be overlooked by Judy Moss and her coven."

"Don't we?" I asked her. "I saw the red-haired one—Angel—leaving Lizzy's store last night. She did not look happy. Which means she didn't know Lizzy was here in the city."

"So, let me get this straight. The way you're making this okay in your own mind is by telling yourself that if we take this woman and force her to live with us—if we can even do that—then she will be grateful to us because we will protect her from the witches in the quarter. And in return, she'll fall to her knees before you and offer us her own magic—and maybe even her *life*—in return. Is that about right?"

It didn't make as much sense hearing her lay it out like that. Sinking down onto the edge of the bed, I rested my elbows on my knees and ran my hands through my hair. "Tell me then, Kenya. Tell me what the fuck else I'm supposed to do."

She was quiet for a long time. And then she pulled my hand from my hair and held it in her lap.

I lifted my head and met her eyes.

"You could just let me go."

Anger filled me. "That's not an option," I told her again.

"Killian..."

"No, Kenya. Shite! That's not a fucking option. Lizzy will come here, and she will help you. And I will do whatever I have to do to make her do it." I stood and made my way across the room.

"Then why haven't you done it already?" Kenya called after me.

I paused with my hand on the doorknob as she fell into a coughing fit. Then I opened the door and walked out.

6

KILLIAN

I thought about what Jamal and Kenya had said all the way to the Quarter. Were they right, then? Would Lizzy only end up hating me if I forced her hand?

But even if she did, so what? Why the hell did I care?

The funny thing was, I hadn't even realized I was seriously considering doing it until I'd spoken the words out loud.

Parking the car at Crescent Park, I turned off the engine but didn't get out right away. Cloaked by darkness, I scanned the area around me before I opened the door, calming my emotions and reaching out with my senses. Distracted as I was, I didn't want to be taken by surprise and be the next one lying in my death bed. Striking down someone as sweet as Kenya was no doubt the witch's way of warning us.

But for what? That was the question I had no answer to.

I stayed vigilant as I climbed out of my Tesla, but I felt no eyes on me, no magic in the air. Only the muddy smell of fish from the Mississippi river.

There were still some stragglers in the city from the Halloween celebration and the path leading to the French market was crowded, even at this time of night. That was good. I drew less attention that way. I could blend in with the tourists while keeping an eye out for any who may not be happy to see me.

When I got to Lizzy's store, she had already closed up for the night. The door was locked the lights were out. Feeling unusually tired and restless, I heaved a sigh and turned around, my eyes scanning the crowd. I realized I didn't even know what time it was. The Quarter would be awake until the early morning hours, so it was hard to tell. Pulling my cell phone out of my pocket, I saw it was just after ten. Lizzy must be home by now.

Trailing behind a group of young guys celebrating what appeared to be a bachelor party by all the talk of this being his "last chance," I made my way to her apartment. The windows were dark, and there was no movement inside.

I stood undecided for a long time. I could track her like an animal, or I could stop obsessing and go check on my club. Lizzy would still be here tomorrow. And, the gods willing, Kenya would still be alive. The bad thing about the spell that was cast on her was that it was long and drawn out and made her suffer. The good part was that it gave me much needed time to make a decision that would impact my coven. One way or the other.

The Quarter was alive with humans, young and old, enjoying the city. Drinks in hand, they stumbled up and down Bourbon street in small groups and large. The women pulling up their shirts for cheap plastic beads that rained down on them from the balconies. The men ogling them like they've never seen a pair of knockers before in their life. It was a city of mystery and celebration and very few inhibitions, and I fed off the energy around me, letting it revive my spirits and feed my hunger.

Making my way around one large group blocking the middle of the street, I saw the purple neon lights of The Purple Fang, my club. And one of the few male strip clubs in the Quarter. With a nod at Kenny, my human bouncer, I went inside. My eyes quickly adjusted to the darkness, lit only by purple and white laser lights that danced across the stage before flaring out to light up the people filling the tables on the floor. In the back room, black leather booths with high sides made up the perimeter of the room, spaced apart for plenty of privacy, with room in the center for dancing.

Dae-Jung was up on the stage in nothing but a pair of cowboy boots and rip-away jeans, a group of women at his booted feet waving dollar bills. With a wink at the one who held the largest wad of cash, he turned around, showing off the massive green skull tattoo that covered his muscular back, surrounded by red flowers and vines. And when he ripped off his jeans, there was a collective gasp even over the deep beat of the music. Hands reached for the flowers that continued down his body, covering his left hip and disappearing beneath the strip of cloth covering his cock, tendrils of vines and flowers hanging down his thigh to just above his knee.

Dae gave me a smile when he spotted me. Dropping to his knees, he tightened his abs for his admirers and allowed the women to tuck their money into his G string. One girl reached up and ran her hand down his arm, admiring the sharp cut of muscle. I couldn't say that I blamed her. Dae worked really hard to keep his physique the way it was, and it got him a lot of private dances in the back room. Which meant plenty of blood for him to feed on. Of course, the women didn't remember this. They only remembered that he showed them a hell of a time, and came back for more.

"Hey, man," Elias said from behind the bar. "Whiskey?"

I gave him a nod. "Growing out the beard again, are ya?"

He smiled an evil smile. "The females like the feel of it between their legs." He poured two fingers into a glass and slid it across the bar top. "Do you need anything else?"

Yes. I need to find a witch before I go mad from thinking of her. "No, thank you. Take care of your customers," I told him. There was no need to raise my voice. He could hear me loud and clear even over the deep bass thumping through the speakers.

"Gotcha, boss." He turned away, flashing his fangs to the delight of a pretty little thing with bright brown eyes and skin as dark as Elias's smile. Like the others, she didn't know they were real, but thought they were part of a year-round costume. All part of the show.

Elias would dance tomorrow night. Kenya normally tended bar, along with keeping track of the books, but with her in the condition she was in, the guys were taking turns covering for her. Whiskey in hand, I leaned back against the bar to watch the show as I waited for Dae to get done with his dance so he could give me an update.

Three whiskeys later, I finally had my chance. He grinned as he met me at the bar, his dark eyes dancing in his smooth face, fully dressed—sort of—his skin flushed with new blood.

"Hey, Killian! How's our girl?" He took the beer Elias offered him and drank it down in three swallows.

"Hey." I watched Jamal as he turned on the charm on stage. A side of him I only got to see when I was here. "You have a minute to go over the books?"

A shadow crossed his happy features when I didn't answer his question about Kenya. He hadn't seen her in about two weeks, and knew it could only mean one thing. "Yeah, sure. I just balanced everything last night."

Once back in the office, I took a seat in front of the desk and waited for him to grab the receipts and other info to show me.

"Seriously. How is Kenya?" he asked again once we were alone.

"No better than the last time you asked," I told him. "Maybe a wee bit worse."

"I'm sorry to hear that. I know she's a favorite of yours."

"She's not my favorite. She's just..."

"She's your favorite."

He grinned when I had no argument for him. "Yeah, so, maybe she is," I told him.

"It's okay, man. No offense taken. We all love her."

I knew Dae well enough to know that was true as far as he was concerned. For the most part, he had taken to vampire life better than any of the others, and had carried over his happy-go-lucky personality from his human life. Every once in a while, though, I'd see something dark and heavy reflected in his eyes. He never offered to tell me what it was about, and I never asked him. Whatever it was, it never affected his loyalty to the coven. Or to me. And that's all I truly cared about.

"So, how are things going here?" I asked him. "I know I haven't been around much."

"It's all good. You've been needed somewhere else more, and this place practically runs itself now." He pulled a thick, black book out of the drawer and pulled up a spreadsheet on the computer monitor. "Just don't tell Kenya that," he added as he handed me the book and turned the monitor around so I could see the screen. "She'll be crushed."

He was right. This club ran like a well-oiled machine. Business had been better than normal with it being Halloween. A vampire bar and strip club only added to the general ambiance the city provided to its visitors. "No problems with customers getting out of hand?"

Dae gave me a smirk. "As if any of us would complain if they did?"

"Where's Brogan?"

"Taking a break. He told us he had something to do. Said he'd be back by the time he was needed on stage."

I raised an eyebrow. Brogan should've taken the main stage before Jamal.

"It's all right," Dae said when he saw my look. "Elias, Jamal and I have the place handled."

I nodded. Jamal may hate me, but I could always count on him to carry his weight. And Dae, Elias, and Brogan were staying here at the club, which meant I didn't have to hunt any of them down to remind them about their shift.

Usually.

"I hear you found someone to help Kenya. One of the witches? How did you manage that?"

"She is a witch," I hedged. "But not one of our witches here in the quarter. She's new in town."

"But you know for sure she is one?"

"Yeah. I've met her." I didn't need to say anything else. Dae knew as well as any other vampire that we could sense the magic within the witches, once you knew how to recognize it. And we were around them enough that it had become second nature.

"She agreed to help her? Just like that?"

"Not exactly." I admitted. "But I'll talk her into it. Or not. Either way, she'll help Kenya."

"Maybe I could convince her. I do have a certain animal magnetism with the ladies."

How he said things like that with a perfectly straight face I would never know. Still, even though I knew he was only messing around, my gums burned as my fangs lengthened, instant fury rising within me. I caught myself right before I hissed a warning.

What the hell was that?

I ducked my head and pretended to study the books to hide my reaction. "Thanks for the offer, but I'll handle it."

"All right. But just let me know if you change your mind. I'm always available." He sat back in his chair, but I felt his eyes on me, watching me more closely than he was trying to let on. "What if you can't talk her into it?"

"Then I won't give her a choice."

He sat forward again and slapped his hand down over the page I was pretending to study. "Man, you know we can't do that to a witch. The rest of them would be on us like flies on a carcass. They'd make our lives miserable...chase us out of the city. Or worse. What are you trying to do to us here, Killian?"

Slowly, I raised my eyes to his. I knew his reaction was out of worry and not meant as a direct challenge, which was the only reason his head wasn't on the other side of the wall right now minus the rest of his body. "There won't be any trouble," I told him. "Honestly, I don't think they'd give a rat's ass." I shrugged. "Maybe they'd even be grateful to us for removing her from their territory. By bringing her to join us, it would, in reality, protect her just as much as it would help us."

He sat back again, his hand sliding off the book and across the desk until it fell into his lap. "Where is the witch?"

"Not sure. I went by her store and her apartment before I came here. She wasn't at either place. I'll go check again after I leave here."

He made a quick sideways movement with his head. Dae's way of conveying his approval. "Well, good luck with that."

"Thanks," I told him. "I'm going to need it."

An hour later, I headed back over to Lizzy's apartment. This time, I knew as soon as I got there that she was home. Even before I heard her thoughts I sensed her there. Smelled her scent. Heard her blood singing through her veins.

I was at the front door of her building without realizing I'd moved. My body hardening, muscles tensed to the point of pain. I touched my tongue to the sharp points of my fangs, desperate for a taste of her. It seemed every time I was around her, I became more sensitive to the essence that was Lizzy. It made me wonder if she had, indeed, cast some sort of spell on me.

Closing my eyes, I inhaled deeply in an attempt to differentiate the smells in the air as I tried to get a grip on myself. It was only then I recognized it.

A wisp of smoke coming from Lizzy's apartment building. And not from someone burning a late night meal. I'd smelled this before, many years ago.

When someone had tried to burn down our home.

7

LIZZY

EARLIER THAT DAY

"Hello! Aunt Jude, are you home?" I let myself into the backyard, knowing that's probably where I would find her at this time of the afternoon, winterizing her garden.

My Aunt Judy was my father's sister and my only living relative on either side. At least as far as I knew. I'd called her "Aunt Jude" since I was little, because apparently, three syllables were one too many to say.

She and my mom hadn't had a very good relationship when she was alive, but when I'd needed to leave New York my aunt had welcomed me back with open arms, even though we hadn't really spoken since I was twelve. That was when my mother had taken me out of Louisiana and moved us both to the northeast, eventually settling in New Jersey and, later, New York City. At first, I'd been too young to think of asking for my aunt's number or if I could call her, more concerned with fitting in at my new school and whatever guy I had the latest crush on. And later, when my life had been consumed with acting and dance classes and vocal lessons, I'd always meant to get back in touch but just could never find the time. It wasn't until my mom passed that I dug up her contact info from my mom's stuff and called her.

She'd come to the city for the funeral, but only stayed long enough to make sure I had everything handled before she had to go home. Buried in grief, I didn't realize how much I'd missed her. But when I'd needed a place to go, she was the first one I'd thought of.

"Oh! Hi, honey," she greeted me when she saw me there. Sure enough, she was bent over one of her raised beds with a little shovel in one hand and what looked to be a bulb of some sort in the other. Her short, salt and pepper hair was covered with a hat, and her pale blue eyes were protected with sunglasses. "Where's Wiggles?"

"Napping," I laughed. My old boy was always napping these days. "I didn't want to wake him up."

"He'll probably still be right where you left him when you get home."

"Probably. Whatcha planting?"

"Just a little garlic."

As I got closer, I could see by the small army of popsicle sticks with "Garlic" written on the ends she was actually planting quite a lot. "Trying to keep the vampires away?"

She gave me an odd look. "Something like that." Patting down the soil around the last clove, she straightened up with a groan. "I'm gonna have to have somebody raise these beds a little higher."

My aunt was a good six inches shorter than I was, which put her at around five feet tall. But she had grown a little older, and a little rounder, since the last time I'd seen her. Hence, the raised beds. "I'm sure you'll be able to find some young, strong, Louisiana boy who could use a little extra cash."

She smiled. "Shouldn't be too hard around here."

I grinned back at her, then stood there obediently as she took in my appearance. Apparently unsatisfied with what she saw, she started to head into the house. "Come on, I'll make some lunch."

"It's three in the afternoon."

"So? I'm hungry."

Obediently, I followed her up the steps and onto her little back porch, then through the screen door that led into her white kitchen.

My aunt lived in the lower Garden District in a little one-story, three bedroom, two bath house. The outside was painted a pale aqua-green and boasted a bright red front door and four white columns that held up the roof of the front porch. Inside it was clean and bright, with a gray formal front room that opened up into a combined living and kitchen area. Down the short hallway on the left were two spare bedrooms with a shared bath, and at the end was the master bed and bath. Nothing fancy. And exactly the kind of house I'd like to own one day.

"Whatcha hungry for?" she called from the kitchen sink, laying her hat and sunglasses on the counter before she washed her hands.

"Really. You don't have to make me anything."

"I know that, but I'm starving, so it's no trouble to make a little extra." She eyed me again where I stood on the other side of the bar across from the sink. "And you're looking too thin."

Actually, I was about fourteen pounds over my "ideal" weight. Not being on stage was really doing a number on my metabolism. But I knew from experience she'd feed me whether I wanted something or not. It was useless to pretend otherwise. "Well, what are you making?"

She fought back a smile, knowing she had won. "I was thinking some BLTs. And I have a little leftover gumbo in the fridge."

"Gumbo and BLT's?"

"Sure," she said with a little roll of one shoulder. "Why not?"

"It actually sounds wonderful. Thanks." At least this way I wouldn't have to worry about dinner.

I helped her by heating up the gumbo while she made the sandwiches. Her cat, Ted, watched me from his perch on the counter. Ted had apparently gotten his name from the actor Ted Danson, who Aunt Judy had a huge thing for. But unlike the handsome actor, Ted the cat was an overweight gray tabby. They did, however, share the same blue eyes. "You'd better watch it," I told him. "Get much closer and I'll make *you* into gumbo."

Ted blinked lazily and swished his tail.

"He'll never believe you," my aunt said. "He knows he's the king of the house."

This was true. He also knew I was all talk. I already loved that fat cat almost as much as I loved Wiggles. Once our food was ready and Ted had his lunch, we sat down at her round kitchen table and dug in.

"So, what's going on with you, Lizzy? I'm sensing some tension happening here." She waved one hand in the air, encompassing my entire physical form and overall aura.

"I had a weird interaction with a customer," I admitted, knowing after only a few visits with her that she'd drag it out of me one way or another, so I might as well spill. Besides, the voodoo store had been hers before I'd taken it over. From what she'd told me, she'd worked there for most of her life, maybe she'd had strange requests like this before and could give me some pointers on how to handle it.

"What sort of interaction?" Her eyes rolled back in her head at her first taste of the gumbo. "Damn, this is good."

I had to agree. My aunt was a helluva cook. "A man came in a few nights ago. Tallish. Light brown hair. Dresses like the guys in the European magazines. He seems to think I'll be able to help his friend who's sick. I told him I knew nothing about medicine or healing, or voodoo for that matter, that I just ran the store. I mean, Mike is the one who knows about all of that shit." I took a bite of my sandwich. It was still warm from the bacon. "He didn't believe me," I told her with my hand over my mouth, "and showed up again on Halloween night to walk me home and try, again, to convince me to help his friend. I honestly don't know how much more blunt I can be. I've told him over and over I can't help this person, but he said he was coming back, and he expects that I'll have changed my mind by then..." I trailed off as I noticed my aunt sitting there completely motionless, her eyes glued to me.

"What was this man's name, honey?" she asked me.

"Killian...something." I rolled my eyes and shrugged.

"Killian Rice?"

I put a spoonful of gumbo in my mouth, then nodded. "Mm-hmm. That sounds right."

Aunt Judy set down the half sandwich she'd been about to eat and sat back in her chair. She stared at me, chewing the inside of her cheek.

"What? Do you know him?" It wouldn't surprise me. She'd lived in this city her entire life. And, from I could guess about Killian, so had he.

Leaning forward, she laid her hand on my arm where it rested on the table. "Lizzy, Killian is...well, he's not the normal kind of guy that wanders into a voodoo store."

She wasn't wrong there.

"He's..." Her eyes wandered the room, looking for the words she wanted to say.

"What? From Ireland? A thief? A woman abuser?"

"He's not a good guy, honey."

Even though I'd thought that very thing myself, hearing the words out loud pulled all of the air from my lungs. "Yeah, I kind of got that feeling about him. Something...I don't know. Dangerous."

"And that's putting it lightly."

I got up to rinse off my dishes and make some tea. "So, how do you know so much about him?" I asked as I picked up her empty bowl and took it to the sink.

She glanced up at me. "Make me some of that tea and we'll talk about it some more."

I did as she asked, setting her cup on the table in front of her before taking my seat. Blowing on my tea, I waited for her to get her thoughts together. This was the first time I'd seen my aunt this serious about anything. I was starting to get nervous. Was this guy a rapist? A murderer? Jesus, he practically knew where I lived.

"What do you know about our family, Lizzy? Did your momma ever tell you anything?"

The question, so far out in left field of what I'd been thinking, completely threw me off. "What?" I thought we were talking about Killian.

"Our family," she repeated. "You were barely a teenager when she took you away, and even before that, she'd never let anyone but me see you. And that was only because I swore to keep my mouth shut about our family's...eccentricities. So, I'm just wondering, what, if anything, did your mother tell you?"

I thought back to our conversations about my father and his side of the family, which was pretty easy since my mom didn't like to talk about him at all. "She didn't really like it when I asked questions about Dad, or any of you."

Aunt Judy nodded, her expression thoughtful. "Don't blame her for the first part. Your father was a piece of work."

"But, you know, if there are some deep, dark secrets I need to know about, you can tell me. I'm not a kid anymore. I'm thirty-eight, and quite mature for my age." I smiled at my joke.

Aunt Judy's blue eyes lit up as she chuckled. I now knew where I got my goofy sense of humor.

"I'm also single and alone, so you don't have to worry about me telling anyone anything. You're the only one I talk to. Except for Mike at the store, but I don't make it a habit to confide in him about personal stuff." I thought about it for a second. "And Wiggles, but you know, he's a dog. And he's old and deaf, so he doesn't hear anything I tell him."

"Typical male."

"Pretty much."

I could see her teetering back and forth, trying to decide, and then she slapped her hands down on the table, rattling the salt and pepper shakers. "Well, since your mother slacked off on her parenting duties—no offense—"

"None taken. She was flaky."

"I suppose it's up to me to pass down your heritage to you."

Heritage? "You mean, like, money?"

"No, honey." She laughed again. "Hell, if we had money I'd be living in one of those million dollar houses down the street."

"This is true. Unless, of course, you didn't want anyone to know you had all that money."

"Lizzy, do you want to hear this or not?"

Actually, I'd prefer to hear what she had to say about Killian. But maybe one had something to do with the other. "Yes, I would."

She took a sip of her tea. "You know I don't believe in beating around the bush."

I didn't, really, but I just nodded.

Looking me dead in the eye, she said, "Lizzy, you are descended from a family of witches." Immediately, she held up her hand before I could say anything. "Not voodoo.

There's a difference between their magic and ours. But witches."

I asked the first question that came to my mind. "Then why did you own a voodoo store?"

She sighed and moved around on her chair, getting into a more comfortable position. "I don't know. I guess because it was familiar in a way. And it's all really interesting, don't you think?"

"I don't really know. I don't know much about it."

"With all of those books you sell? You never picked one up and read it?" Pursing her lips, she waved her hand in the air before I could answer. "Never mind. That's neither here nor there right now." She took another sip of her tea, then set her cup on the table and stared at me so intently I couldn't look away. "Get comfortable, hon. I have a long story to tell you."

Two hours later, I was on my way home, my head buzzing with the tale Aunt Judy had just told me. I didn't know if I believed her. But, then again, how could I not? I'd always felt there was something different about me. In any case, she'd asked me to meet her at the store on Sunday when we were closed.

And she said there would be others with her.

8

KILLIAN

"LIZZY!"

Her name was ripped from my throat as though by unseen hands. Precious seconds ticked by as panic froze me where I stood, staring up at her apartment windows. A few stragglers glanced at me uncomfortably, probably thinking I was a drunk boyfriend or some sort of abusive husband, but I had no time to ease the minds of humans. By the time I forced myself to move, smoke burned the inside of my nostrils.

Fuck it.

Thoughts of my own safety never entered my mind as I opened the door to the residences above the cafe that took up the first floor of Lizzy's building. "God dammit!" I needed a code for the elevator. Trying a few random numbers that didn't work, I punched the steel doors in sheer frustration and went back outside, jogging around the end of the block to the alley behind the building. What I was about to do was not for human eyes to see.

With a quick glance around, I removed my sweater and hung it over the Dumpster. Testing the tread of my boots on the brick, I quickly scaled the outside of the building to the second floor. The first set of windows were dark. Inside, I saw black, leather couches and an oversized television.

Not Lizzy's apartment.

Crawling over to the next set of windows, I saw a gray couch with a matching chair. On the wall hung posters of popular Broadway shows. The Phantom of the Opera. Wicked. Hamilton, and others. The smell of smoke was stronger here, and I could see the flickering shadow of flames around the corner. My fist went through one pane of glass and then the other. Blood ran down my hands, but I felt no pain as I ripped out the wooden grilles in between the panes and then did the same to the rest of the window until I had made a large enough hole for me to fit through without shredding myself into bloody ribbons. I hefted myself up and through the opening, landing silently on the hardwood floor.

A thick gray haze hung in the air, swiftly filling the space between me and the 14-foot ceilings. Crouching low, I tried the door nearest me. It was a closet. Moving swiftly through the living room, I circled to the right, heading toward the flames.

Icy fingers crept along my spine, remnants of magic that crawled along my skin like ants.

I shivered in the heat that seared my lungs as I turned toward the kitchen. I'd forgotten not to breathe. A fire was swiftly building from absolutely nothing in the center of the room. It had already burned up what must have been a rug. Parts of it were now licking at the wooden cabinets. Once they caught, it would spread fast.

I saw a closed door to my right across from the kitchen, midway along the inner wall. Her bedroom. It had to be. I eyed the encroaching flames as they crept toward that door. The smoke was turning black, thick enough it made my eyes water.

I sucked in a breath. "Lizzy!"

Immediately, I began to cough so hard I was surprised pieces of my lungs didn't spew out of my mouth. Again, I eyed the flames edging closer to her door, judging the distance between. If something blew, I would be engulfed in the flames. And vampire or not, there was no way I'd live through being burned alive.

But I couldn't leave her there to burn.

As I made my way to her room, hugging the wall, I tried to will the flames away with my mind. I don't know if it worked or not, but somehow, I made it to the door without becoming a pile of ash myself. I concentrated on slowing my heartbeat to keep my mind off of the urge to breathe. I didn't really need to breathe; it was just an automatic process of my body that had never stopped after I had been turned.

Once I got to the door, I placed my palms against the wood, feeling for heat, just in case. But it was impossible to tell with the inferno just behind me. Without thinking, I grabbed the doorknob. The heated metal seared the skin from my palm, exposing the muscle in the split second it took me to let go again. I roared in pain, my upper lip pulling back from my fangs. There was only one way I was going to get into that room.

Backing up a step, I kicked the door just below the latch. It flew open, banging off the wall behind it. I threw my body into the doorway before it could shut again.

The bedroom I found myself in was small and rectangular. To my right was a small seating area near the windows. Just a lounge chair and a table with a lamp. Her dog was on the chair, lying on a blanket. A corner of it covered his face.

To the left was a queen-sized bed. Lizzy was there, the blankets kicked off of her. She wore a gray T-shirt and loose, black shorts and her dark hair was pulled up to the top of her head. She was lying on her stomach with one leg bent and one arm reaching toward the edge. It almost looked like she was trying to crawl off before she passed out.

Moving quickly, I reached under her arms and rolled her over, then pulled her up and off the bed. Throwing her motionless body over my shoulder, I headed toward the door. There, I paused. The flames had crept closer in the few seconds it had taken me to find her. Colors flashed within them, variations of blues and greens, feeding the spell that had started it.

"Shite."

My fangs ached to sink into this thing that was threatening her, but I couldn't drain the lifeblood from fire. Rage burned through me for the second time that night. Someone had set her apartment ablaze, had purposefully tried to harm her. But there was nothing I could do about it right now.

I laid her back on the bed and rushed to the windows. Pushing the chair out of the way, I busted through the glass much as I had to get in. There was no way I'd be able to get through the fire now, it was too close. So window it was. Luckily, this side of the apartment also looked out over the alley below.

As I went back to the bed to get her, I couldn't help but think she deserved so much more than a cheap flat that looked out over an alley filled with dumpsters and the buildings across the way. I checked that she was still breathing, then threw her back over my shoulder. At the window, I held on to her with one arm and used the other to steady us as I climbed out.

Once I had a steady hold and felt her weight balanced across my shoulder, I released her legs, reached in, and grabbed the dog.

Tucking him under my arm, I held onto both of them as I used my free hand to climb down. On the ground, I laid her down on the pavement and put the dog beside her. They were both unconscious, but still breathing. I retrieved my sweater, moved the dog to her stomach, and picked them both up in my arms.

Sirens grew louder as they came closer. It seemed the saviors had finally been called, and I needed to be long gone before they arrived. Leaving the alley, I ran full speed to our home. Not the swamp. Our actual home in the Quarter. I thought of nothing but getting her someplace safe and warm, and since we'd abandoned it after the attack on Kenya, the house was empty right now. If the witches have been watching, they'd know we're not staying there. Lizzy should be safe enough there.

No humans saw me. The streets were finally emptying out. And even if there were any stragglers, I moved too fast for any of them to track. At most, I was a blur. A breeze that ruffled their clothes. A ghost that flew past them in the night. After all, New Orleans was known for its many hauntings, especially this time of year.

About a block away from my home, I ducked into a doorway. Taking a deep breath, I scented the air, but smelled nothing except the warm scent of Lizzy's skin beneath the smoke that clung to her clothes and the dog's fur. She started to stir in my arms. I needed to get her inside.

I went through the narrow gate on the side of the house that led to the back courtyard. My nerves were strung tight, but I felt nothing threatening. No menacing forces. Inside the house, I immediately took them both to my room. Gently, I laid her on the bed and took the dog from her stomach, laying him beside her. As I pulled the comforter over her, she started to cough, her eyes flickering open.

"It's all right," I told her as I brushed escaped tendrils of her hair back from her forehead. "I'll get you some water. Stay here."

In the kitchen, I found a glass and filled it with filtered water. As an afterthought, I pulled a small bowl from the cabinet and did the same.

I didn't examine why I had done what I had, risking my own life to save a human. And not just any human. A witch. I didn't examine it, because I knew the reason. I needed her to save Kenya. Lizzy should have burned tonight. Now, she owed me a life.

Actually, she owed me two.

When I got back upstairs, she was sitting up in the middle of my bed, tears streaking down her dirty face as she pet the dog.

Had I been too late? "Is he..."

She didn't seem surprised to see me. Actually, she didn't even look up. "No." Her voice was raspy and raw. "He's breathing."

I set the bowl of water on the nightstand and handed her the glass. She looked up at me then. "Thank you," she said. She took a sip, then covered the front of her throat with her hand, wincing. "That hurts," she mumbled.

"You were in a fire," I told her. "You seemed to have inhaled a bit of smoke. Both of you." I nodded at the dog.

When she looked up at me again, her eyes were red and raw. From the smoke? Or from tears? "You got us out," she said in disbelief. "It seems I owe you."

"Yes, you do." I didn't need to explain what my payment would be. She had never struck me as a stupid woman. She knew what I wanted from her.

But, does she?

"I need to take Wiggles to the vet." She started to get off the bed. "He probably needs oxygen, or...or...something." On her feet, she looked around my room, confused, then started coughing. "Do you have a phone?" she asked when it stopped.

Yes. And she should probably be at a hospital. But that plan wasn't going to work for me. I'd just gotten her here. I had risked my life to do so. However, I could see by the determined look on her face she wasn't going to let this one go. So, a little bit of influence it was. "The bathroom is right there." I pointed to the door. "Why don't you go rinse your face and I'll see if I can find a number for an emergency vet and a blanket to carry him in."

"Okay. Thank you, Killian." In a sort of daze, she wandered into the bathroom and shut the door.

I looked at the dog passed out on my bed, his dirty little body ruining my comforter. Wiggles, wasn't it? "All right, boy. Let's get you fixed up." My fangs tingled in anticipation as I brought my wrist to my mouth. With a moan, I sank them into my own flesh, the coppery taste of my blood teasing my tongue. Grabbing the dog gently by the muzzle, I pried his mouth open and dripped a little of my blood down his throat. When I thought he'd had enough, I licked my wound closed as I massaged his throat with my other hand to force him to swallow. I didn't have a lot of time. Lizzy would be back in a second. "There you go, fella." She would now have her old dog for a few extra years.

I glanced at her water glass, wondering how badly her lungs were damaged. But sharing my blood had consequences I didn't think either of us were ready for. As it stood now, as long as the dog was with her, I'd be able to find her anywhere.

And maybe he wouldn't growl at me anymore.

But what if she was damaged?

I watched as his eyes blinked open. He stared up at me for a moment before his tongue fell out of his mouth and he started panting happily. Before I could make up my mind about whether I should do the same for her, Lizzy came back into the room. As soon as he saw her, the pup tried to sit up, so I sat on the bed and helped him get his stubby legs beneath him. "It looks like he's coming around," I told her.

She rushed over to us. The confusion was gone from her face, her eyes once again sharp. "Oh, thank God!" Running her hands all over him, she searched for other injuries as he licked her face with enthusiasm.

I laid my hand over one of hers, stopping her frantic movements. "He's all right, Lizzy. He's not hurt. Just took in a bit of smoke, like you. Luckily, your bedroom door was closed. And I was able to get to you both before the fire spread." Wiggles lived up to his name, wagging his back end and twisting around to lick my forearm.

An unfamiliar warmth filled my chest at this unexpected affection. "You're welcome," I told him quietly.

Lizzy glanced up at me. She'd taken my advice and washed the soot from her face, but her eyes were still red and her voice still raspy. She also smelled like a campfire.

And yet I couldn't keep from taking in every inch of her I could see like a male starved.

She sat down on the other side of the bed and I put Wiggles on the floor with his water bowl. He had half of it gone by the time I straightened up.

"Um, don't take this the wrong way," she told me. "I'm very grateful to you for getting us out of there. But, what exactly were you doing at my apartment? I never told you where I lived."

My answer, when it came, was honest. "Do you think that would keep me away from you, Lizzy?"

9

LIZZY

Somehow, I knew it was true. This man had me on his radar, and by the way he was looking at me, I didn't think I'd be coming off of it anytime soon.

I should have been scared. That was the normal reaction, right? If a man I barely knew basically told me he was a stalker, I should be breaking out into a cold sweat and feeling around for my phone to call the police. Except that my phone was probably a puddle of melted plastic and glass right now.

But if it wasn't, that was what *should* be happening in a situation like this. But with Killian, my reactions were far outside anything that was normal. I still had a brain in my head, though, even if it was a little hazy right now. "I appreciate you risking your life to save us. I truly do. But I need to go to the hospital. Or home. I have a home." I lost my track of thought as his black eyes caught mine.

"Not anymore. Lizzy, your entire kitchen was nearly in flames by the time I got you out. And the fire trucks were still blocks away. I don't see how they could've gotten there and put it out before most of your place was lost. I'm sorry," he said after a pause, but it didn't feel sincere.

It struck me then, at just that moment, that he was probably right. My apartment and everything in it was probably gone by now, and the only thing keeping me from freaking out was the fact that Wiggles was here and alive, and that I didn't really own much. I had left my life behind in NYC, and that included anything that held memories of my past. The little bit of furniture I'd had was second-hand. Just something to sit on. My bed had been cheap and uncomfortable, and I could replace my clothes. But I couldn't replace my best friend.

"But, I still don't understand. How did you get in?" My throat burned and my lungs ached with every breath. Talking was like trying to force words through a cheese grater. But I had questions. Questions I needed answers to now that my brain seemed to be coming back online. "The only way to get upstairs is by elevator, and you need a code. The stairway is also locked. And why didn't you wait for the firetrucks?"

I took in the bedroom I was in as I thought of questions. It wasn't huge, but it was luxurious enough to let me know we weren't in some tiny apartment. The huge painting of a green countryside on the wall above the bed probably cost thousands of dollars alone. "Where are we? Is this where you live?" I fell into a coughing fit, effectively ending my line of questioning as I bent over and tried to hack up a lung. Or maybe both of them.

"This is my home," he told me when I finally stopped. I noticed he'd stood up, one hand reaching toward me as though to try to help. I waved him off as I caught my breath, and his hand dropped back to his side, clenching into a fist as he took a step back. "But it's empty at the moment. I've been staying with my friend, the one who's sick. I'd like for you to stay here until you're recovered."

It wasn't an offer. It was an order.

Killian took off his sweater and laid it on the bed. "I can find you something clean to wear if you'd like to shower. And food. You're going to need food."

I wasn't sure if he was talking to me or himself with that last part. "You're not going to answer my questions?"

He studied me, his brow furrowed in thought. I noticed he was wearing all black again tonight. Standing the way he was, in this room, his obsidian eyes so intense, he seriously could've just walked off of the pages of a men's magazine.

But I would not let myself be swayed from my course. "Do you need me to repeat them?" I was sort of being a bitch. It wasn't really like me. Or hell, maybe it was and it had just taken me until I was almost forty to find this out about myself.

"No." He sighed. One hand absently rubbed the front of his right thigh. Then he proceeded to answer my questions in the order I'd asked them. "I got in through a window around the back of your building. Broke the glass and climbed through." He shrugged. "Nothing anyone else wouldn't do. I didn't wait for the fire trucks and ambulance to get there because I wanted to take care of you myself."

That last statement took me aback. But before I could think of anything to say, he continued on.

"As I said, this is my home. We are still in the Quarter. It's a...family home that is currently empty, and it would ease my mind greatly if someone were here. And if that someone had a killer watchdog"—he smiled at Wiggles, who wagged his butt when he noticed Killian's attention on him—"then that's even better. Um, let's see. What else?" He put his hands on his narrow hips, his head dropping forward in thought.

"I asked how you knew where I lived," I reminded him quietly.

His head came up. "Mmm. That." He took a step toward me. "I watched you go inside the night I walked you home."

Okay. That was entirely possible, even though I'd tried to make sure he wouldn't, but I could have easily missed him with so many other pedestrians. "But, why were you there tonight? In the middle of the night?"

Slow and careful, as though he didn't want to frighten me away, he took another step toward me. "I wanted to see you."

"Why? Because of your friend?"

"Partly."

"But I already told you I can't help her."

"I said 'partly'."

I stared at him, my heart pounding in my chest and my legs feeling more wobbly by the second. "Why did you want to see me?"

"To do this."

Killian was suddenly right in front of me, his delicious smell overtaking my senses. My hands went up, gripping the front of his shirt. Vaguely, I wondered why he didn't smell like smoke. He'd been in the apartment. He'd saved us. He should stink like I did.

As if in slow motion, his head dipped down close to mine. I closed my eyes, feeling like I couldn't catch my breath, and it had nothing at all to do with the smoke inhalation. He nuzzled the side of my neck, his lips warm as they brushed against my skin. I knew I smelled awful, but I couldn't bring myself to move away. I was completely frozen where I stood. And *so* very conscious of the large bed right behind me.

His breath feathered against my neck as he moaned in my ear, the sound so erotic I had to lock my knees to remain standing. Something scraped the side of my throat where my pulse beat a rapid staccato. "You smell so good," he whispered.

"I don't," I told him. "I need to shower."

He froze, then slowly straightened, turning his head away before I could see his face. "I'll get you some clothes." And then he walked out of the room.

The air rushed out of me so fast my head swam and I felt behind me, looking for the bed, before I ended up on the floor. My fingers scraped along the edge of the mattress and I let my knees give out with a grateful sigh.

Killian reappeared a few minutes later with an armful of clothes. "I think these should fit you. You're about the same size."

"Whose clothes are they?" From the colors, they appeared to be women's clothing, and I felt something sharp and painful stab me in the chest.

"They're Kenya's. My friend who's sick," he clarified. "She won't mind."

His *friend*. Whose clothes were at *his* house, even though he was currently staying at *hers*.

Yeah, got it.

I suddenly found myself wanting to burn her clothes in the fire. "Thank you, but I can just put my own stuff back on."

He looked at me as if I'd lost my mind. "Don't be ridiculous. Even if you washed them, I don't think you'd get the smoke smell out." He laid the borrowed clothes on the bed beside me.

I could tell he was waiting for me to say something, but I couldn't even bring myself to look at him for fear he would see the pettiness in my expression.

"All right, then," he said. "I'll leave you to it." When I still wouldn't look at him, he added, "I'll leave a key and the code for the gate on the table in the kitchen. Please make yourself at home. No one will bother you here. I'll come check on you tomorrow night, after you both get some rest."

He touched my hair, still in a messy knot on top of my head to keep it out of my face when I slept.

I finally got a grip on myself. "Thank you—" I started to say as I raised my head.

But he was gone.

A wave of weakness washed over me and I sank down onto the bed, staring at the plush carpet and breathing deep until it passed. Eventually, I wandered out of the bedroom, Wiggles on my heels, turning lights on as I went. "Killian?" But there was no sign of him.

I discovered I was on the first floor of the house. The bedroom I was in was at the end of the hall. Next to it was a full-sized study with bookshelves lining the walls. It contained a simple desk that held a large computer monitor. A simple leather chair was behind it, the seat turned as though someone had just been sitting there.

Wiggles sniffed around the desk, but finding no crumbs, he plopped himself down in the middle of the floor and watched me as I walked over to the closest shelf. My attention was immediately grabbed by what looked to be an ancient edition of Bram Stoker's *Dracula*, set inside a glass display box. Pulling it carefully from the shelf, I admired the tan cloth cover. Stamped on the front was a color image of Dracula's mountaintop castle. There were a few stains on the binding, but overall it was in excellent condition for something that looked so old. I was tempted to see if it was signed by the author, but I didn't want to risk damaging it.

Carefully putting the box back on the shelf, I walked the perimeter of the room, trailing my fingers along the spines of Killian's collection and trying very hard not to think about what had happened to me tonight. Because if I did, I feared I would break apart, and there was no one here to put me back together.

He had an eclectic library, ranging from what appeared to be first edition classics to more modern bestsellers both in the horror and suspense genres. There were even a few well-known romance novels thrown in.

The hall opened up into the kitchen, and as promised, I found a key and a piece of paper with the code to the gate on the redwood table. He'd also left me a note, written in neat, old-fashioned handwriting:

> Lizzy,
>
> I meant what I said. Please stay as long as you wish.
> You and Wiggles are safe here.
>
> Killian

I set the note back on the table with the key and checked out the kitchen. Once again, the room wasn't overly large, but it was built of the finest materials: hardwood floors, wooden cabinets with fancy little designs carved into the doors, stainless steel appliances, and a large island in the middle. The counters were the color of wet concrete with red-brown veins that matched the cabinets.

The refrigerator was completely empty, as was the pantry. In the third cabinet I found a bottle of mango flavored vodka. "This will work." I opened doors until I found a glass, filled it with ice, and took that and the bottle of vodka back into the bedroom. Tomorrow, I'd explore the rest of the house and figure out how to get my life back together. Right now, I was exhausted, suffering from smoke exposure, probably a little bit in shock, and I needed a shower. And so did Wiggles. But his would have to wait until I could get some doggy shampoo.

I thought I would feel weird sleeping in his bed, but that wasn't the case. Finally clean, with wet hair and dressed in a long T-shirt I'd found in his dresser—because I couldn't get past my own weirdness about wearing that woman's clothes—I put Wiggles on a towel on the bed, climbed in, and drifted off as soon as my head hit the pillow, my glass of vodka on the nightstand beside me.

For tonight, I would sleep. Tomorrow I would face the rest of the world.

The rest of the world being my aunt.

10

LIZZY

I was late getting to my store the next day. Wiggles and I had both been dead to the world until well past noon. Since there was no coffee or food in the house—something I needed to remedy later today—I stopped at Cafe Du Monde.

Geared with a stomach full of beignets and a fresh cup of coffee in my hand, I unlocked the door to my shop to find my aunt was already inside. "Hey, Aunt Jude. I didn't realize you still had a key."

She shrugged a round shoulder. "Just in case," she told me with a partial smile.

With her was a good-looking guy with olive-colored skin and short dark hair and eyes, plus three other women not much younger than me. Including the woman with the red hair who'd been hanging out with Mike the other night.

The other two were equally as pretty. One was tall with long, straight, black hair and pale green eyes. Her left eyebrow was pierced with a silver bar capped with red gems, and both of her ears were pierced with diamond studs all the way to the top. She wore ripped jeans and a long-sleeved, black shirt with a glittery green skull on the front.

The other was a little bit of a thing who probably looked much younger than she was. She had dark, honey-blonde hair that fell in soft waves down past her shoulders and deep brown eyes with hints of gold. Her loose, burgundy dress and brown ankle boots were the perfect complement to her guileless face and excited smile. Her style appeared to be a mix of Oliver Twist and The Handmaid's Tale.

Closing and locking the door behind me, I decided to try with the redhead again. "Angel, wasn't it?"

"Yeah." The word was heavy with attitude I didn't understand, but at least she had the decency to respond. She even managed to look slightly chagrined when my aunt gave her a disapproving look.

Aunt Judy met me in the middle of the store and I bent down so she could give me a kiss on the cheek. "How are you, hon?"

"I'm good. Just wondering what's going on," I told her honestly.

"Where's Wiggles?

"He's...home. Napping. As usual." Actually, I'd left him sleeping contentedly in the sun on a chair in Killian's room. I was kind of surprised when he didn't snuffle around for his food bowl that morning, but also grateful as I'd had nothing to feed him. Maybe the exposure to the smoke was messing with his appetite. I'd have to give him extra treats tonight after I stopped at the store. "Who are all these people?" I asked just loud enough for them to hear me, and then tilted my head discreetly toward the people gathered around the checkout counter. I would tell Aunt Jude about the fire later when we were alone. I was sure she'd invite us to come and stay with her until I found something else, and I'd already decided to take her up on her offer. I wasn't even going to tell her where we stayed last night. I'd just say we were at a hotel. There was no need to worry her. Nothing had happened with Killian and...

Well, nothing that needed to be mentioned, anyway.

A shiver ran down my spine. I could still feel his teeth grazing my throat.

My aunt took my hand and walked me over to make introductions, pulling me from my memories. "Lizzy, I'd like you to meet Alex, Alice, Talin, and it appears you've already met Angel?"

"I did," I said. To Talin I joked, "Looks like you and I are the odd balls out."

She frowned, her eerie green eyes flickering between me and my aunt.

I pointed back and forth between us. "Lizzy. Talin. The only ones without an 'A' name..." When she just looked at me I gave up and turned to Angel.

"You met up with Mike the other night, right?"

She gave my aunt a sideways look before giving me a simple, "Mmm-hmm."

"Mike?" Aunt Judy asked. "Your assistant?"

"That would be him." There was a lot of subterfuge going on here I didn't really understand. My aunt didn't look happy about Angel's new friend. "He's a great guy," I told her, feeling the need to defend him, even though I didn't know why. But what I was really wondering was who these people were to her and why she would even care. "So, what's going on? Why the super-secret meeting?" I meant it as a joke, but no one even cracked a smile.

"I'm kind of wondering that myself," Alex told her. His voice was deep, and just raspy enough to sound more "sex" and less "I drink too much and scream at strangers in the street".

Aunt Judy came to stand beside me. "Everyone, I'd like you to meet my brother's daughter, my niece, Lizzy...Smith."

I noticed the slight pause with the last name I'd chosen for myself in my attempts to separate myself from my past as much as possible, but didn't have time to wonder about it as all eyes were suddenly on me. I read varying levels of emotions in those looks, from pleasantly surprised by sweet-looking Alice to downright hostile from Angel.

"And, so...what? She's your niece so you expect us to just bring her into the fold?" Angel asked her.

"She has as much right to be here as any of you," my aunt told her.

"I agree," Alice said. "I felt it as soon as she walked in. Alex?"

His eyes were thoughtful as they assessed me. "Yeah, I felt it."

"Talin?"

She'd been quiet up until now, and when she finally spoke, I could hear just the slightest bit of distrust in her voice. "Yes, it's there."

The tension in the room had just shot up a crazy amount, and I tried to bring it down to a suitable level. "Does this mean I get to be in the knitting club, or...?"

Angel gave me a look of disgust. "She doesn't even take this seriously. How do you expect us to accept her?"

"She's family," my aunt told her. "That why we're all here."

"Why are you just bringing her around now?" Talin asked.

"Because she didn't know about our history until just the other night at dinner. You all are probably too young to remember, but her mother took her away when she was twelve. She never told Lizzy about any of you. The only reason I was allowed to see her was because I promised I wouldn't talk about it." She rubbed my back in what was meant to be a comforting gesture but just made me feel like a child again. "She didn't know she comes from a magical family, or that she herself has any abilities."

"Maybe we should keep it that way," Alex said. "It could be too dangerous to bring her in now." He turned his attention to me. "You're like, what? Forty?"

"I'm thirty-eight," I informed him. He looked around the same age as me, so I couldn't imagine why I was being discriminated against. I've lived with whatever was inside of me as long as he's lived with whatever was inside of him.

"She's too old," he said. "How will she ever learn to control it?" He glanced around at the others, who seemed to be in agreement for the most part.

"That's exactly why she needs us. What will happen if she doesn't?" my aunt asked them all. "We're lucky she hasn't accidentally turned someone into a toad in the middle of Manhattan." There was laughter in her tone at the thought, but I could see she was also perfectly serious.

Everyone started talking. At my aunt. At each other. Anywhere but at me.

I listened for a full minute before I'd had enough. Setting my coffee on the counter, I threw both hands in the air, palms out, effectively getting everyone's attention. "I would really appreciate it if you all would stop talking about me like I wasn't here. I'm a grown woman, not a child."

They all turned to me like they just remembered I was there.

Aunt Judy was the only one who had the decency to look ashamed. "You're absolutely right, Lizzy. I'm sorry. This is your decision as much as it is ours."

"Maybe if we showed her," Alice suggested.

"I agree," Aunt Judy told her. Then she took my arm and turned me toward the back of the shop. "Come on, honey, there's something I need to show you."

Angel stepped to the side, blocking our path. "I don't agree with this, Judy."

"Noted," my aunt responded. "Now, get the fuck out of my way."

For a moment I was too shocked to move. Not because of what she'd said, but because of the authority and strength in her tone. And by the way Angel's eyes widened in fear before she obediently moved aside.

"Come on, Lizzy."

My curiosity was piqued as I followed her back to the storeroom, both about this relative I thought I kinda knew and what she was about to show me. The rest of the group fell in silently behind us. Aunt Judy flicked on the light, then made her way between the shelves filled with boxes of items for the store. For a minute, I thought she was leading us out the back door, but instead, she squeezed between the wall and the end of a rack of shelves.

"Alex?"

He stepped around the girls and took a hold of the other end. Together, they moved it away from the wall. My aunt took a key from her pocket and inserted it into a lock in the wall I'd never noticed before. Only it wasn't *only* a lock, it was a door, perfectly disguised within the wall.

"Judy..."

My aunt's head whipped around. "Hush, Angel! This is happening. It *needs* to happen before she accidentally hurts someone. Lizzy has been out of our reach for too long. And if you can't get on board with that, then you are welcome to leave."

I had the distinct feeling she meant something much more than just leaving the store, for what little color Angel had in her face drained away until she was as pale as a ghost. No one else dared to protest that ultimatum, and after that Angel kept her head down and wouldn't look at me.

Great. As if she didn't already hate me enough. Not that I really cared. But it would make things even more uncomfortable if she was going to make a habit of meeting up with Mike here.

Aunt Judy turned to me. "Lizzy, all I'm asking is that you keep an open mind and hear me out. Then you can make your own choice about what you want to do with the information I'm about to give you. Deal?"

"Deal," I agreed. There was no way I was missing whatever big family secret I was about to be exposed to.

I didn't see her open the door, but suddenly I was looking into the inky blackness of some sort of secret room. My aunt walked into the darkness and candles flared to life, revealing a long rectangular room that ran parallel to the side wall of my store. It was wide enough for everyone to fit inside, yet narrow enough that it wasn't a noticeable flaw in the building from the street.

"Come on, Lizzy."

I looked up to see Alex beside me, waiting for me to proceed him into the room. The others were already inside standing to either side of my aunt. There was a table against the far wall with a chalice in the center. A wooden bowl and pestle sat beside it. Dried herbs hung from the ceiling. Large white candles lined the back, the light of their flames casting shadows on the brick wall behind them.

Next to the big table was a smaller table. A large, black, hardbound book took up most of its surface. The other side of the room contained a few high shelves with more candles and jars filled with various items. I couldn't even begin to try to guess what was inside of them. "What is this?" It looked like some kind of séance room. All it was missing was the Ouija board and Tarot cards. Or maybe a crystal ball. I couldn't believe this had all been back here all this time and I didn't know it.

"Lizzy, this rowdy crew I brought here with me today is your family. Cousins, to be exact. Alex and Alice are your first cousins from your Aunt Charlotte, my sister. Talin and Angel are more distant, but still family, nonetheless."

Family. The word meant little to me. As I'd learned from my mother and father, blood did not make you family. My father had never been in my life. He left us when I was an infant and no one knew where he was now. And my mother, though she had loved me and I her, had always kept me at arm's length. We never really connected, and it had only gotten worse the older I'd become. I'd mourned her when she'd died, but I'd never really missed her. I didn't feel guilty about it, it just was the way it was. And I think she would understand.

So, this big reveal did not have the shock value on me I think my aunt was expecting. It didn't flood me with emotion, or hope, or some kind of instant love. "Okay. Nice to meet you all again." I didn't know what else to say. But they were all staring at me so I felt the need to say *something*.

Aunt Judy tilted her head, her expression thoughtful. I was beginning to feel like I didn't know her at all, and that bothered me. Out of every relative of mine, she was the only one I'd ever felt remotely close to, even with all the years we'd spent apart.

"I'm going to be blunt with you, hon. I think that will be the best way to do this."

"Please," I told her. But once that was decided, she appeared to be at a loss for words. "So, I assume this room isn't some Halloween joke? A tourist attraction? Some weird séance meetup place?"

"No, hon. This room is warded against anyone who might want to overhear what we're doing in here. We could literally be screaming our heads off and no would hear us."

"Not even if they were standing right there in the storeroom?"

Aunt Judy shook her head. "This is the safest place to have these kinds of discussions."

I rubbed my forehead and pushed my fingers into my hair. "Ok, so, I get that you think you're all a bunch of witches—"

"Not just us. You, too," Alex said.

My arms fell to my sides as I barked out a short laugh. "I'm sorry to disappoint you, but I'm no witch. I can't even keep a cake from collapsing in the oven."

"There's a spell for that," Alice told me.

I stared at her, half wondering if they were all crazy and half wondering if the spell would really work because I really liked cake.

"Ever set fire to anything without matches?"

I met Angel's hostile look with one of my own. The question wasn't hypothetical.

Motherfucker. She knew about me. Knew what I'd done in New York, and apparently to my own apartment last night while I was sleeping. I looked at each of them in turn. None of them were surprised by the question. "You all know about me." But that was impossible. I'd never told anyone anything about the fire in New York, and my apartment had just burned down last night.

Alice and Alex exchanged frowns. Then they did the same with Talin before she shook her head. "We didn't know anything about you until just today."

"If we had, it might have made all of this easier." Although the statement was directed at me, Talin was looking at my...*our* aunt.

She didn't rise to the bait. "No one knows anything about you, Lizzy. Not even me. Not really. Your mother took you away from us before any magic you might possess became apparent. And that's exactly what we're here to discover."

"I don't understand how my mother knew about all of this. About all of you," I pointed to my newfound cousins. "And never told me."

"She did," Talin told me. "I remember my parents talking about her. I use to wonder about this 'secret' cousin of mine." Leaning back against the table, she crossed her arms over her chest. "At least when I was a kid. Honestly, I'd forgotten about you."

"Thanks."

She shrugged. "I was thirteen. I had other things to worry about."

"Like what guy you were going to fuck that weekend?" Angel asked her.

"Fuck off," Talin responded. The words were said almost automatically, like they'd had similar exchanges so many times before the passion behind it was gone but she still told her off out of habit.

Alice smiled at me. "I'd love to get to know you now, Lizzy."

Her sincerity was a bit overwhelming for me. To stabilize myself, I focused on my aunt, but she was watching the others.

"We're getting sidetracked here," Angel said. "You never answered my question."

"Or, did she?" Talin asked her.

"Lizzy?"

I looked back at my aunt. There was no way in hell I was going to admit what had happened in New York. I didn't trust any of these people. I didn't even know if I trusted my aunt after all of this.

As if she could see my indecision, she said, "You need to tell us, Lizzy."

No. No, I didn't. I would end up in jail. Or worse. A mental facility.

I was suddenly angry. "If you're so concerned about all of this, why are you waiting until just now to say anything?" I asked my aunt. "I would think if you were so worried about me and what I could or couldn't do you wouldn't have waited until I was almost forty to throw all of this at me."

"Lizzy..."

"You know what? I think it's time you all got out of my store. And I'd like my spare key back, please."

No one moved.

"I mean it. I own this store now. It's mine. And I want you all out."

My aunt studied me for a moment. "Do as she says," she told them.

Angel and Talin flounced out of there like they couldn't wait to leave. Alex trailed behind them, with Alice being the last to go.

The light from the storeroom streamed in though the open door, and Aunt Judy murmured some words I couldn't quite hear. The candles all went out simultaneously.

The hair stood up on the back of my neck, but I still had the presence of mind to hold out my hand for the key as she walked past. "'The key to this room, too," I told her.

After a brief pause, she dropped it into my palm, along with her key to the store. "Call me when you're ready to talk some more about this," she said. Then she followed the others out.

Once I made sure they had all left the store and I'd locked the door behind them, I went back into the storeroom and shut and locked the door to the secret room. Then I yanked and tugged the rack of shelves back into its place against the wall.

I stepped back and stared at the wall.

There was no sign of a door or a lock that I could see.

11

KILLIAN

I knew right away she was still at my house. The small amount of my blood I'd given her dog led me to them both like a lighthouse in a storm.

The forceful rush of relief I felt, when it came, was a surprise to me. Because I had the uneasy feeling it had very little to do with the reason I was here again.

Kenya was getting worse every night now. I'd gone in to see her before I left the house. The spell had progressed to such a point that for the first time, I felt true fear she would leave me before I could return with the witch.

But when she saw the determination on my face and I'd told her I was planning to come straight here, she'd begged me to try to convince Lizzy once again to help her willingly, instead of going with my original plan. I was tired of this game. There was no time to play nice. Not when I could see the life draining from Kenya's eyes with every hour that passed. But, nonetheless, I'd agreed.

After checking I wasn't being watched by any curious eyes, I let myself in through the side gate and walked through the courtyard to the back door. I was momentarily surprised to find it locked. Although I don't know why. What did I expect? That she would have the door open wide and be waiting with open arms for me to kidnap her?

I debated breaking it down out of sheer frustration for about half a second. It would take very little effort on my part. But it would also mean replacing the original door with something more modern. And I liked my house the way it was. Removing my hand from the doorknob, I backed up a step, took a breath, and rapped gently on the wood. "It's me," I called when I heard her footsteps on the other side of the door.

When she opened the door, I unconsciously backed up another step. I thought I'd prepared myself for the hit the sight and smell of her would have on me. But I'd completely forgotten how potent it was on both counts. Staring at her standing there, my fangs shot down and every muscle in my body tightened as the predator inside of me took over before I could get a handle on it.

And then she smiled, and I lost my breath, not catching it again until it faded uneasily from her face as her eyes took in the tightness of my jaw and my fists clenched at my sides.

"Hey," she said.

I could hear the nervous tremor in her voice, still the slightest bit raspy from the fire. It snapped me from my trance. "I just came to check on you." I mumbled the words to keep my fangs hidden.

She was dressed in Kenya's clothes I'd brought to her the night before, black knit pants and a soft winter pullover. Pink and white plaid. It complimented the blush in her cheeks beautifully. With her dark hair and eyes, she looked so innocent. Young. Vulnerable. Despite the fact she had to be in her thirties.

As my eyes traveled over her, she looked down at the clothes she was wearing. "I'll go shopping and pick up a few things tomorrow," she said. "I didn't have time today."

"You don't have to worry about all that," I told her. "Kenya is more than happy to share with you. She has tons of clothes."

"Still, they're not mine." She stood, undecided as to whether or not to invite me in. I didn't need an invitation to enter my own home. It was one of the reasons I'd brought her here. But I let her work it out for herself. It didn't take long. "Would you like to come in? I was just making something to eat."

Now that she mentioned it, something was burning. "I think you might want to go check on that."

She blinked rapidly a few times, then suddenly turned and rushed over to the stove, leaving me standing on the other side of the threshold.

I let myself in and closed and locked the door behind me. As I watched Lizzy move around my kitchen as though she'd lived here for years, my throat burned with thirst and my fangs ached to sink into the taut flesh of her throat.

However, with Kenya's plea still ringing loudly in my head, I decided I would give her this last chance to decide to help me. If, by the end of the night, she still refused to try, I would make the choice for her. If I planned it right, I could have her bound and gagged before she had a chance to cast her magic on me. I just had to get to my bedroom closet.

I heard a bark to my right and looked over to see Wiggles trotting toward me. When he got within a few feet of where I stood, he stopped abruptly, cloudy eyes staring up at me intently as he tried to make out who I was. "Hey now, buddy. There's no need for any of that."

He inched forward cautiously until he could get a good whiff of my leg, and then he yowled, ending it on a happy little whine as his entire chubby body began to wag back and forth. Something caught in my chest as I bent down to give him a pet. His black fur was short and soft beneath my palm, his little heart pounding with excitement. Pulling the nearest chair out from the kitchen table, I picked him up onto my lap. After he got over his excitement, he gave me a few good extra licks on my chin, then found a comfortable position and settled down for a snuggle.

My eyes stung a bit as I rubbed his satiny ears. Apparently, all it took to have the unconditional love of a pet was to give it a little of my blood. I only wished it worked that easily with my vampires.

When I looked up, Lizzy was watching us silently from her place in front of the stove, a stirring spoon suspended from one hand. Her eyes caught mine.

"What?" I asked her.

She shook her head. "Nothing. He just doesn't usually take to men very well."

"Maybe he's just grateful I got him out of the fire, and saved his favorite human while I was at it."

"Maybe."

My reward for that answer was another smile.

"I know I said this last night, but thank you again. You really did save us. And now you're letting us stay here in your beautiful house and everything." She waved the spoon down the front of her body, again pointing out the borrowed clothes she was wearing, and drawing my eyes to her luscious figure. Lizzy had a body that was made to be loved, and loved well. Combine the sight of her with the sweet scent of her blood and it was a wonder I could stay sitting here at all.

I gave myself an internal shake. I needed to concentrate on why I was here. And the first thing to do was get her to open up to me. "I was wondering if you'd still be here. I know you have family in town."

She gave me an odd look before she turned around to check on her dinner. A stir-fry if my sense of smell was correct. "My aunt and I had a disagreement. Staying with her would be uncomfortable right now, to be honest."

"Your aunt?"

"My Aunt Judy. She lives here in town."

So, she *was* one of them. There was only one "Judy" I knew of that she could possibly be related to. Judy Moss, the high priestess of the witch's coven. The thing with Angel I saw must've been something within the coven. "Then I'm very glad my place was available for you."

Pulling the pan from the burner, she turned off the heat, then walked over to the sink to wash her hands. She moved with the elegant grace of a dancer. I discovered in that moment how much I loved to watch her. The natural sway of her hips, the curve of her spine, the slight bounce of her breasts, the confident way she held her head. Even the way her long hair slid like silk over her shoulder when she turned her head to look at me.

"Killian? Did you hear what I said?"

I had, I'd just ignored it. "I won't take your money, Lizzy."

"I insist," she argued. "I can't pay much, but I can pay you what my apartment cost me in rent. It should at least take care of the water and electricity I'm using, plus a little extra."

"The water and electric were already on. And I doubt one person would use very much at all. You'll be at your store most days, anyway. Am I right?"

"Killian."

I could tell by the set of her jaw and the glint of steel in her eyes she wasn't going to take no for an answer. I sighed and gave her a slight roll of my eyes. "Fine. You can pay me. Starting the first of the month if you both are still here." As it was the beginning of November, I could guarantee the only way she'd still be here by then is if she cured Kenya and became one of us, something that seemed much more farfetched now that I knew who her family was. I ran my hand over Wiggles, enjoying the texture of his silky ears on my fingertips, and wondered what Lizzy's skin would feel like to my sensitive touch.

"Please, allow me to pay you now, Killian. It would make me feel less like a...like a..."

"A pauper?" I inserted playfully, playing my part.

"I was going to say mistress, but I guess what you said is more accurate."

Mistress. Images of Lizzy naked and writhing beneath me flooded my head. My blood surged into my groin and I closed my eyes to hide the hunger I knew she'd see. My jeans were suddenly horribly uncomfortable, the zipper digging into my swollen cock.

How I hungered for this woman. Her blood. Her body. Even her mind. I wanted it all.

Lizzy studied me intently and I quickly dropped my head. Breathing through my mouth, I concentrated on petting my new friend until I could control the lust screaming through my body. Reminding myself over and over of my promise to Kenya not to be forceful with her.

"Would you like some of this? It's just a stir-fry. There should be enough. If not, I have some other stuff in the fridge I picked up earlier. I could whip something up."

I interrupted her before she started rattling off a list. "I'm not hungry." Not for what she was offering. "But I would love to keep you company while you eat."

As she found herself a plate and filled it with her dinner, I put Wiggles on the floor and got a couple of wine glasses out of the cabinet. Kenya always kept some good wine in the bottom of the fridge, and she did not disappoint me. Alcohol didn't affect us. Our metabolism burned it away as quickly as we could consume it. But she loved the taste, as did I, along with a good whiskey. I poured us both a glass. When I turned around, Lizzy was sitting at the table.

Her eyes dropped to my cock, still hard and quite obvious in my jeans. Her lips parted, and I heard her quick inhale before she searched out my face.

A low growl formed in my throat, but I caught it before I showed her exactly what she should be worried about.

"Um, you have dog hair all over your jeans." She popped up out of her chair. "I have one of those sticky roller things."

Dog hair was not what she was thinking about. And that scared her, because she didn't trust me. "Lizzy."

She froze.

"Sit down and eat your dinner. Please," I added.

Keeping her eyes carefully on my face, she sat.

Carrying over both glasses and the bottle, I set one of the wineglasses in front of her and took a seat on the other side of the square table, directly across from her so I could watch her expressions as we talked. Though she picked up her fork, she just held it in her hand as her eyes shifting around the table. Looking for a weapon, perhaps? I listened in on her thoughts for a moment. Yes, that's exactly what she was doing. "You don't have to be scared, Lizzy. I'm not going to hurt you." And I wouldn't. Not yet. "But I can't control my body's reaction to being so near a woman such as yourself." I held my arms out to either side. "I am just a male, after all."

She didn't try to deny her fear or play it off with false bravado. She also didn't act like some fearful virgin. She was just a woman who was prepared to defend herself if she had to. I admired that about her.

"Is my aunt right about you?" she blurted. "That I should stay away from you. I haven't even told her what happened last night. Or that I'm staying here."

Good. I hope she kept it that way. "You told her about me, did you?" I was strangely flattered.

"Yes, after you came into the store and walked me home."

So, Judy didn't tell her what I am. "What do you think?"

"Well, Wiggles has taken to you. So, you can't be all bad."

That brought a smile to my face. If she only knew the reason behind his sudden change of heart. "I guess you'll just have to make up your own mind about that, then."

She took a bite of her dinner, her expression thoughtful. "So, you're from Ireland."

"I am." I swirled the wine in my glass before taking a sip. Kenya truly had fine taste in wines.

"What's it like there?"

"Cold," I told her. "And wet. And very green."

"Is your family still there?"

So we were doing *this*. "Not anymore."

"Where are they? Are they here with you?"

"The family that matters is, yes."

"Like your friend who's sick."

Rolling the stem of the wine glass between my palms, I nodded. "Yes. Like her."

A flash of something flew across her face. But it was there and gone before I could catch what it meant. I tried probing her bent head with my mind, but there were no clues there, either. Actually, she was singing a song to herself.

I almost smiled. She was catching on to me. Whether she truly believed it or not.

"Why did you leave Ireland?" she asked after a moment.

"Because it was too cold and too wet, and I was too poor." That was not a lie. "So, I came to the land of opportunity." I held up my glass in a toast, then drained it before refilling it.

Setting down her fork, she picked up her wine and leaned back in her chair. "You make it sound like you came over here in the nineteenth century."

I mimicked her posture. It made humans feel more comfortable when you acted more like they did. Breathing. Moving your limbs every once in a while. Even though it was easy for me to sit completely motionless for hours at a time. "Perhaps I did."

"That would make you over a hundred years old."

It was time for a change of subject. For now, anyway. "Tell me why you left New York."

The only sounds in the quiet of the kitchen were the soft snores of her dog, the beating of her heart, and her own steady breathing. A clock ticked in my office. And outside, a group of people discussed what restaurant had the best Hurricanes as they walked by.

She frowned slightly, looking down into her glass. "I told you why the night you walked into my store asking me a bunch of questions and begging me to come heal your friend."

"Yes, but now I would like to know the entire story." I'd caught flashes of things she hadn't said that night, but I wanted to hear it from her lips.

"Why? What does it matter?"

That was a very good question. "I think you know things, Lizzy. About yourself. Things you don't share with anyone."

"And you think I should share these things with you?"

"I do."

"What makes you so special?" The words weren't said with malice, but with a genuine curiosity.

I had to laugh a little at that. "Nothing, except perhaps that I can help you not be afraid of who you truly are." A memory flashed through her mind. Something recent. She was in a room lit with candles. Others were there, but it was gone before I could identify them.

Interesting.

"What do you know about your family here?" I asked her.

"Oh, I'm finding out more and more all the time," she told me as she grabbed the wine bottle to refill her glass, sarcasm dripping from her voice. She didn't sound like the reunion was all she'd hoped it would be.

"Tell me about New York."

A wistful smile teased the corners of her mouth. "I loved New York."

"Then why leave?"

She pressed her lips together as she swirled the wine in her glass, tilting it this way and that and holding it up to the light to see the legs it left on the glass.

I could pull the story from her mind, however, doing that would not only reveal she was right about my mind reading abilities but it would also break what fragile trust I'd managed to build so far. "You can trust me, Lizzy."

"I don't know that that's true."

"Touché," I told her. Setting my glass down on the table, I leaned forward and laced my fingers together. With a casual shrug I told her, "I already think you're a witch. I don't know that there's anything you can tell me that would surprise me, or make me think badly of you."

"You're not the only one who thinks I'm a witch," she mumbled quietly. So quiet, I knew it wasn't meant for my ears. After a pause, she said, "But I guess that's true enough. And honestly, it'd be nice to have somebody to talk to about it."

"So, tell me," I told her. "Tomorrow we can blame it on the wine and laugh it off as a night of telling tales. No harm done." I felt something within her click as she stared at me.

"Well, in that case," she said. "Pour me another glass."

I did a she asked, then went to get another bottle from the fridge and poured one for myself.

And then I waited.

12

LIZZY

I don't know what I was thinking.

In the bright light of the morning sun the following day, my head aching from all the wine I'd drank, I could easily blame my loose tongue on the alcohol as Killian had suggested. But the fact of the matter was, it wasn't just the wine that made me open up to him.

Maybe it was because I sensed some type of kindred spirit. Or maybe I just needed to tell someone who wouldn't think I was crazy. Someone other than my aunt who was trying to recruit me into her cult. Someone who would listen without judging me, for I sensed that no matter what I told Killian, no matter what I'd done, he wouldn't judge me. Because there was a darkness in him that spoke of things far worse.

Maybe I just needed to confess my sins.

As I started to tell him about my time in New York, my aunt's warning drifted through my head. And maybe she was right. Maybe I was crazy to trust him. But then again, maybe not.

"My mom moved us to New York when I was twelve," I told him. "First upstate and then down to the city. My father ran off when I was young, and she spent way too many years waiting around for him to come back. When she finally realized that wasn't going to happen, she decided to leave the south and start new somewhere else."

"But you had family here," he'd said. "I would imagine that would be helpful when you are a single mom on your own."

"Not really. The only family she allowed me to see was my aunt. Of course, I didn't know that. I only recently discovered I have a slew of cousins I'd never known about." My soft laughter was hurt and awkward.

"Why didn't she let you see your family?"

"At the time, I had no idea about them so it didn't matter. Now, I know it was because they're all fucking crazy."

He laughed, the sound rich and warm, heating my insides much more efficiently than the wine. "I can understand that." There was a thread of familiarity in his tone. But before I could explore that further, he brought the conversation back around to my life growing up. "So, you grew up in New York City."

I nodded.

"What made you decide you wanted to be on Broadway?"

"Oh, well, that one's easy," I told him. "Shortly after we got to the city, my mom took me to see *The Phantom of the Opera*." I remembered every minute detail like it was yesterday. "And from the very first opening notes, when the chandelier lights exploded and the music started, I was in love. The stage, the sets, the music...it all gave me chills." I paused as I remembered. "It was completely overwhelming and yet, I'd never seen or heard anything more beautiful. I decided right then and there I wanted to be one of those people who could create this feeling in people. So, I begged my mom to put me into dance lessons. And she did. I eventually added voice training and acting lessons. I worked my ass off all through high school and into my twenties."

"So you've always been a student of the arts."

"Yes and no. I also got a degree in business because that's what my mother wanted me to do. She was an executive, and assumed I would do the same once I'd burned out this crazy idea. She always told me getting her degree was the one smart thing she'd done in her life. I landed an entry level job at a tech company, gradually working my way up through the company. And, in the meantime, I started auditioning. I landed some very minor roles here and there on a few of the smaller shows. Nothing to brag about." I stopped for a sip of my wine. "Up until she died, my mom never supported that part of my life. She told me I didn't have 'it'. Told me I was too old. That if I hadn't gotten a part yet, no one was going to give me a chance, and blah, blah, blah. I was starting to believe her." I looked up to find I had

Killian's complete attention. "And then I landed a major role in a new musical."

I sat there lost to my thoughts for a while as I remembered the thrill of getting the callback. I must have sat there for a long time, because he nudged me on with a soft, "Go on."

"My best friend had gotten a part, too," I told him. "I was so excited we were going to share the stage. Debbie, not so much. We'd both auditioned for the main part. And for the first time, I was the one who got it, and she was placed in a role with less stage time. When they finished casting, a bunch of us went out to celebrate. Me, Debbie, and five of the other actors. We hit the town hard. We drank. We danced. We dined. We drank some more, and danced some more. And somewhere in all of that, I had the bright idea to share something with Debbie, something I'd kept hidden from everyone but my mom, who had told me my entire life I would get locked up if I started running around showing people my true self."

"What's so wrong with being yourself?"

My heart ached as my mother's face, twisted in disgust and fear, flashed through my mind. "Everything, apparently." I finished my wine and held my glass out for more. "But I was tired of hiding. So, in the middle of the dance floor of a crowded New York City club, I, in my drunken state of mind, stopped dancing and did the one trick I'd figured out how to control. I opened my fist to reveal a flame dancing on my palm."

"But it wasn't a trick."

I shook my head. "No."

Something flickered behind his eyes. There and gone so fast I wondered if I'd imagined it. "What did your friend do?" he asked.

"At first, she laughed. When I showed her another flame in my other hand, she stopped dancing. Then her blue eyes bugged out and she grabbed my wrist and dragged me over to the rest of the group. 'Show them,' she demanded. 'Show them what you just showed me.' Five sets of bloodshot eyes turned my way as I tried not to fall in the heels that I'd had no problems dancing in a minute ago." I laughed self-consciously and held my hands out, palms up. "I held my hands like this so they could see nothing was there."

I closed my fists and thought about fire. First just a spark. Then the way the flames flickered. I felt a flare of heat dance across my palms and focused it into the center. Then I opened them again.

In the centers of both of my palms were little, flickering flames.

Killian glanced down at the fires briefly, then back up to my face. He showed no shock, no fear, no reaction at all.

"They freaked out. The guy closest to me shoved his chair back and stood up. 'Holy shit,' he'd said. 'How the hell did you do that?' There were other things I could do, too. New things I discovered every day. But I didn't want them to think I was a complete freak. So, as Debbie laughed hysterically beside me and the rest of them stared in horror my palms, I closed my fists," I closed them tight and lowered my arms, "and put out the flames. I tried to play it off to them, realizing my mistake too late. Finally, I just offered to buy everyone drinks and Debbie and I headed off to the bar. Other than some odd looks here and there, the rest of the night was fairly uneventful."

"But that wasn't the end of it, was it, Lizzy?"

"No." I shook my head, then frowned when it took a few seconds for everything to come into focus again. "I'd thought it was. I thought nobody would remember. We were all so, so drunk. Or, if they did remember, they would just think it had been some kind of amazing trick I'd done and they'd been stupid to believe it. I really thought they would all forget about it. But I was wrong."

"What happened?"

I looked up to find Killian staring at me intently. "I guess I overestimated their loyalty to me," I told him. "Two days later when we started rehearsals, no one would talk to me. The group I'd gone out with—people I'd known for years as we all auditioned for the same shows—acted like I was some sort of pariah. Even Debbie. Everywhere I went, I heard whispers behind my back." I laughed again, but this time it was ugly. "It was like being in high school again. Only worse, because this was my career. This was something I had fought for. Something I'd poured blood, sweat, and tears into. And sooo many blisters."

"What did you do?"

"The only thing I could. I ignored them. I went to rehearsals. I danced and I sang and I played my role. I ignored the looks and the whispers and the rumors that were spreading about me. Gradually, it all started to die down. And I thought to myself, 'Thank God. Now we can all get on with our lives and they can find something else to gossip about.' But I was wrong. They weren't done with me, yet. Debbie, the person who I'd thought was my best friend, and the one I'd always supported every time she bagged a role, was not so gracious when the shoe was on the other foot. Apparently, she was out and out pissed she hadn't gotten the part. And had only gotten more so when her attempts at ostracizing me didn't get the results she'd wanted. So, at our last rehearsal before opening night, she shoved me near the edge of the stage, and I went sideways down the stairs. It was impossible to catch myself, I was going too fast. The momentum was too much. And in my efforts to stop my fall, my foot caught on the edge of one of the steps and I twisted my knee as I landed hard on the other, banging my head off the floor. She timed it just right to look like an accident, but I felt her hands on my ribcage. I felt her push me."

A low growl filled the room, making the tiny hairs on the back of my neck stand straight up, and I looked around the room for Wiggles, wondering what he was grumbling about. But he was sound asleep on the cold tile floor. I started to ask Killian if he'd heard it, but when my gaze clashed with his, I lost all track of thought.

His eyes were blacker than I'd ever seen them. His jaw clenched so tight I could see the muscles clenching. In my wine induced haze, I think I smiled.

My dark, vengeful angel.

"Don't worry," I told him. "I got back at all of them."

"And how did you do that?"

Picking up my glass of wine, I stared down into the ruby red liquid. "I burned the entire motherfucking place down." I tipped the glass up to my lips and swallowed it down.

His answering smile was evil. "I think I would have done the same." His smile faded. "Was anyone hurt?" he asked. "Or more importantly, how badly were *you* hurt?"

"I heard no one had anything more than a few bumps and scrapes as they all fell over each other trying to get out," I told him.

"And what about you, how did you get out? Did someone help you?"

I shook my head. "No, they left me lying there like Carrie in the middle of the prom, blood dripping down my head as I destroyed the place around me. But I managed to crawl to the emergency door and get myself out of the building." I took a deep breath as I fiddled with my glass. I didn't like to think about that night. About how they'd just left me there to die. Even if they hated me, who *does* that? Was my existence that worthless?

Sometimes, I thought maybe it was. "I'm going to hell, aren't I?"

"I seriously doubt that. It sounds to me like they completely deserved it."

I thought about that. "But I *am* a witch." The truth of that statement filled me to the point I couldn't deny it anymore. Much as I would like to continue to make excuses as I had all my life. When I was young, I thought I was a superhero. When I got older, a freak of nature.

"Yes."

I let that sink in for a moment, then continued with my story. "Of course, I couldn't get a part anywhere after that. You wouldn't believe the reach of the rumor mill in a city as big as New York. I stayed another five years, but my budding career as a Broadway star was over."

"It doesn't surprise me at all," he told me. "And I wouldn't have done anything differently."

As I'd expected, there was no judgment in his tone. But what did surprise me was the lack of fear in his eyes. "Aren't you afraid of me now?" I asked.

"Should I be?"

I studied him for a long time. "No," I told him.

He reached across the table and laid his hand over mine. "I'm glad you came back to New Orleans," he told me. "And I'm very glad I got to meet you, Lizzy Smith." Then he stood.

"Where are you going?"

"I need to go check on my club."

He walked over to the sink and rinsed out his glass before setting it on the counter. He appeared a little disconcerted, but if I had to guess, I would say it wasn't my big revelation that had done it.

"Killian."

He turned back toward me.

"You believe me, don't you?"

"Completely," he answered with a small smile. "Goodnight, sweet Lizzy."

As he headed toward the door, I called out to him again. "Killian?"

With his hand on the knob, he stopped and looked back over his shoulder.

"I'd like to come meet your friend."

He stood frozen for a long moment.

"I don't think I can help her, but I'd still like to meet her."

His chin dropped. For someone who was so gung ho to get me there, he seemed hesitant. But then he lifted his head. "I'll take you to her tomorrow. I'll be here at sunset."

Sunset.

I walked into the front sitting area with my coffee and looked out the window. That was only...what?

Hours.

It was only hours away.

But first I had to deal with work. Staring at my reflection in the window, I knew, deep down, Killian had been right all along.

I'm a witch, aren't I?

Yes.

13

KILLIAN

"You're bringing her here," Jamal stood outside the small bathroom and pointed at the floorboards of the house to emphasize his point. "Here, to this house," he said again. "To the swamp."

"Yeah. Yes," I told him when he just looked at me. "She's coming to see Kenya." I didn't tell him what I'd discovered the night before. I was still bringing Lizzy here. She doesn't know everything she's capable of. She may be able to help. It wasn't unheard of for a fire witch to have healing powers. Just more rare.

"She's not going to help us, man. She's a witch."

I stopped shaving and set down my razor, spinning around to face him. "What else do you expect me to do then, Jamal?

Let Kenya die? Without doing everything in my power to keep that from happening?"

He had the good grace to look disgusted. "No, of course not."

"Well?" I threw my arms out to the side "What, then? Because me carrying a sick vampire through the streets of the French Quarter will surely get a lot more attention than one lone witch coming out here."

"How do you know she won't be leading her coven right to us?"

"She's not even talking to her family."

"That you know of," Jamal said. "What if she's the bait and this is just a trap for them to find out where we are?"

I turned back around and continue shaving. I was done with his questions. "It's not a trap."

"But how do you *know*, Killian?"

"I know," I told him. "All right? I know."

In the mirror, I saw him cross his arms over his chest. "So you've been poking around in people's heads again," he accused.

"Of course I have. How else am I to find out anything?"

He was quiet as I finished shaving my face, rinsed the razor, and set it on the sink. "Look," I told him, grabbing a towel. "I'm bringing her here to see Kenya because I don't think it would be wise to try to move her."

He gave me that bland stare that never failed to get under my skin and crawl around until I felt like screaming. "I'll erase her memory," I promised. "She won't remember where we are."

"And if you forget?"

I gave him a look that would whither a lesser man on the spot. "Shite, man. I won't forget."

"Just like you didn't forget to erase mine, huh?"

I turned around and leaned back against the sink. Mimicking his pose and crossing my ankles, I stared him down—my first friend who was now my sworn enemy because he was never going to forgive me for what I had done to him. Eventually, he lowered his eyes in deference to me. I hated making him do it, but the survival of our coven depended on a hierarchy, and he needed to remember who was at the top.

With a sigh, I dropped my arms and pushed away from the sink, rubbing the old wound on my thigh unconsciously. "I don't have time for this right now, Jamal," I told him as I pushed past him.

"Of course you don't." He dismissed me with a wave of his hand and disappeared into his room.

I'd completely forgotten he wasn't going into the club tonight. After ghosting us for two days, Brogan had reappeared last night with four full bags of new Hawaiian shirts—his apparel of choice—and a cocky grin splitting his face. He'd told Jamal he'd cover for him to give him a break and sent him home early. AKA, he needed to feed. I wasn't sure what was going on with that one, but at least he'd found his way home.

I supposed I would have to have a talk with him about his habit of running off without so much as leaving a proper note, but like everything else in my life right now, it was going to have to wait.

Checking in on Kenya before I left, I found her sleeping restlessly in sweat-soaked sheets, her expression tightened with pain. We were running out of time. If Lizzy tried to back out on me tonight...

But that wasn't going to happen. Because I was done giving her a choice. I'd already wasted too many days doing as Kenya wished, being the nice guy so as not to upset the witches who would surely be angered if I harmed one of their own in any way, whether she was ready to join them or not.

I shut the door quietly behind me. The sun had barely sank beneath the horizon, but it was safe enough for me to be out. Still, I wasted no time getting into the car to drive to the Quarter.

When I got to Lizzy's, she was waiting for me outside in the courtyard while Wiggles did his business before we left. I took her in, hearing her heart beat steadily in her chest and breathing in her scent. "Is he going to be all right here by himself?" I asked her.

"He'll be fine," she told me, "as long as I'm home in a few hours."

Though she was concentrating very hard on watching her dog sniff around a patch of grass, I caught the undercurrent in her tone. She was basically telling me I had to bring her back or the dog would suffer.

Lizzy was catching on to my weaknesses way too easily.

I waited outside while she took the dog into the house and made sure he was settled. When we left the side gate, she stopped and looked around.

"My car is down at Crescent Park," I explained. "It's better than wasting time circling around the block looking for a spot."

"That's what I like about living in here, there's no need for a car unless I want to leave the city. Which I rarely do."

I grunted my agreement.

"You're quiet," she told me a few minutes later as we walked.

I purposely avoided the busiest streets, wanting her all to myself. Or, as much as I could.

I glanced over at her. Her long hair was pulled back in a low ponytail tonight, and she was dressed in what appeared to be new clothes. They were casual attire—jeans and sneakers with a heavy green sweater—and remembering the reason why she'd had to purchase them, I was suddenly infuriated. "Have you heard anything about your apartment? Do they know how the fire started?" I knew how. I'd felt the magic creeping along my skin. But I wanted to see what she would say.

She shook her head. "No. They have no idea. But the police officer who called said I could go back there tomorrow to salvage what I can."

"I don't think it would be wise for you to go there alone."

She was quiet for a long time. "I think it was me." The words were no more than a whisper amongst the chatter of the other pedestrians and wailing of jazz horns, yet she might as well have screamed them in my ear.

"You?"

She glanced over at me in surprise, then quickly stared straight ahead again. Obviously, she hadn't meant for me to hear.

"It wasn't you, Lizzy."

"How do you know that? I showed you...last night...maybe I was dreaming or something."

I grabbed her arm and pulled her to a stop, forcing her to look up at me. "It wasn't you." A few people looked over at us as they passed, concern marring their features, and I released her arm.

"How would you know? You weren't there when it happened."

"I wasn't. But I was there right after and I felt it. I felt the magic. It wasn't yours."

She stared up at me as though I'd lost my mind.

"Don't look at me like that. I'm not crazy. It wasn't you."

"You can feel magic?"

More people were sending nervous glances in our direction and I realized we were standing toe to toe. I took a step back. "Let's walk."

Glancing around as though she just remembered we were standing in the middle of the sidewalk on a public street, she fell in beside me.

Neither of us spoke again until we got to my car.

"A Tesla, huh?" She seemed surprised as she eyed my black Model S.

"Doing my best to save the environment and all that," I told her. I held her door open for her and waited until she'd slid inside the synthetic leather interior before I jogged around to the driver's side.

As soon as I was inside and the doors were shut she began to bombard me with questions. Which was good. It distracted me from the way her delicious scent filled the small space.

"What do you mean you can 'feel' magic? Are you a witch, too? Uh...warlock? Is that how you knew about me?"

I laughed. "No. But I've been around them long enough to be familiar with their ways."

"So, you know my family, then?"

I pulled out onto I-10 and headed northwest toward the swampland. "I've known them for a long time. Since your aunt was nothing but a wee child."

"But how can that be? You can't be more than...what? Thirty-five? Forty?"

"I was forty-two," I told her distractedly as I changed lanes. Too late, I realized my slip.

"Aunt Judy is in her sixties. It's not possible that you knew her then."

Dammit. I tried to play it off. "Many things are possible if you believe in them." She would find out what I was, sooner or later, but I was suddenly averse to telling her. I didn't know why. It would only help my cause for her to have a little fear of me.

But the truth was, I didn't want her to be afraid. I wanted her to long to be near me always. Not run away.

Frustrated with myself and my rollercoaster of emotions, I drove faster than I ought, speeding down the highway and weaving in and out of traffic. From the corner of my eye I saw Lizzy's hands clenching the sides of her seat and it only angered me more. Easing off the gas, I tried to calm myself. I didn't know what it was about this woman...this *witch*...that caused such extreme reactions in me. But gods, I ached to be close to her again like the first night I'd brought her to my home.

I was a vampire, and yes, when I was first reborn, just like my heightened senses of touch and hearing, my emotions had also become something to be reckoned with. It had taken me a long time to learn control, and at times I'd felt like a five-year-old lad again, throwing tantrums when I didn't get my way. But, eventually, it had gotten better. I'd grown older and more used to this new body. More used to the force of my anger, the delirium of my joy, and the animal need of my lust —both for blood and for sex.

But the gods help me, Lizzy brought all of it to entirely new levels.

"Are you angry with me?" Her voice was quiet but firm, as though my rage made her nervous, but not enough for her not to question me about it.

I exhaled fast and hard, the sound loud in the quiet of the car's interior. "No. I'm not angry at you."

"So, now I'm kind of wondering what the car did from the time we left the Quarter until now."

I frowned, looking over to find her lips twitching with mirth. Instantly, my mood changed from frustrated anger to complete and utter joy just because her dark eyes were dancing. I didn't care that I was the brunt of her joke, only that she was happy.

For Christ's sake. What the hell was the matter with me? Shaking my head, I faced the road again. "We're almost there."

That drew her attention back to the narrow road we were on and the moss covered cypress trees draped over it, their trunks underwater. "You're living on the swamp?"

"Only temporarily."

"But why?" she asked. "Why live out here when you have such a beautiful home in the Quarter?"

I debated making up some passable excuse, but then reconsidered. I was going to wipe her memory of this place, and that would include anything we discussed since we'd left the highway. There was no reason I couldn't tell her the truth. Truths she wouldn't recall tomorrow. I just needed her to try to heal Kenya, and if being straight up with her would help her trust me, then I was all for it.

"Because we believe it was one of your family who cast this spell on my friend that's killing her, and we brought her here, where they can't find us, so they don't find her and rush the job."

"That's what you meant when you said it was one of my own kind."

"Yes."

"But why would they want to hurt her?"

The old house came into view, and I sighed with relief when I felt the weight of her stare leave me to take it all in. From the front, the weathered wood gave it the impression of being a large fishing shack. And the inside wasn't much better. But it had a big back porch we would occasionally find a gator sunning itself on, and watching Jamal wrestle it away made for some good entertainment.

"We're here," I told her.

She was distracted enough by the unsightly mess that she was quiet as she got out of the car and followed me to the front door. I felt a sense of rightness when she walked into that old swamp house. Almost as though she belonged there.

The same thing I'd felt having her grace my home in the Quarter. But that was insane.

Lizzy didn't belong in a place like this. She should be surrounded by expensive things and draped in jewels and clothing you couldn't buy off the rack. Things that would enhance her beauty, not make her the diamond in the rough.

Jamal was waiting in the living room when we walked in. He turned off the crime show he was watching and stood up when he spotted Lizzy. She stopped abruptly as she took in all six foot two inches of him.

"Jamal, this is Lizzy. Lizzy, this is Jamal. My friend." I looked at him as I made the introduction, half expecting him to deny it.

She gave him a timid smile, one he returned. "Good to meet you," he told her. "Thank you for coming here."

"I don't think I can help your friend," she blurted. "But Killian insisted and..." She lifted her hands in a helpless gesture.

"Yeah, he's stubborn like that." He gave me a warning look, which I returned with one of my own. Jamal was one of the few who could get away with something like that with me, and it was only because of our long history. But that didn't mean I liked it.

"Don't sell yourself short," I told Lizzy. "We won't know until you try."

She asked if she could use the restroom and I pointed her in the direction of the hallway. "First door on your right."

"Thanks. I'll be right out." Taking off her sweater, she folded it over her arm as she walked past the kitchen and down the hall.

When she was gone, Jamal stepped in closer to me. "You know she doesn't believe it's a spell. How is she going to heal Kenya if she doesn't even believe in it?"

"I'm well aware of that," I told him. "But I'm hoping that when she sees Kenya she'll... Shite, I don't know. Feel something. Sense something. And maybe she'll be able to work off of that."

Jamal started to say something else, but snapped his jaw shut when Lizzy came out of the restroom.

"We'll talk later," I told him, then joined Lizzy to lead her back down the hallway. "This way."

I placed my hand on the small of her back. The warmth of her skin seeped through her clothing to heat my palm. Before I realized what I was doing, I had her T-shirt gripped in my fist. Quickly, I released what I was doing and dropped my hand before she could notice.

"I apologize for the stench," I told her quietly while we were still in the hall, knowing that Kenya would hear me if she was awake and not wanting to embarrass her.

Lizzy acknowledged my apology with a "there's no need" and waited while I knocked softly on the door. I stuck my head inside. "You have a visitor."

14

KILLIAN

Kenya's eyes fluttered open when we entered the room, dazed with pain. It was the only acknowledgment I received. Her face was drained of all color, her lips cracked and dry, each labored breath rattling loudly in her chest.

Momentarily forgetting about Lizzy, I rushed into the room and felt her forehead. She was burning alive from the inside out. "Jamal!"

Kenya reached for me and I took her hand, pressing it to my lips. "I've got you."

I heard Jamal's boots run down the hall and then he was on the other side of the bed. He froze when he saw the condition Kenya was in, so much worse than just a few hours before, then fell to his knees beside the bed. "What the fuck is happening? She was no worse when I checked on her earlier."

Kenya's entire body suddenly stiffened, hard and flat as a board.

"Kenya? Kenya! Look at me!"

Her wide eyes were filled with tears when they found mine, then they rolled back in her head. But before I could order her to stay with me, to stay alive, her lips drew back in a hiss of pain and her body began to convulse on the bed. Her mouth opened on a silent scream, her fangs fully extended.

"What the fuck is happening?" Jamal shouted.

I grabbed Kenya's jaw to hold her still and bent down to her ear. "Don't you bloody leave me, do you hear me, Kenya? I won't let you. Fight!" I ordered. "Fight this!"

As suddenly as they'd began, the convulsions stopped and Kenya's eyes drifted shut in exhaustion, only the tight grip she had on my hand letting me know she was still alive.

Jamal leaned back, sitting on his heels. "I swear, man, she was not like this an hour ago."

"For Christ's sake, Jamal. I believe you," I reassured him. Jamal might have it out for me, but he loved Kenya as much as the rest of us did. We were like the pack of older brothers she'd never wanted. Only scarier.

There was a scuffing noise behind me and I belatedly remembered Lizzy's presence. When I looked over at her, she still stood much as I had left her, frozen by the door, only now her eyes were wide and she was even paler than Kenya. And not because of her lighter skin.

Her eyes skittered over to mine. "What happened to her?" she asked.

My patience worn thin, I snapped, "I <u>told</u> you, it's a witch's spell." Immediately, I regretted my stern tone. But I pushed the sentiment down. I had no time to babysit her feelings.

"Witches can really do stuff like this?"

"Can you help her?" Jamal asked before I could rage at her some more.

Lizzy's eyes shot over to him. A moment later, she edged over to where I sat. Releasing Kenya's hand, I stood to give her room.

She leaned in just as Kenya moaned and flashed her fangs, her body fighting the spell even in her unconscious state.

Lizzy jumped back from the bed. "What the hell?"

"She needs blood," Jamal stated.

"Don't you think I know that?" I asked him. "She can't keep anything down." Raking my fingers through my hair, I tried to think as I studied Kenya's prone form. "Lizzy, would you just try. Lay your hands on her or something. She won't hurt you. Or...or..."

"Wait. You didn't tell her?"

My head snapped up.

Anger twisted Jamal's features. "She doesn't know what we are? Seriously?" He pointed behind me.

Lizzy stood there watching, her back pressed against the sheet of metal that made up half of the wall. Her eyes were filled with horror as they bounced between the three of us.

As I took in her terrified face, the pounding of her pulse drummed loud in my ears. The flow of her blood rushing through her veins, full of adrenaline. Much like it did when I stood too close to her.

Her blood...

"Killian." My name was a warning on Jamal's lips. "No. Don't do this, man. Nothing good will come of it. I can go to the city and find someone. A homeless person. Somebody who won't be missed."

"There's no time," I muttered.

Jamal raised his voice. "Killian."

Lizzy's eyes flew to me. Her hands flew out in front of her, palms out toward me. "What are you doing?"

I'd taken a step toward her. Hesitated. I knew what I had to do, but I was having a hard time making myself do it.

"Killian! We can't do this! She's one of *them*, man! They'll hunt our coven down and annihilate all of us if you sacrifice her for one of us."

Like a rabbit caught in a briar bush, Lizzy watched me, her expression wary, her eyes on my mouth. Not my mouth. My fangs. It was only then I realized my upper lip was pulled up in a snarl.

"Killian. Please."

My name on her lips was so sweet I had to momentarily close my eyes.

"Please," she pleaded. "Don't."

I heard Jamal move to stop me and gave up all pretense of appearing human. Faster than she could track, I had her back at the bed, her back against my front, one arm around her to hold her there and the other forcing her bleeding wrist to Kenya's mouth. "Drink, Kenya."

Lizzy's blood dripped onto her parted lips.

"DRINK!"

Distantly, I heard Jamal pacing near the door uttering curses. But he didn't dare stop me. Not now. As much as he loved to defy me, he knew as well as I did Kenya wouldn't make it another hour without blood in her system. Fresh, human blood. Not the animals or bagged shite we've been bringing her.

If Lizzy couldn't save her with magic, she would fucking save her with blood.

I was about to reopen the wound on Lizzy's wrist to increase the flow when I saw Kenya's tongue flicker over her bottom lip. "That's it," I encouraged. "Drink, Kenya."

Lizzy's entire body was shaking against me so hard I felt it all the way to my bones, even as she tried to pry my hand from her waist and pull away. But at least she didn't scream. She didn't cry. I tightened my grip, forcing her wrist closer to Kenya's mouth, blood lust raging through my body as my starved friend finally bared her fangs and latched on.

It had been a while since I'd fed, and watching Kenya drink combined with the sweet scent of Lizzy's blood was my undoing. Her ass pressed into my hardening cock, made worse with her struggles. With a moan, I licked the drops left on my own lips when I'd bitten her wrist.

Like a drab of strong Irish whiskey it shot through my system, burning my insides with sweet fire, flooding every single one of my cells. A violent shudder wracked me and my low growl filled the room as her lifeblood merged with my own.

MINE.

With only that tiny taste, the knowledge flooded my mind and soul, as old as time and as fickle as the fates.

This witch had been born for me. Bound by her blood. And I for her.

My eyes darted to Kenya. Her eyelids had fluttered open and she was staring up at me as she drank. One of her hands was fisted in my sweater and the other had a death grip on my arm. I knew what she was feeling. The desperation. The need. The *hunger*. Because it was the same thing that made my muscles tremble and my throat burn with thirst.

Kenya cried out, the sound muffled by Lizzy's wrist as I tried to pull it away from her. Frowning, I yanked Lizzy's arm closer, giving my friend what she needed to live.

No! She is MINE.

"Killian? What's happening, man?"

Jamal was again on the other side of the bed, watching us carefully. His eyes traveled back and forth between Lizzy, still struggling against me, and Kenya.

I bared my fangs and hissed at him in warning. Lizzy whimpered in my arms, and I pulled her closer against me. Tucking my face into her neck, I breathed in her warm scent before I ran the sharp tip of one fang over the pounding pulse in her throat, drawing a thin line of blood. I tasted her, teasing myself.

Jamal stepped toward us and a deep growl rose up within me as I tracked his movements. He pulled back as stunned realization slowly dawned across his face. "No way."

Lizzy let out a sound that was something between disbelief and fear as she craned her head around to see my face. "Please," she begged. "Let me go. I'll find someone who can help her. I'll get my aunt."

Let her go? Ha! No. That wasn't going to happen. This witch was mine. The one I'd been waiting for. The one I'd longed for without the knowing it until just this very moment. Every instinct inside of me told me so. I was barely hanging onto my sanity watching another vampire feed from her.

"Killian?"

Jamal was leaning over Kenya, trying to get my attention. I pulled Lizzy in even closer to my body, away from the other male, then buried my face in her soft hair, shutting him out. She smelled amazing. So fresh. So clean. Hunching over her protectively, I made my way back down to her throat, beyond grateful she'd had the foresight to wear a ponytail. "*Acushla,*" I whispered against her skin.

My pulse.

She trembled beneath me.

"Don't be afraid," I told her. "I would never hurt you." I don't think I could, even if I wanted to. This woman was mine. My mate. A gift from the gods. I now knew what it was that had kept drawing me to her. This explained so much. Why I'd been so bloody patient with her. Why I'd never taken another to satisfy my body's needs of either kind since I'd met her.

"Killian, I feel like I'm going to pass out," she whispered.

I pulled back, my eyes searching her face and then traveling over her body for the cause of her distress. When they fell on Kenya, her mouth sealed around Lizzy's wrist as tears slid silently down her temples, a homicidal rage such as I'd never felt before exploded inside of me and the world turned red. With a roar of fury, I ripped my mate away from her and pushed her behind me. There was no logic to the action, no emotion, only an animalistic instinct to protect Lizzy from the rival vampire who dared to take any part of what was mine.

The life light that had briefly filled Kenya's eyes faded away as she watched me, knowing death would soon be coming for her. And it wasn't the witch's spell that would take her out. Even as a part of me knew I cared for her and didn't want to hurt her—that it had been *me* who had offered Lizzy up in the first place—as a mated male, I was now ruled by my vampire instincts. And those instincts told me to protect Lizzy at all costs.

My upper lip pulled back, baring my fangs as my muscles tightened, hardened, and my focus zeroed in on the vampire in the bed.

"Son of a bitch."

The words came right before I was hit head on by a very large object, the force of it throwing me back through the wall behind me and out into the overgrown yard. I landed hard, Jamal on top of me. Before I could gather myself, he grabbed a large rock and bashed me in the side of the head.

"Snap out of it, you fucker!"

I hissed at him through a haze of pain as I tried to throw him off of me.

"What the hell are you doing? You're going to kill him!"

I immediately sought out that voice, drawn in ways I couldn't explain if I'd been asked. Lizzy was leaning through the hole we made, the concern in her voice flowing over me like a warm breeze.

"Nope," Jamal called back. "But I am going to keep him from killing Kenya. Our *friend*," he shouted in my face.

I growled at him and flipped him off of me and into the swamp, a hundred feet away.

As I got to my feet, I heard a noise behind me and spun around, sinking into a fighting stance and baring my fangs.

Lizzy's terrified face greeted me, her body poised to run. Her eyes traveled over my face and body, as though she couldn't quite believe what she was seeing.

Hunger hit me swift and hard.

Her eyes grew wide as she noticed the change in my posture.

Don't run. Don't run.

She spun away and ran back into the house.

"Killian, don't!"

Jamal's shout barely registered as I took off after her, leaping back through the hole. From the corner of my eye I saw Kenya, awake and more alert than she had been in days, and felt a vague sense of relief I couldn't quite process.

I caught Lizzy in the living room, three feet from the front door. Grabbing her up in my arms, I spun her around and slammed her against the wall, my hand behind her head to protect her. "You shouldn't have run, *Acushla*."

"Killian, please." Her eyes closed. "I don't feel well."

Lizzy's face was pale, her skin moist to my touch.

"You can't feed from her, Killian. She's already lost too much blood. You'll kill her."

Jamal was getting on my very last nerve tonight.

"I want to go home," Lizzy whispered. "I need to go home to Wiggles."

The dog. He was home alone.

"Please, I need to go home."

Although the hunger was still there, there was another part of me—a saner part of me—who was beginning to come back now that I had her safe in my arms away from the others.

A heavy hand landed on my shoulder. "Why don't you let me take her home?"

My eyes never left her face. "Get your fucking hand off of me. I'll take her home."

"Killian, I don't know that you're in any condition to do that."

He was trying to help her. I knew this. And it was the only reason I didn't kill him on the spot. "She is mine, Jamal."

I heard him sigh. "I know you think you need your own witch, just like you thought you could make your own family, but I still say—"

"You're not hearing me," I told him. "She is *mine*."

15

LIZZY

Jamal let out a deep sigh. "I know."

I couldn't take my eyes from Killian's face. It was different. The changes in his eyes and his bone structure slight, but there. And the way he was staring at me. Like I was a...a...possession. Or something to eat.

But no, it was more than that. He stared at me like I was his entire life, like I was the only thing in the universe for him.

And when he spoke, I could see the points of his teeth. They hadn't been like that before.

It scared the hell out of me.

"What do you mean I'm 'yours'?" I tried to look around him to Jamal. "Jamal? What is he talking about?" My nerves were shot. My heart was pounding. That woman in the bed had just fucking *fed* from me, for God's sakes. And Killian was the one who had bit me! Then licked my blood from his lips with a moan like it was the most delectable sauce or the finest wine.

Even Jamal, the one who seemed to be the most level-headed and in control, had the same look to him as the other two. The sharpened bone structure. The black eyes that seemed to glow. The long teeth.

It was all I could do to hold back the screams bubbling up inside of me. But I instinctively knew it would only make things worse if I fell into a pile of hysterics on the floor. Now that he had me where he wanted me, which apparently was pinned against the wall and away from the other two, Killian had calmed down and was making some sense again. I had the feeling he would stay that way as long as I did the same and nothing else happened to set him off. "Jamal?" My voice was shaking. *That* I couldn't help.

"Killian, you need to tell her what's going on, man." His voice was also calm. Resigned.

Killian rubbed the back of his knuckles against my cheek. "So soft," he murmured.

I turned my attention back to him. "Please tell me what's happening here," I whispered. "I'm so scared."

In the blink of an eye, his entire appearance changed from predatory to horrified. He dropped his head, touching his forehead to mine. "Shite. I'm sorry, Lizzy." Then he glanced over his shoulder. "You can go," he told Jamal.

"No," I protested out of some sense of self-preservation. "I want him to stay."

Killian's eyes narrowed and he bared his teeth—his *fangs*—for a brief second before he pushed away from the wall and gave me some space. Not much. But some.

I took a deep breath. My head was swimming. "I need to sit down."

Taking my arm without a word, he led me over to the sofa. "Do we have anything for her?" he asked Jamal.

"I think there's some juice in the fridge. I'll grab it."

"Check on Kenya, too, please."

I sank down onto the sofa gratefully, and when I lifted my head again Jamal was handing me a glass of orange juice. "Kenya is doing better," he told Killian. I took it from him, wondering if I'd passed out or something for a minute. But then I remembered how fast he'd leapt over the bed when he'd tackled Killian in the bedroom.

And how effortlessly Killian had thrown him into the swamp.

Lifting the juice to my lips with a hand that shook, I paused, then pulled it away and peered into the glass.

"It's just juice," Killian told me. "Drink."

I did as he said, sipping the sweet drink slowly while the two of them watched me. After a few minutes, I started feeling better. Not quite as woozy, at least.

"Better?" Killian asked me.

I nodded.

"She needs food," Jamal told him.

"I'll take care of her," he growled in response.

I glared at the both of them. "I can take care of my own damn self." My fear was fading fast now that they were both acting somewhat normal again. "Now, please tell me what the hell is going on. And especially why that woman"—I pointed down the hall—"just *drank* my *blood*."

Killian exchanged a brief look with Jamal before he sat down beside me, turning his body so he faced me. He reached out to touch my arm, the gesture more like something to soothe his own needs than mine, but I pulled away. With a frown, he dropped his hand to his leg and rubbed his thigh, something I'd noticed him doing before when he was feeling stressed.

"Kenya drank your blood," Again, he looked angry and flashed his fangs even though he'd been the one who'd forced her to do it, "because she is a vampire. And so am I. And so is Jamal."

A vampire. The word didn't shock me as much as it probably should have. But with everything that had happened to me in my life and all of the revelations I've had since moving back here, somehow it didn't seem that farfetched. Witches. Vampires. This was New Orleans, after all. We had ghosts, too.

And, well, call me crazy, but it all made so much more sense now. Why I only seemed to see Killian at night. The way he moved, or didn't move at all. How I'd never seen him eat. Hell, even the way my aunt had warned me to stay away from him. And the look on her face when I'd first mentioned his name.

"You don't seem surprised," he said.

I glanced over at him. "I'm not. Not really."

"Does it scare you?"

"Yes." Then I shook my head. "No. Not when you're acting normal."

"Like a human, you mean?" Jamal said.

I looked up at him. "Yes."

"We're not human, Lizzy," Killian told me. "Not anymore. We live in the dark. We're hunted like animals at times. We have the strength of fifteen men. Our senses are beyond what any human could ever conceive of." He paused. "And aye, we drink blood. I can hear yours racing through your veins right now, and it's driving me near insane."

My heart had finally started to slow to its normal pace, but it suddenly sped up again.

Killian smiled a predator's smile.

"Are you going to kill me?"

He shook his head. "I can't."

"Why not?"

"Because you're mine."

I set my empty glass down on the floor beside my foot and pushed the loose strands of my hair out of my face. "You keep saying that."

"Because it's true."

"Killian, stop messing around and just tell her."

Killian never took his eyes from me. "Mind your own fucking business, Jamal."

With a roll of his eyes, Jamal crossed his arms over his chest and wandered over to the opposite end of the couch, taking a seat on the arm. As far away from me as he could get.

Gathering my courage, I angled myself to face Killian. "I want to know what it means. Tell me what it means. In plain English. Not all this secretive vampire bullshit."

He smiled as his eyes traveled over my face. "You are truly something, *Acushla*."

"Why do you keep calling me that? What does it mean?"

"It's an Irish endearment. It translates loosely to 'my pulse'."

His pulse. His heart. The thing that keeps him alive. I took a breath. "Okay. I guess that's not so bad."

He shook his head.

"So, tell me why you suddenly think I belong to you."

He rubbed his thigh again, his expression thoughtful. "There's a story that's been passed down over the centuries.

A story about us. It's said that vampires, if they're very lucky, will meet the one who is meant for them—our soulmate, if you will—that we will know it."

I was getting a very bad feeling about this. "And how do you know?"

"From the moment I tasted your blood."

We weren't speaking hypothetically anymore. "My blood told you this."

"It did."

This couldn't be true. "I don't believe you."

"It's true, *Acushla*. I knew it even from the tiny bit I tasted on my lips. My entire body, everything inside of me, felt it. Like a shockwave from a nuclear blast. You're mine, Lizzy. A gift from the fates." He searched my face. "And I am yours."

Mine?

"What if I don't want to be in this relationship?"

"That can't happen," Jamal said from behind me.

But Killian motioned for him to be quiet. "Then you don't have to be."

I tried really hard to wrap my head around this. "You're immortal."

"I am."

"And I'm not. What will you do when I die? Just find another mate? I mean, it's going to happen. Probably in about forty or fifty years if I'm lucky enough to live that long."

Jamal got up and squatted on his heels in front of me, careful not to get too close. "That's the cool part for you, Lizzy. You don't have to die."

"Of course, I do. Everyone dies. Well, every human, anyway. And that's what I am. And what I want to remain." I glared at Killian meaningfully.

"I don't want to turn you," he assured me. "I couldn't feed from you if I turned you."

He must've seen the flash of an idea in my face for he was suddenly there pulling me up off the couch. "Don't even think about it," he told me. "No one would dare touch you."

"Because you would kill them?"

"I would rip them limb from limb and throw their body parts to the gators without an ounce of remorse."

"You really get the better end of the deal in all of this," Jamal tried to reason with me.

They were both crazy. "The 'better end of the deal'? Is that what you call this? I get to be his feeding bag and that's supposed to be my life now?"

"Lizzy..."

"No." I threw my hands up as Killian came toward me. "Stay away from me."

"I'm sorry, *Acushla*. I can't do that."

I walked away, over to the other side of the room by the kitchen. I just needed some space. I needed to think.

But he kept coming.

I threw my hands up again. "Stop!" I screamed.

Killian froze. "Lizzy..." There was a warning in his tone. "Release me."

Jamal stood up. "What are you doing?"

"God dammit, Lizzy. Let me go!"

I had no idea what he was talking about, but he was starting to scare me again. Suddenly, it all just became so overwhelming. Killian's angry face blurred as my eyes filled with tears.

"Ah, shite. Lizzy. Don't cry. Don't cry."

My arms fell useless to my sides as I felt myself start to crumble. And then Killian was there, wrapping me up in his strength, holding me against him. One hand in my hair and the other stroking my back.

I buried my face against his chest. It was crazy. Seeking comfort from the man who'd just told me my life as I knew it was over. But I couldn't hold it together by myself anymore.

"She really is a witch," Jamal muttered.

Oh, my God. I was so tired of all of this nonsense. Witch or no, I had no idea what to do with any magic I might possess.

The only thing I could do was destroy everything I loved with fire. "I just want to go home," I whispered into his shirt.

"I'll take you," he said into my hair. "Shh. It's all right, *Acushla*. You're safe with me."

"No, I don't think I am—"

The floor disappeared from beneath my feet as he scooped me up into his arms like I weighed less than a feather and strode toward the front door. My head swam at the sudden motion.

"Call me if anything changes with Kenya," he told Jamal.

Tired of fighting and drawn by something I didn't understand, I curled up in the arms of my vampire and let him take me away from this house.

16

KILLIAN

Lizzy was silent all the way home. I let her be with her thoughts. It was a lot to take in, I knew, because my own head was a mass of tangled shite as well, filled with both her thoughts and my own.

My mate.

This explained so fucking much. From the moment I first saw her walk out of the back room of her voodoo store, something had drawn me to her. Something much more powerful than mere physical attraction between a male and a female. And when her scent hit me...I hadn't felt thirst like that in over a hundred years.

Since that night, wherever I went, I would feel her presence before I would see her. Entered her mind with my own smooth and easy without the normal barriers humans normally presented. And, most importantly, I could never bring myself to force her to do something she didn't want to do. Something I'd thought was just me trying not to be a complete and total monster for Kenya's sake, but it wasn't only that. It was something more.

It wasn't until she'd *asked* me to bring her to see Kenya that I was able to do so, even though I showed up every night with the intention of dragging her there whether she wanted to go or not. I'd saved her dog. Not because I cared so much about the animal, although I did like dogs, but because I knew it would break her heart to lose him.

And I wouldn't be able to live with myself if I was the cause of her pain.

Even now, as I glanced over at her sitting so still beside me in the car, I wanted to touch her. Comfort her. Taste her. If I thought she'd accept it I would offer her my blood to help her renew her own. I wanted to make her feel good, hear her moan with pleasure in my ear. I would kill the next twenty people who crossed my path without so much as a thought just to feel her hands on me. I wanted to fuck her until she remembered no male but me. Sink my fangs into her throat and drown in her sweet blood.

Lust, pure and raw, flared within me.

But she wasn't ready for that. Wasn't ready for me. And so I would wait as long as I could.

We arrived in the Quarter. Instead of leaving my car at the park as I normally did, I found a spot half a block from the house. It was dangerous leaving it so close to my home. If the witches saw me here they'd be on me like the bloody banshees they were, but I couldn't make Lizzy walk all that way, and carrying her would draw too much attention. So, it was a chance I'd just have to take. If need be, I'd come out and move it after I got her inside.

Her head was propped against the window and her eyes were closed. "Lizzy, we're home."

Home. I liked the sound of that.

Her eyes fluttered open and she looked around in somewhat of a daze. When she saw the house just ahead, she stared at the two-story structure like I was asking her to walk through the gates of hell. "I can't stay here anymore."

"What are you talking about? Of course you can. You can stay as long as you'd like." *You will stay until the day I no longer exist.*

She reached for the door handle. "No, I can't. I just need to go get Wiggles." Before I could stop her, she was out of the car and walking toward the house faster than I would have thought possible in the state she was in.

I got out and locked the car, catching up to her easily. "You don't have to leave. The house is empty. You're welcome to stay as long as you want. I told you this."

"That was before."

"Before what?"

"Before tonight," she spit at me.

Her hatred hit me so hard at first I thought it was a spell of some sort. Another consequence of our mating. She was angry. But at least she wasn't scared now that she was back on her own stomping grounds. I started to reach out to her with my mind, wanting to know everything she was thinking, but pulled back at the last minute. I didn't need to invade her privacy to figure out what she was feeling. It was quite obvious by her body language.

We reached the side gate and I punched in the code, holding it open for her. "I didn't know this would happen, Lizzy."

"Didn't you?"

What the hell was that supposed to mean? "No," I told her. "I didn't. No one ever knows until it happens. I explained this to you."

At the back door she stopped and pulled out her key. The one I had given her. She wouldn't look at me. "I can take care of myself now. You can go. I'll be out of here by morning."

She was dismissing me?

I don't bloody think so.

Reaching into her mind, I twisted her thoughts to be in accordance with my own. "You will stay here. You need food. And rest. You can barely stand up."

She spun on me so fast she almost caught me by surprise. "And whose fault is that?" she railed, weaving on her feet. "Who did this to me, Killian?" She thrust her wrist into my face. Kenya's and my bite marks were still quite obvious beneath a streak of blood.

My fangs shot down and I breathed in through my mouth to control the thirst.

Lizzy's eyes widened, then flew back and forth between my mouth and her wrist before she lowered her arm and stuck her hand behind her back. "I don't want this," she told me.

I tried to reason with her. "You came here to start a new life."

"Not this life."

At least her anger was putting some color back into her face. Honestly, I was unsure how to handle the situation from here. My mate was staring up at me with fire in her eyes, denying me what was mine. Her blood. Her body. Her company.

Her love.

Anger flooded through me. I didn't need her fucking love. I just needed her to behave. Lizzy was mine. More so than Jamal or Kenya or any of the others. More so than any who had come before her. And she needed to get that through her thick head. And the sooner she did the better off she would be. "It's not a choice, *Acushla*. This *is* your life now."

"No, it's not."

"Lizzy, I understand this is a lot to take in, but you will accept it."

"Or you'll do *what*, exactly?"

I smiled at her. It wasn't a nice smile, and by the way her heartbeat picked up it got my meaning across perfectly.

Wrapping my hand around her throat, I forced her to look up at me.

She met my stare with a rebellious one of her own. Even weak from lack of blood she stood up to me. It was admirable. And foolish. But what she didn't realize was that I *liked* it.

Lowering my head, I nipped at her lips. So soft. So perfect. She didn't say anything. Didn't touch me. But she didn't have to, because her body gave her away. The musky scent of her desire rose between us, eliciting a growl from my throat right before I took her lips with mine. She froze for a brief moment before her lips parted to let me in, an invitation I wasn't about to refuse. I gave her no time to think, only to feel as I possessed her mouth, just like I would possess the rest of her. Mind, body, and soul.

And when she moaned softly, when I heard that sound I'd so longed for, I nearly fell to my knees. "Lizzy..." The wanting was there in my voice, raw and eager. I felt her hands press against my chest, fisting in my shirt. "Yes, *Acushla*," I whispered against her lips.

Pain, fierce and swift as she bit down hard on my lower lip and shoved me away from her. "I'm not yours," she told me. "I belong to one person and one person only. And that's me."

A low growl rose up inside of me. I took a step toward her. She would submit to me tonight if it was the last thing she did.

"Stop!" she yelled. "I don't want you!"

Just like before, I couldn't move my arms or legs. I flashed my fangs at her. "Release me, Lizzy."

Her eyes travelled over me, frozen in mid-step. I watched as understanding dawned across her face. She'd just discovered a new power.

"Lizzy..." The warning was clear in my voice.

She turned and unlocked the door, then slipped inside. I heard the bolt slide into the lock as she barred me from my own home.

Suddenly, my foot slammed down onto the pavement as I broke free and stumbled into the door, the force of her magic dissipated. I raised my fist to punch through this feeble barrier, but stopped myself. "Fine, then," I spit out. "You don't want me? That's fucking fine. I will live without you, witch." Turning on my heel, I slammed out the gate and hit the streets of the French Quarter. I left my car where it was. Let the witches find it. I was in the perfect mood for a fight.

But in the meantime, I would prove to that woman, and to myself, that I could—and would—live without her. I didn't need a temperamental witch as my mate. One who didn't appreciate everything I could give her. Everything I could offer.

For Christ's sake! She could be immortal. Other humans would give their limbs for such a chance.

Maybe she just doesn't want to be with you. Just like Jamal. Just like every other person you've brought into your coven.

Even Kenya will turn on you. She's probably terrified after the way you acted tonight. It's only a matter of time.

As I stalked through the Quarter, jazz coming at me from every corner and humans stumbling over themselves to get out of my way, I couldn't get the truth of that out of my head.

She didn't want me. It was as simple as that. She wasn't even willing to give me a chance. The only saving grace to it all was the fact that I wouldn't have to suffer long, because I would be dead before long if I couldn't feed from the one who was meant to nourish me.

Or, would I?

There was only one way to find out if the stories were true, or if telling a vampire he or she could only feed from their true mate—once they'd found them—was nothing but a tall tale to add to the lore...

Five hours later, I sat with Wiggles in the chair in the bedroom of my home, petting his soft fur as I watched Lizzy sleep. Despite the fact she hated me so, the predator inside of me was comforted by her presence. I would just have to be content to wait. To snatch what tiny figments of sustenance she would give me until she came around and learned to accept her fate.

I'd prowled the streets of the city all night, drinking whiskey that did nothing to numb my pain, all while silently cursing Lizzy to the gates of hell and back again. It hadn't taken long to attract the attention of an ideal group of humans. As a vampire, everything about me was irresistible to them. My looks, my smell, the way I moved. They sensed the danger I presented, but it was easily overridden by the weapons nature had given me. It was why we were the top predator of the species over any other supernatural creature. Humans couldn't resist us.

Except for one, apparently.

Three college students approached me on the street, two females and one male. They asked me if I was a local, and before long I'd wooed them away to the cemetery, far from prying eyes. I could've taken them to my club, but I had no desire to go there and let the others see me in the state I was in. Besides, bringing people there by fucking with their heads was against the rules. I never would've heard the end of it.

There, behind the crypts, we drank my whiskey, we toasted the dead, and then I ripped open their throats.

The first one I attempted to feed on was the young man. Tall and muscular, he probably came along on the trip thinking he could protect the two girls he was with, and maybe get into one or both of their pants, and he'd put up a valiant effort. But in the end, I'd taken him down easily, his blood like tar in my mouth.

Gagging, I threw him to the side and grabbed the blonde. It was much the same with her.

By this time, the last one snapped out of her horrified shock and had the intelligence to run, her dark hair—much like my Lizzy's—flying out behind her like a flag. I smiled as she dodged around the graves, desperate to escape me, and to her good fortune, she did.

I was running parallel to her, focused solely on the hunt, when the red-haired witch appeared in my line of vision. Ducking behind a tall tomb, I remained perfectly still, watching as she turned her head this way and that. She sensed me here, just as I would have her if I hadn't been so distracted by my games with the humans. Exposed and with nowhere to run, I waited for her to find me. I'd gambled with my life tonight, and if she found me, I would lose. And for what? To prove something to myself? Something I knew instinctively wasn't true?

After only a few seconds, she spun on her heel and walked swiftly out of the graveyard. But it had been enough time for the human woman to get away. Mother fucking shite! I went back to the other two bodies. I needed to remove them before the witch came back with reinforcements. Throwing one over each shoulder, I gave them a proper burial in the Mississippi.

Now, my thoughts as dark as the moonless sky above me but my blood lust calmed, I watched Lizzy sleep. The scent of her mixing with the disgusting smell of human remains on my clothes, diluting it so I could breathe.

Wiggles, after a cautious sniff or two, had turned his face away from me but stayed close enough that I could scratch his back end. My hand shook as I trailed my fingers through his fur. It was all I could do to remain sitting quietly in that chair while the female whose warmth I craved more than anything in this world or the next lay in my bed not six feet away.

Never taking my eyes from her, I gave my new friend one last pat on the head and stood up. I needed to leave. The longer I stayed here the more tempted I was to join her in that bed. I hungered for her to the point of physical pain. For her blood. For her body. For something as simple as her smile.

As I walked across the bedroom, she stirred beneath the sheets. "Killian? What are you doing here?" The fierce anger she'd shown me earlier was forgotten with sleep, replaced with curiosity.

Gods, I craved her. Every muscle in my body ached with the effort it took me to stay where I was.

Lizzy *would* be mine.

17

LIZZY

Killian was standing in my room—his room—watching me as I'd slept. Though it was still dark, there was a tiny bit of light coming in off the street and I recognized the silhouette of his body right away. I wasn't scared, and I was too tired to be angry. I was just surprised to find him there.

"How long have you been here?"

Briefly, he looked away toward the window before coming back to me. I had the feeling he wished he'd used that window as an escape route before I noticed him. "I was just leaving."

His tone was off. And not because he was angry. It was something more. I struggled to unwrap myself from the blankets and sit up. They felt like they weighed a thousand pounds. But then I realized it was the atmosphere in the room weighing me down, filled with such tension and agony the air practically pulsated with it. And there was a strange smell. One that hadn't been here before, so strong I tasted copper on my tongue. "What's wrong? What's happened?"

He didn't answer me for a long time, and when he did, there was a rawness to his tone that made me distinctly uneasy. "Nothing. Go back to sleep."

There was a small lamp beside the bed. Reaching over, I clicked it on just as Killian raised his hand. "Don't!"

I blinked against the light as I swung my bare legs over the bed. I was only wearing the T-shirt I'd pulled out of his drawer. Shivering, I grabbed the blanket off the back of the chair Wiggles had claimed, wrapped it around my shoulders and turned to face him. "Oh, my God!"

Killian's face and hands were covered in drying blood. And I could see large, dark spots on his clothes, that if I were to guess, was even more blood. "What the hell did you do? What happened?" I took three steps toward him before I realized he was standing absolutely still, staring at the shirt I was wearing with a strange look on his face.

"You're wearing my shirt." His gaze clashed with mine. Hunger, dark and desperate, reflected in his eyes. But for what, I didn't know. My understanding? My blood?

I pulled the blanket tighter around me. "I won't get my clothes back until tomorrow, if they didn't all go up in flames," I told him as explanation. "And I forgot to buy anything to sleep in." He didn't need to know that it comforted me to wear it. "Now, tell me what happened. Are you hurt?" I was amazingly calm through all of this. Maybe my body had had enough surprises for one day. Maybe I was just getting used to New Orleans and all of its supernatural surprises.

"It doesn't matter."

I realized his entire body was shaking. In spite of my better judgement, I was starting to get concerned. Was he hurt? "Killian..." I stepped closer to him.

"If I were you, I wouldn't come any closer."

The warning was clear. I stopped just out of arm's reach. "Are you hurt?"

His lips twitched. "No. Not like you think."

I had no idea what he meant by that. "You need a shower."

"Aye."

"You can take one here if you want."

His eyes traveled over my face, searching for something. "Thanks." There was the slightest bit of sarcasm in his tone.

"Just one question," I asked him as he walked over to his dresser and started pulling out some clothes. "Did any of them live?" There was so much blood, and if he hadn't been attacked, that left me with only one other possible conclusion.

I didn't think he was going to answer me, but at the bathroom door, he stopped.

"One of them did."

Then he shut the door. A few seconds later I heard the shower come on.

My hand flew to my mouth to hold back my gasp of shock. Oh, my God. I was right. He'd killed people tonight! Why? Was it because of me? Because I'd pushed him away? Or was this something he always did?

I shouldn't flatter myself. Of course, it was something he always did. He was a fucking vampire.

I heard the water shut off and looked around for something more to put on. I found Wiggles sleeping on my clothes where I'd laid them on the chair. There was blood on the arm where Killian must've rested his arm. The sight of it brought me up short. It was just a few seconds, but it was a few seconds too long.

The door opened behind me and Killian came walking out wearing nothing but a pair of dark blue jeans, his shirt in his hands. He looked better. A little less shell-shocked, at least. But still not his normal self. There was something dark going on inside of him. Something I couldn't begin to understand.

As I watched him come into the room, I realized this was the first time I'd seen him without layers of clothes covering him. And my God, he was truly like something out of a magazine. Lean and cut, the muscles in his arm and chest bunched and released as he ran a hand repeatedly through his wet hair, pushing it back off his forehead. His abs were ribbed with bands of muscle, all the way down to the sexy "V" that disappeared into his jeans. Without the long sweater he always wore, his hips were narrow, his legs powerful, but perfectly proportioned to his frame. There wasn't an ounce of fat on him.

Desire pooled lazily in my core as my pulse sped up in anticipation. I froze beside the chair, devouring him with my eyes. I couldn't help it. I was thrown. I couldn't stop looking at him. And I didn't know what was wrong with me. I'd seen plenty of good looking men in my life. I'd even had a few in my bed. But none had ever arrested my attention like Killian.

He appeared in front of me, moving too fast for my eyes to track, his hands in my hair and his shirt on the floor near our bare feet. "Don't look at me like that, *Acushla*."

"I can't help it," I told him honestly.

I felt him tug on my hair as his eyes roamed over my face. "I discovered something interesting tonight."

Gripping the blanket tight in my fists, as if it could possibly protect me from him, I asked, "What was that?"

He closed his eyes briefly when he heard the huskiness of my voice. "I discovered the lore about us is true. Now that I've had even just that tiny taste of your blood, any other tastes like sludge in my mouth. I can't feed without gagging. I have no desire to fuck anyone else." He paused, his eyes roaming over my face and hair. "I killed two people tonight trying to prove it otherwise."

It was hard to think with him standing so close to me, his clean skin radiating warmth and that delicious scent that was completely and utterly him. There was a hint of whiskey on his breath. Even as I struggled to resist my attraction to him, a flash of something ugly and jealous seared my insides at the thought of him being this intimate with someone else. "I thought you said they got away?"

"I said one got away. The other two weren't so lucky."

"So, you *are* a killer." I should be bothered by this confession, but like everything else when I was around him, the feeling was there and gone before it could take root.

"Not usually, no. But it wouldn't matter even if I was."

"Why not?"

"Because, Lizzy, you are *mine*. And good or bad, I'm yours."

I saw a flash of his fangs just before he captured my lips, taking what was his without asking. Without apology.

Overwhelmed by everything that was Killian, I gave him access. He moaned deep in his throat when he felt my surrender, invading my mouth much like I knew he would invade my body. My soul. If I allowed it to happen.

And, oh God, despite my fear and my anger and the other tangle of emotions he roused in me, I wanted this to happen.

Honestly, I was beginning to wonder if I'd ever really had a choice. Or if what he and Jamal had told me earlier, what he was telling me now, was my only path. As much as my mind tried to fight him, my body had other plans. It welcomed him, betraying my better senses with glee. Even now, as he kissed me until I forgot who I was, forgot who *he* was, I wanted to lean into him so I could feel his warmth and his strength. Wanted to feel his hands on me. His mouth on my breasts. Between my legs.

Wanted to feel his fangs puncture my flesh.

And I wanted to touch him in return. I had to ball my hands into fists around the blanket to keep from doing just that.

"Touch me, Lizzy." He whispered my own thoughts against my mouth. "Please...touch me."

Gently, he tugged the blanket from my fingers and pushed it off my shoulders, letting it fall back onto the chair as he rained kisses on my lips, my cheek, my jaw.

"Touch me," he begged in my ear.

Somewhere in the back of my mind, I knew I shouldn't be doing this. People had died tonight because of him. Innocent people who'd had their entire lives before them. It horrified me.

Yet...my fingertips trailed down his chest and over his stomach, feeling the muscle tightening beneath them. He hissed softly, a different sound than when he was angry, but still causing chills to break out all over. Then he was kissing me again, moaning into my mouth with his hands wrapped in my hair to hold me still, pulling it from its bun to fall around my shoulders.

I flattened my palms, feeling the smooth texture of his skin, the soft, curly hair in the middle of his chest. I followed it with two fingers as it tapered into a trail that took me all the way down to the waistband of his jeans. Empowered by his groan of disappointment, I ran both hands up to his shoulders and hung on as his kisses became harder, more demanding. Nothing touched but our hands and lips, but the anticipation only made it more erotic.

Suddenly, he tore his mouth from mine and his head fell back on his shoulders, his mouth open on a sharp inhale. Looking at him, I was fascinated by the physical signs of his desire for me. And not just his swollen cock straining against his jeans, but the way his entire body seemed larger, harder, trembling with his need. His fangs were long, the tips needle-like and sharp. The bones in his face more prominent. And when he lowered his head and captured me with his eyes, dark and hungry...

I was lost.

"Killian." His name was a plea on my lips. I didn't know what I was pleading for. Maybe for him to release me from this spell. Maybe for him to keep me in it forever. I wanted him to touch me. And I wanted him to leave. I wanted him to forget all about me, and yet the thought of that actually happening felt like a hole cracking though the bones in my chest.

He touched the shirt I was wearing where it hung loose near my stomach, bunching the material between his fingers. Letting it fall, he watched it fall back into place. My heart was pounding so hard I felt sure I was going to pass out as I waited to see what he would do next. I didn't have to wait long.

Between one second and the next, he had torn the shirt I was wearing down the front, exposing my naked body to his hungry eyes. Surprised, I sucked in a breath and took a step back, instinctively grabbing the sides to cover myself.

"Don't."

The command was sharp and powerful. I paused, then let my arms fall back down to my sides. The way he looked at me...I'd never felt so exposed or so powerful in my life.

His upper lip twitched, then lifted, baring his fangs as he ran his eyes over my throat, my breasts, down my stomach and between my legs. His chest rose and fell as he inhaled, and I saw the tip of his tongue touch the tip of one fang. "You smell so good, *Acushla*. And I never thought it would be possible, but you look even better."

"Not bad for a woman hitting middle age?" I tried to tease, but the joke fell flat.

"You're the sexiest thing I've ever seen in my very long life," he answered with such raw intensity I had no choice but to believe him. With a hand that shook, he pushed one side of the torn T-shirt off my shoulder, then the other. It fell to the floor to join his. Then he held his hand out to me.

I stared at it, but didn't take it. I knew as soon as I did there'd be no going back. I'd succumb to him completely. And I just needed a moment to think...

"Lizzy."

There was no warning in the way he said my name. No demands. Maybe if there was I would've been able to resist him. But there was only an aching pain that I might turn him away, and I couldn't do that.

I took his hand.

With a low growl of triumph, he pulled me to him, wrapping me up in arms and burying his face in my neck as he strode to the bed.

18

KILLIAN

"Lizzy." I said her name like a prayer against her throat. She felt so good in my arms. Perfect. Her soft breasts pressed against my bare chest and her legs wrapped around mine as I carried her to the bed.

Triumph raged through me as I followed her down to the mattress, my muscles trembling as I tried to control my hunger for her. And even though my cock was swollen to the point of pain inside my jeans, I didn't dare take them off, knowing if I did I wouldn't be able to stop myself from instantly burying myself inside of her. And I wanted to take my time. I wanted to taste every inch of her body. Wanted to bring her to her knees with need. To make her crave me as much as I craved her.

But when she opened her thighs so I could fit between them, I couldn't resist rolling my hips against her core. Drawn by the sound of her moans, I found her lips again. She tasted so sweet, the only thing that could drag me away from her kisses was the promise of the rest of her.

Tearing myself away, I kissed my way down her throat. When I felt her pulse beneath my tongue, I couldn't resist sliding the tip of one fang against it. I could smell her blood. Feel it rushing through her artery. Lizzy turned her head away, lifting her hips as she did, inviting me into her in every way, and I very nearly did before remembering she'd already lost a lot of blood that day.

Memories of Kenya feeding from her flashed through my mind, causing my grip to tighten and a growl of possession to rise up inside of me. If I'd known, if I'd had any idea, there was no bloody way I would have offered Lizzy up to her or anyone. Not even to heal someone I cared for so deeply. Because now, I would have to live with that memory for the rest of my unnatural life, and I honestly didn't know what I would do or how I would act the next time I saw my friend.

The urge to possess Lizzy, to fully claim her as mine, grew almost unbearable. Her fingers gripped my hair as I moved down her body to her breasts, holding my weight on my hands so as not to crush her. Taking one hard nipple into my mouth, I rolled it between my tongue and teeth, careful not to break the skin. My control was hanging on by a thread as it was. One taste of her blood and I knew I would lose it completely.

I took my time, learning every texture, every curve of her breasts before I continued on down, nipping and kissing my way over her soft stomach, her hipbones, pushing her thighs apart so I could see her. Running my nose through the soft curls between her legs, I inhaled the sweet musky scent of her.

"Please," she whispered.

Gripping her hips, I pulled her down the bed until I was on my knees on the floor, spreading her out before me in the soft light of the lamp.

She was perfect. So very perfect. Smooth, dark pink folds, wet with her desire. I nipped at the inside of one thigh and she lifted her hips, begging me to taste.

Holding her still, I ran my thumb through her wet heat, pressing it just slightly inside of her.

"Killian, please." The last word ended on a moan as I pulled her up to my mouth.

My eyes closed with pleasure as her taste hit my tongue, and I groaned with need as I licked along the same path as my thumb until I found the hard little nub. I teased her lightly until she was fighting against my hold to get closer to my mouth. Lifting one leg over my shoulder, I held her curvy ass in my hand, squeezing the supple flesh before I found her entrance with my thumb and slid inside. I moaned against her as she tightened around my finger and trembled beneath my mouth.

At the last second, I pulled away. I wanted to be inside of her when she came.

Lizzy cried out, reaching for me.

"Don't fret, *Acushla*. I'll give you what you need." What we both needed.

Pulling off my jeans, I left them on the floor and lifted one knee on the bed, shaking my head when she wanted to pull me down on top of her. "I want to see you," I told her. Plus, I didn't know that I'd be able to control my need for her blood if my fangs were that close to her throat.

Even as desperate as I was to be inside of her, I couldn't resist running my hands over her body one more time—squeezing her breasts, rolling her nipples between my fingers, then sliding them down her soft stomach to her rounded hips. I lifted her higher and lined myself up at her entrance, sliding balls-deep inside of her with one quick thrust. I cried out as her wet heat surrounded me, tightening around my cock, then watched myself slide slowly out of her and back in again. My fangs ached to bury themselves in her vein, to take her blood inside of me as I came. But I couldn't. Not this time.

Ah, gods. I couldn't wait anymore. Grasping her hips between my palms, I increased my thrusts as I found her clit with my thumb. Her own cries of pleasure were sweeter than anything I'd ever heard. She was absolutely stunning, her back arched to take me even deeper, her breasts bouncing and her head thrown back as I fucked her hard.

Then she opened her eyes and let me in to the deepest part of her soul. I watched her lose herself, her emotions crashing over me as she hovered on the edge of her orgasm, and with a roar I buried myself as deep as I could go, feeling her body pulse around my cock, draining my own pleasure from me until I couldn't hold myself upright anymore and collapsed on top of her.

Immediately, I rolled off of her, pulling her with me until she was on top. "I'm not done with you, yet, *Acushla*."

Lifting her until she was straddling my hips, I slid back inside of her.

"Oh, my God," she moaned when she felt how hard I still was.

"Your God isn't going to save you." Bending my knees, I pushed deep.

I awoke to a prickly feeling on my skin. The dawn was coming.

This was the part of being a vampire I loathed at times. We had automatic shutters on every window on this house that locked down automatically at sunrise and lifted at sunset, but I'd disabled them after bringing Lizzy here. I didn't want her to be scared when they suddenly slid down. And since we couldn't have anything underground here in New Orleans because of the water levels, there was nowhere I could go without turning them back on.

Lizzy was sound asleep, her limbs tangled with mine, her head on my chest, her dark hair covering my stomach. I hated to leave her, but I should really go check on Kenya. I could only imagine what she was thinking after what happened last night.

Carefully, I slid out from beneath my new mate, taking a second to admire her naked form before I pulled the blankets over her. I got my wallet from my jeans and found the rest of my clothes, needing to pull my shirt out from underneath Wiggles where he'd made himself a bed on the floor. I replaced it with the blanket Lizzy had worn and gave him a face rub before I kissed Lizzy on the head, gathered up the bloody clothes I'd ruined, and went out to the kitchen to leave her a note.

It occurred to me then that she didn't have a cell phone. That she hadn't had one since the fire. At least not that I had seen. And I'd never even asked if she had money, or needed anything other than the very basics of food, water and shelter. Apparently, she had enough to buy some food, but just in case, I pulled some cash out of my wallet and left it with the note.

I arrived back at the swamp just as the first rays of the sun were coming up over the horizon. Tossing my bloody clothes into the swamp for the gators to fight over, I rushed into the house.

Jamal was in the kitchen, the shades closed and the blackout curtains drawn. "Hey," he greeted me when I walked in. "How is Lizzy?"

I didn't miss the undercurrent to his tone. "She's fine. I left her at the house. She's staying there, by the way. Someone tried to burn her apartment down the other night, with her inside of it."

"What?" Water hissed on the stove and he turned around to shut off the burner. "Who the fuck did that?"

I leaned up against the refrigerator door, crossing my arms over my chest. "I only know it was a witch. I felt it as soon as I got inside."

His eyebrows lifted. "You actually ran into a burning building to save her?"

"Lizzy and her dog, yeah."

"When was this?"

"A few nights ago."

"Huh." He grabbed a cup out of the cabinet and poured some boiling water over a tea bag. "Who'd have thought."

I eyed his broad back. "I would do the same for you, you know."

He looked at me over his shoulder. "Yeah, I know. It doesn't change anything between us."

"I wish I knew what would."

Turning around to face me, he said, "You do."

I met his eyes with my own. "I can't do that, Jamal. And I wish you'd stop asking it of me. Truly."

Coming over to me, he handed me the tea cup. "You should take this to Kenya. She's scared shitless you're going to rip off her head when she sees you again. She's probably in there freaking the hell out."

I was glad for the change of subject. "How is she?"

"Go see for yourself." With a halfhearted smile, he walked away. I heard his door close a second later.

Following him down the hall, I knocked on Kenya's door before I opened it.

She was sitting up in bed, her thick-rimmed glasses on her face, reading a book Jamal must've snagged for her from somewhere. Or, she had been reading. It was face down on the bed beside her and her hands were twisted together in her lap. I could tell she wasn't cured, not by a long shot, but Lizzy's blood had bought us some much-needed time.

"How are you?" I asked as I brought her tea in to her.

"That's what I was about to ask you," she told me.

I joined her on the bed and gave her a shrug. "I'm mated to a witch who hates me."

"Funny you say that, because I can smell her all over you."

"Parts of her hate me," I amended. "Other parts, not so much."

She laughed a little, then became deadly serious. "Killian, I'm so sorry. If I had known she was yours..."

"I didn't even know, how could you have?"

"I should've stopped feeding. I was just so thirsty, and for the first time it tasted so good...I just couldn't stop."

I grabbed her hand. "Kenya, it's all right. I made you do it. I forced you both to do it. And I'm glad. Looking at you here, now, I'm so glad I did."

"That's good," she told me. "I don't think I'm quite ready to be *dead* dead just yet. I've had this feeling that something is coming my way. Something good. And I don't want to miss out."

"Well, we'll have to make sure that you don't."

"Thank you." She gave me a smile, and I returned it.

"Is there anything else you need before I go try to get some sleep?"

"I would love a shower," she told me. "I don't suppose you'd be willing to lend me a hand?"

"I could do that," I told her. "If you feel up to it and, of course, you don't mind my seeing you in all your glory." I grinned at her and she grinned back.

"You're the only one I would trust implicitly right now. Because if you've found your mate, and the lore is true, there ain't nothing on this body that will do a thing for you. Especially because I'm kinda gross right now."

"You are at that," I teased her. "Let's get you cleaned up, then." I found her some clean, comfortable clothes then went back to the bed to help her get to the bathroom. "You're going to have to help me with the hair," I told her as I slipped an arm around her and steadied her as she stood. "I know absolutely nothing about black hair and all the stuff you use in it."

"At this point, I'll just be glad to have it clean."

Jamal opened his bedroom door as we passed. "I'll get some clean sheets on the bed while you guys do that."

"I don't deserve you," Kenya told him.

He winked at her. "You got that right. I had to pause my show for this."

I got Kenya stripped and in the shower in record time. Once she was steady enough for a few minutes, I got her towels and took off my shirt, then got in with her to help her get cleaned up.

"You're right," I told her as I helped her wash her hair.

"About what?"

"I'll readily admit, you're a beautiful woman, Kenya, but I don't feel one damn stir of lust looking at you."

"I'll try not to take that personally."

A short while later, she was clean and back in bed. That small act had taken most of her energy though, and her eyes were already closing as Jamal and I got her settled and gathered up the dirty laundry.

"I love you both so much right now."

"We know," I told her. "Get some sleep."

"And don't expect this to be a daily thing now," Jamal said.

"Every other day, maybe," I teased, but she was already drifting off.

Back in my own shite room, I peeled off my wet jeans and put on some lounge pants. I wanted to call Lizzy. But she didn't have a phone. She was probably still asleep, anyway. And I was glad I'd been here to help Kenya and calm her fears about what had happened. Giving in to my own exhaustion, I climbed into the cheap bed and tried to get some sleep.

But something was scratching at the back of my mind.

Something that was telling me I should've stayed with her.

19

LIZZY

I woke up to an empty bed, my entire body sore, like I'd been in an accident or something. With a groan, I rolled over. It took me a minute to remember.

Sitting up, I looked around the empty room. "Killian?"

No response.

It was morning, and the sun was shining through the windows. Maybe he'd just gone to a different room. He couldn't be in the sun, could he? I didn't think so. I'd only ever seen him at night.

Surely, he didn't just slink off after everything that had happened.

Only, I kind of wished he had. I needed time to process everything I'd seen and heard yesterday. Because right now I wasn't sure what to think about it. How to feel. I felt like I was walking on a thin plate of glass that could shatter at any moment, and there was nothing for me to grab onto, nothing to stop my fall.

I got out of bed and went into the bathroom to take care of my first urgent need. Then I brushed my teeth and found a new T-shirt to wear.

"Come on, boy." I rubbed Wiggles' chubby body until he woke up and saw me there. "Come on, buddy. Let's go outside."

In the kitchen, I called for him again. "Killian? Are you here?" I turned on the coffee machine and grabbed a cup from the cabinet, then went to the backdoor to let Wiggles out. The sun was deceiving. It was pretty cold outside.

As I waited for him to finish his business, I spotted a note on the table. Beneath it was a wad of cash.

> *Lizzy,*
> *I needed to go check on Kenya. We'll talk tonight.*
>
> *Killian*
>
> *PS- The money is for you.*

He left me money?

Picking it up, I thumbed through it. I had to admit this was the first time I'd ever been paid for sex. Anger rose, unbidden, heating my face and chest. Did he think he could just throw cash at me and I'd do as he said like a good little girl? Was this what being his "mate" would be like?

Yeah, fuck that.

Wiggles barked to be let in. "I know you've grown attached to that chair in the bedroom, buddy, but it's time to pack our things. We're done here."

It occurred to me that I might be acting irrationally. I knew I was feeling rather...sensitive these days. But honestly, I didn't really care. I just needed to get back to my real life, where everything was orderly and sensible and no one was springing life altering surprises at me.

An hour later we arrived at Ancient Magicks. I'd left Killian's key under the mat by the back door. Mike was dealing with a customer when I came in, so I went into the back to check Wiggles' food and water bowls by his nap spot and take a quick look around our inventory while he finished up. When I heard the door chime, I went back out.

Mike had my dog's old face between his palms, rubbing his ears and telling him what a good boy he was. It warmed my heart, and made me feel better about what I was about to do. "Hey," I greeted him. "Sorry I'm late."

"No worries. You're the boss." He smiled up at me and then did a double-take. "Are you okay? You look kind of...off."

"I feel kind of off," I admitted. "I need to do a few things today. Do you think you could watch him for me for a while and handle the store?"

"Of course. Is everything okay? Can I do anything?"

I shook my head. "Um, no. Not really." I started to walk away, then stopped. "Uh, I haven't told you this, yet, but there was a fire in my apartment. I've been staying with a...friend. Today, I need to go back and see if there's anything I can salvage, and also run by the bank and get a new debit card so I can get a hotel room."

He straightened up from the floor, his expression etched in concern. "Lizzy, if you need a place to stay, I've got a second bedroom—"

I cut him off. "No, no. Thank you, but no." I wasn't sure how Killian would react to my staying with another man, but I was sure it wouldn't be good, and the less drama I could bring into my life right now, the better. "I'll be more comfortable in a hotel. Honestly."

"I'm really glad you guys got out okay. How did the fire start? Was it the apartment manager's fault? If so, he or she would be responsible for helping you find a new place to live."

"I'm not really sure," I told him. "But I don't think it was anything wrong with the apartment. It started in the kitchen. I probably just left a burner on or something."

I couldn't tell him my new vampire mate swore up and down and sideways he had sensed it was magic that started it. Magic that wasn't mine.

"Anyway," I said as I gave Wiggles some love and headed toward the door. "I should be back in a few hours. I might stop and pick up some new clothes if I need to while you're watching him, if that's okay? I just hate to leave him alone these days."

"Yeah, yeah. Of course. Take all the time you need, Liz. I'll be here till you make it back. Wiggles and I will hang."

"I don't deserve you," I told him.

He gave me a weird smile. "Seriously, take your time."

At the old place, I sifted through what was left of my clothes. The fire had done quite a job, and there wasn't much that hadn't been ruined, but by some miracle, it hadn't spread to any of the other apartments.

Icy fingers ran up and down my spine as I bent over the pile of my things. Was it possible Killian had been right? Did someone purposefully try to hurt me? But who? And, more importantly, why?

When I was done, I'd managed to salvage one dress, a few pairs of jeans, some underwear, and a couple of summer tops. They all reeked of smoke so bad I had no idea how I'd ever get the smell out.

I left empty-handed and went to the bank. They were very sorry to hear what had happened and managed to get me a new debit card right then and there. I took that card and rented a pet-friendly room just down the street, then did a little shopping and got some new clothes and bath items and a few things for Wiggles. I also went and got a new cell phone with a new number. I'd been wanting to change it since I'd gotten here to avoid any calls from New York. Not that I was expecting any, but this way there'd be no reminders of that life.

Dropping everything off at the hotel room, I changed into some of my new clothes and the pair of comfy walking shoes I'd found that would match just about anything I'd bought. I put my borrowed clothes and shoes in a bag to take to Killian's house. I'd just leave it hanging on the door. I still knew the code to the gate and no one should bother it back there.

I spent the afternoon and early evening back at the store helping Mike.

The sun was just setting when I locked up. It was early, but I really didn't want to deal with Killian tonight, and I'd let Mike go home early. I planned to run (or walk as fast as Wiggles would go) back to my hotel and hide out for the night. We'd order delivery and spend the night binge-watching something on Netflix. I needed to just be me for a night.

I was a block away from my new home when I spotted Jamal on the street. Ducking my head, I tried to turn down a side street, but Wiggles chose that moment to find a particularly interesting smell and would not be budged no matter how hard I tugged on his leash. For a little dog, he had some weight to him.

"Lizzy."

Reluctantly, I looked up at him. Jamal was a good-looking guy, tall and clean cut, and he smelled almost as good as Killian. And vampire or not, there was something in his deep, brown eyes that drew me to him. A kinship, maybe.

"Hi."

He gave me a tight smile. "Look, I can see you're not wanting to be found tonight. And that's cool. I totally get it. But as long as I ran into you like this, I'm thinking maybe we should talk."

"Oh, you couldn't be more wrong. The last thing I want to do is talk, Jamal."

He laughed. "I hear you. But this is important. Where are you headed?"

"I got a hotel," I told him.

Both eyebrows rose. Then he grinned so wide I was afraid he was going to crack his face. "Killian's gonna fucking hate that."

"I don't care."

His eyes ran up and down my body. Not in a perverse way, just checking me out. "I think I like you, Lizzy."

Wiggles finally finished obsessing over whatever he'd smelled and noticed we had company. The hackles rose on the back of his neck and he growled deep in his throat as he inched forward to check out this stranger.

I let him do it, knowing he'd burst into protective mode and bark ferociously at him until I pulled him away, making it impossible to talk.

Imagine my surprise when he only leaned way out, sniffed Jamal's leg, and then sat down on the sidewalk, his tongue lolling out of his mouth.

Jamal reached down and gave him a rub on the head, which only made Wiggles more excited.

"What did you guys do to my dog?"

"He's a great dog. What's his name?"

"Sir Wigglebutt. Wiggles for short."

"Hey, Wiggles. How you doin', boy? Are you a good boy? Yes, yes, you are."

It was getting darker. I really needed to get to my room before Killian or one of my aunt's minions found me out here. "Look, I really need to go."

He gave Wiggles one last pat and straightened up, the smile gone from his face. "I'd really like to talk. We can do it somewhere public if you'd like. Or we can go back to your hotel. I promise no harm will come to you. And, like you, Killian is the last person I want to see tonight."

I sighed. "Look, Jamal. I really just want to have a night to myself."

"Lizzy, I want to help you, if I can." He paused, biting on his full lips as he glanced around.

The movement seemed casual, but standing this close to him, I could see it was anything but. With that one quick look, he could probably tell me exactly how many other people were on the street with us, what they were wearing, and if any of them were a threat.

"I've been where you are, Lizzy." At my puzzled look, he corrected himself. "Well, not exactly where you are. Killian didn't claim me as his mate, but he did claim me, nonetheless."

"How long ago was this?"

"It happened in 1877."

Stunned, I could only stare at him. I mean, I knew the myths about vampires, how they were immortal, and I remembered everything Killian had told me last night, but I guess it just hadn't really hit me exactly what that meant.

"You look good for your age."

He barked out a laugh. "Which way is your hotel? Or would you rather go somewhere else?"

"No, the hotel is fine." I trusted Jamal. More so even than Killian. I didn't know why. It was just an inert feeling.

I signed to Wiggles it was time to go and started walking. "I don't want to see Killian tonight."

"I don't want to see Killian tonight, either, as I said. But I have a feeling I'm going to. Especially when he can't find you."

"Is he always so...intense?"

Jamal shoved his hands into the front pockets of his jeans. "Yup."

We were both quiet until we got to my room. "I was going to have a pizza delivered or something. Did you want anything?" I asked as he followed me inside and I released Wiggles from his leash so he could explore.

"Maybe just a soda? Or whatever you're having to drink."

I studied him a moment. "So vampires just drink stuff, but don't eat."

The room I'd gotten had a small seating area when you first walked in. There was a loveseat, a second television, and a small table and chairs. Jamal pulled out one of the chairs and took a seat. "Pretty much."

I acknowledged his answer with a "Hmm" and looked through the flyers lying on the dresser back by the king-sized bed. I found one for a pizza place nearby and called in an order. "Sorry," I told Jamal when I hung up. "I'm starving."

"No worries, Lizzy. You gotta feed yourself."

After I made sure Wiggles had food and water in his new bowls, I joined him at the table. "So, what did you want to talk about?"

He looked down at his hands, laced together on top of the table. After a moment of thought, he looked up. "I wanted to tell you about Killian. Maybe help you understand him."

Leaning back in my chair, I crossed my legs and arms. "What's there to understand? He's an overbearing vampire. He's 'claimed' me," I made air quotes. "And now he thinks I'm just going to change my whole life to live in his."

"Well, hell, girl. Maybe you do know him." Humor made Jamal's dark eyes twinkle.

I shrugged. "What else is there?"

"I hate him," he blurted. The pain in his voice was obvious. Then he sighed. "And I love him."

"I don't understand."

"Killian saved my life. Twice, as a matter of fact. The first time when he was just a kid. Around eighteen, I think? Maybe a little older."

"What happened?"

He stared at me a moment, something ugly and haunting darkening his expression. "I was a slave, Lizzy."

I stared at him with my heart in my throat, not knowing what to say as horror filled my bones. "I'm so sorry," I finally whispered.

"I'm not telling you so you can feel sorry for me. It was fucked up," he gritted through his teeth. "But I think you know that."

"Yeah," I said. "It was."

He studied me for a few seconds before he continued his story. "I grew up in that life. But unlike my parents, I never accepted it. When I was fourteen, I managed to escape. I mean, back then, you were considered a man at that age. And I thought of myself as one. You've heard of the Underground Railroad, right?"

"Of course."

"Killian was one of the people who helped me. He met me at a farm, what they called a 'station' back then, in New Jersey, I think it was. And he guided me to New York."

"That's a long way for a kid."

"It was, but he was a scrappy little shit." He paused. "The second time I saw him he was much as he is now."

There was a knock on the door, and I jumped.

"Delivery!" a girl's voice called.

Visions of the horrible life Jamal must have had running through my head, I got up and opened the door, giving Wiggles the sign to stay. He did his duty and barked anyway, but only until he smelled the food.

Taking the pizza and the bottles of soda, I signed the receipt and with a "Thanks so much!" I closed and locked the door.

Jamal got up and retrieved the glasses from the tray with the ice bucket, unwrapped the protective plastic wrapping, and put some ice in them for us before coming back to the table.

"Thank you," I told him.

He poured some soda for both of us and sat back down. "You eat. I'll talk."

Pulling the box in front of me, I opened it and pulled out a slice.

"I had a hard time figuring out how to live my life as anything other than a slave. I got in trouble a lot. People in the north weren't always as tolerant of us black people as we were led to believe. I ended up in jail for a lot of years. It was mostly my own fault for not controlling my temper—"

"That's bullshit. You have as much right to express your emotions as anyone."

His smile was sad. "You would think so, wouldn't you?" He scratched at his nose. "Anyway, I was probably on my way back there when I met up with Killian again. I recognized him right away, even though it had been over twenty years since I'd seen him last. I was in bad shape, and he took me into his home. Gave me food. Gave me shelter. Helped me find work." He took a sip of his soda. "We got to be good friends."

"Was he still human the second time you saw him?" I was trying to figure out how they'd both become what they are now.

"No," Jamal said. "He was a vampire. A young one."

"How did it happen?"

"You should probably ask Killian that."

"I'm asking you."

He shook his head.

But I wasn't backing down. "I'm asking you, Jamal."

He took another drink of his soda, eyeing me over the rim of his glass. "All right. But don't tell him I told you this."

"I swear," I promised, grabbing another slice of pizza.

"Apparently, it all went down because of a woman."

I rolled my eyes. Of course, it had to be that.

Jamal laughed. "I know what you're thinking, and you're absolutely fucking right. It was like a bad movie. Killian wouldn't even tell me about it for like, a year."

"So, you knew what he was?"

"After a few months, yeah, he told me. He kind of had to at that point. Sun allergies weren't a thing at that time."

Ah. I was right. "You guys can't go out in the sun."

He rubbed one hand over his short hair. "Nope. Although the older you are, the more you can push it. But direct sunlight is a no go for any vampire."

"You're getting off the subject," I told him. "How did Killian become a vampire? How did *you* become a vampire?"

"Killian confessed his story to me the night I found out he wasn't human anymore. A woman named Olivia turned him one night after..." He glanced up at me. "Well, *after*. He'd met her at the home of a friend. He was enthralled, as anyone would be by such a beautiful and mysterious woman, especially back then. She offered him things he'd never dreamt of having. Money. Power. A chance to see the world change with every decade for as long as you wanted. See new inventions, meet new people. He would never age.

Never die. And if Killian was anything. He was a survivor. But, most importantly, she offered him companionship. So, he took her up on her offer." He paused while he took a drink. "She killed his friend a few months later."

I covered my mouth when it dropped open from shock. "What did he do?"

"He killed *her*."

It was wrong of me, I know, but at that moment, I was glad he'd killed her. As I was quickly finding out, vampires had an attachment to their makers. And, God help me, I didn't want Killian to have any such attachment to another woman.

"What about his family? Other friends?"

But Jamal shook his head. "He came over from Ireland with his parents during the famine. I believe he was fourteen at the time. His mother didn't survive the journey and his father died a couple of years later from an illness. He was on his own over here. By the time he could travel back to Ireland, there was no one there he really knew."

Sadness filled my heart for that young boy who'd had so much struggle in his life. "So, what about you?"

"Me? I'm easy. I got into a fight and got gutted like a deer, though you wouldn't know it now." He lifted up his shirt. There was no scar. Only smooth, brown skin and rippling abs. "Killian healed me. But to do that he had to turn me."

"And I take it that wasn't what you wanted."

"No. I told him to let me die. I didn't want to be like him. I didn't want to be a monster. But he wouldn't let me go." He paused. "He didn't give me a choice. And I'm too much of a coward to have done anything about it."

Now I understand where the hatred came from.

"I wasn't like him," he told me. "He loves being what he is. Loves the power. The immortality. He wanted to become what he is. I was lost. Besides my friendship with Killian, this world hadn't done shit for me."

Reaching across the table, I took his hand. "I'm glad you're still here," I told him. "I'm glad you survived everything you did. For purely selfish reasons, of course." I smiled at him. "I like you, Jamal."

He flipped his hand over and held mine. "I like you, too." He studied me for a moment. "I'm sorry about everything that happened with Kenya. Sorry it freaked you out." He paused, and I could see he was unsure what else to say. "She's my friend, Liz. She's a good person. Thank you for helping her."

"I didn't do anything."

"You gave her time. Time we desperately need. She doesn't deserve what's happening to her. She's a good one."

I believed him. "Thank you for telling me all of this. I really wish I could do more to help her."

"There's one more thing I need to tell you."

"What's that?" Giving his hand a squeeze before I let go, I went in for a third slice. I was not one of those women who pretended like they never ate food.

"How much did Killian tell you about this whole mate thing? The connection between the two of you."

"Nothing really, except that it happened at the swamp."

His face was thoughtful as he nodded. "You might want to ask him about that."

"Can't you just tell me? You're so much easier to talk to."

"I could, but it would be better if you guys had this conversation." Finishing his soda, he got up from the table. "Anyway, I'm late. I've got to get to the club."

Wiping my fingers on a napkin, I got up, too. "Are you meeting somebody somewhere?" I held up my hand, stopping myself right there. "Sorry, it's none of my business."

"Nah. I work there, so to speak. It's called The Purple Fang. You seen it?"

"Oh, yeah." I thought about it for a second. "Isn't that a male strip joint?"

Jamal grinned.

Then his meaning hit me and my mouth dropped open. "You strip there?"

"We all do," he told me as he made his way to the door. "We strip. We feed. The ladies are happy. We're happy. It's a win-

win. You should stop by some time. Check the place out. No one will hurt you."

"That's how you...feed? Aren't you worried someone will tell somebody about you?"

He shook his head. "We wipe their memories. All the ladies remember is a good time was had by all, and no one gets hurt this way. It was actually Killian's idea when he saw what a hard time I was having feeding the old school way. I couldn't terrorize people like that. We've run different versions of this club over the years, depending on what was popular at the time."

"Huh. How many of you are there?"

"Vampires? Six of us counting Killian. I mean it. Come by." He pulled the door open. "Take care, Liz. Lock up behind me."

"I will." Stepping up to him, I wrapped my arms around his big body and gave him a hug.

He hugged me back without hesitation. "Next time, you can bore me with *your* life story," he said.

"Deal." I watched him walk away. Funny how you found friends where you least expected it. And I had a feeling Jamal and I were going to be really great friends. At the door, I stuck my head out. "Oh, hey! Jamal?"

He stopped and turned around.

"Don't tell Killian where I am. Please? At least, not for a few days."

"I gotchu." With a wave of his hand, he was gone.

Locking the door, I took my pizza to the loveseat and turned on the television. But I couldn't have told anyone what I was watching. My head was too full of everything Jamal must have gone through to make him risk his life to run.

And a small, innocent Irish boy who risked his life to help people, only to turn around and steal those lives as a man.

20

KILLIAN

Something was wrong. I knew it before I'd even gotten to the back door and saw the plastic bag hanging from the knob. Looking inside, I saw it was full of Kenya's clothes. The ones I'd given to Lizzy to wear.

I dropped it and tried the knob but it was locked. "Lizzy?" I called.

There was no movement inside. No lights were on, either.

Backing away from the door, I looked up to the second floor to see if she was possibly up there. It was completely dark. I didn't know why I bothered. I knew she wasn't here. But what really worried me was neither was Wiggles. I didn't feel either of them.

Hands on my hips, I tried not to give in to the panic rising up inside of me. Maybe she just went to see her family. It wasn't an ideal situation right now, but at least I knew she'd be safe with them.

So, then, why had she left the bag?

My eyes landed on the mat in front of the door. It had been there so long it had left a dark outline on the brick of the courtyard. Part of that outline was visible, which meant the mat had been moved.

Squatting down, I picked up one corner and found the key to the house I'd given Lizzy. I picked it up, turning it over in my fingers, my mind racing.

She'd left me. There was no other reason for her to have left the key.

But where could she have gone? She had no car, no home of her own right now. There was no way she'd rented a new place this fast.

Or had she?

Fear shot through me as soon as I realized I had no idea where she was or how to get ahold of her, and I had to talk myself down. She still had her voodoo store. Maybe she'd made up with her aunt and had gone to stay with her.

Unlocking the door, I went inside. My note was where I'd left it on the kitchen table, but the money was gone. I picked up the piece of paper to see if maybe she'd done me the same courtesy, but there was only what I'd written.

I crumpled it up and threw it into the trash. In the bedroom, everything was neat and clean. The extra toothbrush I'd found for her was in the trash.

It was almost as though she'd never even been there.

Standing in the middle of the bedroom, I tried to figure out what the hell she was thinking to just take off the way she had, but I didn't have the slightest clue. When I'd left her early this morning she'd been sleeping contentedly in my arms. What could possibly have happened between then and now? What the fuck had possessed her to leave the way she had? Without a by your leave? I didn't care that she'd taken the money. She was more than welcome to it. The gods knew I had more than enough. And I had no idea what kind of access she had to her own since the fire.

Maybe I should've asked.

My thigh began to ache and I rubbed the old wound absentmindedly while I tried to figure out what my next move would be. I couldn't just let her disappear from my life. Not now. It was much too late for that. Our lives, such as they were, were now entwined. Because what she didn't know, at least not yet, was that I would die without her. Literally.

And I wasn't finished with this life.

I went back to my car and got inside, but that's as far as I got. What I was thinking was dangerous. However, Lizzy wasn't giving me any other choice.

Starting the car, I drove to the Garden District, telling myself I just wanted to make sure she was safe. It wasn't the smartest move, coming here. This part of New Orleans was home to the witches. Vampires were strictly forbidden. If I was seen, I could very well end up in the same situation as Kenya, or worse. Our agreement with the high priestess would be considered broken, and the lives of my entire coven would be in danger. The witches were already angry at us about something. What was happening with Kenya was a warning. To rile them up even more was the epitome of stupidity.

I knew this, but I couldn't get myself to leave without seeing her. I just wanted to make sure she was here and she was okay. Once I knew that, I would leave her be and let her get this little act of rebellion out of her system.

She would come back to me.

Pulling up about a half a block from Judy's home, I parked the car and turned off the engine. Hours passed, and still there was no sign of Lizzy or her aunt. I stayed in my car, ducked down low in my seat, keeping one eye on her house and one on the occasional passing pedestrian. If a witch walked by, I was completely fucked. There was no way around it. They would know I was here as soon as they got within twenty feet of me. If they drove past, I might have a chance of escaping their notice.

I was about to give up when a car coming from the opposite direction slowed down and pulled into Judy Moss's drive along the far side of her house. I lost sight of it when she got past the house, and watched anxiously for lights to come on inside.

A few seconds later, I saw a faint light through the front windows.

Getting out of the car, I walked down the sidewalk until I stood directly across the street. From there, I could see into the front room and through another window on the other side set back from the front door. I watched as Lizzy's aunt walked back and forth across the kitchen. Walking up and down the sidewalk, I searched for Lizzy, but there was no sign of her.

Eventually, Judy came into the front room with a mug in her hand. She picked something up—the remote control—and turned on the television. In the blue light of the screen, I watched her, waiting, just to be sure she was alone.

Judy suddenly stilled with her drink halfway to her mouth. A moment later, her head turned slowly in my direction.

I took a step back into the shadows of a large magnolia tree, lowered my head and shoved my hands into the pockets of my sweater. My clothes were dark. There was no way she could see me, not standing where I was. The darkness was too dense.

Yet, she knew I was here.

I knew this because the hair on my arms stood straight up. It was her magic, probing the darkness. With a curse, I ran to my car. It only took me half a second to get there. Turning off my headlights before I started it, I threw it into reverse and backed up a full block before swinging around and leaving the Garden District.

I could only hope she hadn't gotten enough of a read to recognize me.

A few minutes later, I pulled up in front of The Purple Fang. Plenty of time for every single worst case scenario to run through my head. Every horrifying scene of what could have possibly happened to Lizzy to play in front of my eyes.

I'd waited enough.

Every one of my vampires was going to help find Lizzy. I would close down this fucking club if I had to.

With that thought in mind, I charged inside. It was early yet for club goers, which was good. There was only a small group of patrons, a birthday party if I were to guess by the crown one young woman wore and the decorations on the tables.

"Killian? What's up, man? What's happened?"

Elias was behind the bar again.

"My mate is missing. And you're going to help me find her. You all are." I swung my arm in an arc, pointing at Jamal and Brogan at a table near the entrance to the back room where the private dances took place, and Dae on the stage.

"I'm sorry. Your what?"

Elias's face was slack with shock.

"My mate. I'll explain later."

I had his full attention now. "You actually found your mate?" Leaning across the bar, he grabbed my arm. "It's fucking real?"

"Yes," I gritted through my teeth.

"Aww, man. Don't tell me that! I don't need no woman telling me how to live my life."

"Jesus fucking shite, Elias, we don't have time for this now! I'm closing down the club for the night. We have to find her."

"Yeah. Yeah. Of course." He started tallying up tabs. "A fucking mate," he muttered under his breath.

I caught Jamal's eye and indicated for him and Brogan to join me at the bar. Jamal elbowed Brogan and pointed his chin in my direction, never taking his eyes from me.

Something was going on there. I could see it on his face. But I had no time to worry about whatever the hell Jamal was upset with me about now. I had to find Lizzy.

Brogan took one look at me and hightailed it over to the bar, buttoning up his shirt on the way. This one was covered in bright blue birds and pink palm leaves. I don't think I would ever understand this guy's choice of "fashion."

Jamal followed him at a much slower pace, dragging his feet. As soon as he got within five feet of me, I knew why.

Lizzy's scent was all over him.

The world around me faded into an angry red haze, my fangs shooting down as I lunged for his throat with an animalistic growl. Hands grabbed me just before I reached him, two large bodies jumping in front of me and throwing me back against the bar.

One of the girls who'd just wandered up turned and rushed back to her group.

With a surge of strength that came from the darkest depths of my instincts, I threw them off of me. But I only got one step in before they were on me again, holding me back.

"Killian! What the fuck, man?" Brogan shouted. "Why are you trying to kill Jamal?"

There was a roaring sound in my head. I couldn't answer him. All I felt was the need to kill.

"Because I saw Lizzy earlier tonight," Jamal told him calmly. "His newly discovered mate." Taking a step closer to me, he stuck his face right into mine.

I snapped at him, aiming for his throat, but I was pulled away before I could feel my fangs tear into his flesh.

"Why are you instigating this?" Elias asked him calmly. "You do know he'll kill you?"

"Yeah, I know." Jamal ran a hand over his head. "Jesus, Killian. We talked, man. That's it. That's all. I tried to talk to her."

"What in the names of the gods did you need to talk to her about?" Brogan asked.

"And why the hell didn't you just bring her back to...to...wherever the fuck she disappeared from?" Elias added. "This one was about to send us out hunting for her."

"Because she needs a few days to herself and I promised her I would give her that."

Dae's grinning face blocked Jamal from my line of vision. "Hey, man. What's going on?"

"He's trying to kill Jamal," Elias told him.

"Again?"

"I think it's for real this time," Brogan said on a grunt as he dug in his heels and I felt his arm tighten around my midsection. "Apparently, he had the gall to talk to Killian's mate."

"I can smell her on you!" I hissed around Dae's head.

"You have a mate?" Shocked surprise replaced Dae-Jung's usual grin. "Like a real mate? No shit! When did this happen?"

"I would guess recently, since neither Brogan nor I knew about it until Killian decided to take out Jamal tonight."

Dae was suddenly pushed out of my line of vision and Jamal was once again within in my reach. "Let me go!" I roared.

Elias grabbed my chin, turning my face until I looked at him. "We're not letting you kill Jamal, Killian. You'd never forgive yourself when you came back to your senses. So, you might as well just chill the fuck out and maybe listen to what our brother has to say." His eyes suddenly swung around the club as the distant sound of screams came to my ears. "Dae," Elias said. "Take care of that, will you?" Lifting his chin, he indicated the source of the screaming.

"But I'll miss all of this," Dae complained. "They're not going anywhere. I sent Kenny home and locked the door as soon as I saw all of the commotion over here."

"Just do it. I'll fill you in later," Brogan promised.

"Fine." With a heavy sigh, he stomped away. A few seconds later, the screaming stopped. From the corner of my eye I saw seven women heading to the front door, talking in small groups, and gesturing happily. Not one of them looked our way.

Not that I would have cared.

"Jamal, you'd better start talking," Elias told him. "This little Irish shit is stronger than he looks."

My rage focused on Elias for a brief second.

"I meant that in the nicest way," he told me.

Jamal rolled his eyes. "Look, I ran into her and her dog on my way here. I asked her if we could talk. That's it. I just wanted to make sure she was okay."

"Why do you fucking care?" I spit out. "She's not yours to worry about."

He became completely still. "Because she's a person, Killian. She's a person who had no idea we even existed until a day ago. In that one day, she was coerced to the swamp, forced to feed Kenya, saw two vampires fighting it out, and was informed she was one of those vampire's fated mate. She wasn't given a choice, Killian. She was thrown into this world just like I was. Hell, she just barely found out she's a witch!

It's a LOT for someone to take in. And I just wanted to make sure *she was okay*. That's all."

Fighting my instinct to kill this other vampire who had dared to touch my mate, I managed to grit out, "Then why do you have her scent all over you?"

He started to roll his eyes again, and then thought better of it. A smart move. "We talked. We shared. She hugged me goodbye. That's all. I *swear* it."

I let what he'd just told me sink in. Jamal was a pain in the ass sometimes, but one thing he was *not* was a liar. He also wasn't afraid of me as much as he should be. If he said that's what happened, then that's what happened.

"Get me a whiskey," I ordered Elias.

Little by little, he released his hold on me, ready to jump back in at a moment's notice.

I took a few deep breaths, willing my heart to slow and focusing on Jamal and what he'd said. As my irrational anger drained away, Brogan loosened his hold, then took a step back.

When I'd drained the glass Elias had brought me and had a second one in my hand, I looked up at Jamal. "Do you know where she is?"

He nodded. "I do. But I promised her I'd give her a few days to herself before I told you."

I cocked my head. "So your allegiance lies with her now, and not me?"

"She just needs a little space. Let her digest everything."

I swallowed the rest of my whiskey and set my glass on the bar. "I'm not good at waiting."

Jamal laughed. "Don't I know that. But if you don't want her to hate you, you'll do this for her."

Walking around the bar, I pulled out more glasses for everyone. Brogan, Elias, and Dae immediately took a seat and let me serve them. It was my way of thanking them for keeping me under control because Elias had been right when he'd said I'd never forgive myself. At one time, a long time ago, Jamal had been my one and only friend. My best friend. I still loved him as such, and hoped one day we could get that relationship back.

They accepted my apology with toasts and requests for refills, which I obliged. "Sorry I ruined your night," I told Dae as I filled his glass.

"Aww." He waved one hand back and forth as though he was waving away a bad smell. "No worries, man. The ladies will be back tomorrow. And they're bringing more friends."

"How do you know?" Brogan asked.

"Because I 'suggested' it to them as I was wiping their memories of what they just saw here."

"Awesome. I could use the extra." Brogan lifted his glass for another toast.

Jamal still stood behind them, his arms wrapped around this middle as he looked off at the stage without really seeing it. Bringing the bottle of whiskey with me, I joined him. "I—"

He shook his head. "You don't have to apologize. I get it." A thoughtful expression came over his face. "I mean, I don't really get it. But I get it."

I nodded, taking a swig from the bottle before offering it to him. It burned going down, warming me from the inside out and melting away my anger though my mind and my reflexes remained as sharp as ever. "I know she's not at her aunt's. Is she at a hotel?"

"Killian. Let it go. I'm not going to tell you."

Taking the bottle back, I finished it off. "What if she never wants to stay with me?" I asked him quietly as the others goofed off behind us. "What if, like you, she can't forgive me?"

"There's nothing for her to forgive. It's not like you knew this was going to happen. It just...is."

"It wouldn't have happened if I hadn't harassed her into coming to the swamp and then bit open her wrist to save Kenya." I pointed the bottle at him and then back at me. "*This* wouldn't have happened between us if I would've just left her the hell alone like you told me."

Jamal thought about that. "I dunno, Killian. Maybe it would've happened anyway. Eventually. She's your mate. And I get it now. Why you were so drawn to her, I mean."

"I can still smell her on you, and it's driving me mad."

He gave me a wary look.

I suddenly thought of something. "Wait. If we're all here, who's with Kenya?"

"Kenya's okay. Not well, but better than she was. I told her I'd be back as soon as I could."

Turning around, I set the bottle on the bar. "I'll go. You stay here. Or do whatever you'd like to do tonight. You've been stuck at the house enough while I've been chasing Lizzy around. And apparently she doesn't want anything to fucking do with me right now."

"She'll come around, man."

I didn't know about that. "I'm opening the doors, lads," I warned them. "Have a good night, and uh, sorry for the outburst."

As they cheered me out the door, my thoughts turned to Lizzy. I still didn't understand why she'd left the way she had, but I would give her the time she asked for. Because when she came back, and she *would* come back...

She wasn't leaving me again.

21

LIZZY

THREE DAYS LATER

The Purple Fang was exactly what I'd expected. But what I hadn't counted on was seeing Killian up on the stage, shirtless, breaking out moves I had no idea an Irish boy was capable of, to the thrill of the crowd of women clustered around the stage waving five-dollar bills at him.

I made my way over to the long bar at the back of the room. A good looking guy with tanned skin, dark hair, and a short beard was throwing drinks together and flashing his fangs at his customers, much to their delight if I was to judge by the overflowing tip jar. I was sure the customers thought they were fake, and I wasn't about to tell them otherwise. Jamal had assured me no one was seriously hurt by what the vampires did, so even though it didn't sit quite right with me,

I was also grateful none of them were running around terrorizing the city.

I watched the show on stage while I waited for the bartender to make his way to me. I didn't think Killian had seen me walk in, but suddenly his head jerked up, his eyes searching the club until they landed on me. The slow smile he gave me was far from friendly, it was sinful, and made my stomach flip and my heart skip a beat. I watched him dance, trying to play it cool as my blood heated in my veins, and it only got worse as he slid his hands down his flat stomach and beneath the waistband of his jeans, then pulled them back out and rubbed the heal of one hand over his cock as he rolled his hips erotically in time to the music.

Wow.

"What can I get ya, darlin?"

A cold shower would be nice. "Um." Tearing my eyes away from the vampire on the stage, I faced the bartender. "Just a beer. Whatever you have on draft."

He grinned, not even trying to hide those pointed teeth as he grabbed a chilled glass and started filling it. "I'm Elias," he said. "What's your name?" He slid my glass across the bar.

"Lizzy," I told him, handing him my new debit card.

His eyes locked onto my face with new interest. Apparently, he'd already heard of me. "You don't say. Want to start a tab, Lizzy?"

"No, thank you. I don't think I'll be here that long."

With a wink, he handed it back to me along with the receipt to sign and then made his way to the other end of the bar, taking orders as he went.

I took my glass and found an empty seat at a high table that looked like it was unoccupied by any of the women rushing the stage. After that first initial acknowledgment, Killian proceeded to ignore me, playing it up for his "fans." Watching him like this, I realized three things:

One, he was a truly, truly beautiful specimen of a man.

Two, he was a really good dancer. It was more hip-hop than Broadway, but the strength and the control he possessed was amazing.

And third, as I watched him pull a pretty brunette up on stage with him and seat her in a chair so he could give her an up close and personal performance, I was *not* okay with sharing these things—or any part of him—with other women.

Chugging down half of my beer, I almost left him to it. This wasn't high school. I wasn't going to make a scene. I'd only embarrass myself and it wouldn't accomplish anything. However, I also didn't have to sit here and torture myself.

It was stupid of me, really, to be so surprised. I knew he owned the strip club. Jamal had told me where to find him. I don't know why I had it in my head that he only ran the place and didn't participate. He was one of them. He needed to feed just like the others. At least, he had before he met me.

So why was he even up on that stage? I thought I was his "mate." His new one and only. He'd told me he would never allow me to become a vampire because then he couldn't drink from me. So, if he wasn't here to feed, what other need was he planning to fulfill?

Maybe, he'd lied about not wanting anyone else. Maybe, it had only been a way to lure me into his bed. I lifted my glass in a silent toast to myself because it had worked.

And it had been the best sex of my life.

Great sex was great sex. It happened. It was over. Finishing my beer, I left it on the table and stood to leave. But at the last minute, I changed my mind and went back over to the bar, taking the empty glass with me. "Tell me," I nodded toward the stage. "Do you guys do private dances?"

"We sure do, darlin'."

Perfect. How about one more round then before I leave? "How would I go about getting one?"

"Just ask your dancer of choice." The way he grinned told me he most definitely knew who I was, and who my choice would be."

"How much is it?"

"Depends on who you ask." He gave me another wink as he took my glass. "Can I get you anything else?"

"No, I'm good. Thanks."

When I turned around again, Killian's jeans were undone and he was humping the lap of the delighted woman in the chair, the muscles in his thighs and ass flexing to the dark beat of the music, completely visible through the thin material of his pants. Her hands were on his hips, his stomach, his arms...

A fire lit inside of me watching them. I was suddenly burning alive, and not in a good way. Taking a deep breath, I marched up to the stage.

Killian noticed me there immediately. With a kiss on the cheek, he accepted his tip and helped the woman out of the chair and back down off the stage, then he danced his way over to me just as the music changed and another guy in a gaudy Hawaiian shirt and board shorts got up on the stage. By the reaction of the crowd, he was a favorite. And I could see why. The man—the vampire—was gorgeous. And when he smiled, two long, matching dimples appeared in his rugged cheeks.

And he had dance moves as good as Killian.

I crooked my finger at Killian and he dropped to his knees in front of me. "How much for a private dance?" I called up to him.

His eyes were hard. "The price for that is steep," he told me. "Maybe more than you can afford to pay."

He was still angry at me for leaving. That much was apparent. But I was pretty pissed off myself right now. "I have $500," I said. The exact amount he'd left on the table for me.

His eyes narrowed on the wad of cash as I pulled it out of my pocket.

"You left it for me in case I needed anything. This is what I need."

My mouth went dry and my stomach filled with butterflies. The little bastards fluttering around in there like a storm was brewing.

And they were probably right.

He didn't even look at the money. I was about to leave it on the stage and walk out when he reached out and grabbed my wrist, holding onto it as he jumped down from the stage and led me toward an area shut away from prying eyes by a heavy black curtain. Women reach out to him as we passed, touching him with way too much familiarity. I glared them off, even going so far as to push one away when she tried to grab his ass.

Killian, of course, ignored all of this. Which only set my blood to boiling.

He nodded to the guy standing guard. "Make sure we're not disturbed."

"You got it, boss."

Behind the curtain was a room as dark as the rest of the club. Four booths covered in black leather surrounded a small dance floor, two on each side. I assumed for bachelorette parties and such. Two black wooden chairs were set against the wall. He pulled one out and set it in the middle of the floor, then took the money from my hand and tossed it behind him. I watched as it floated lazily through the air.

Some of it landing on top of the booths behind him, some drifting to the floor.

A new song started up, and without a word, he started to dance.

I watched, a bit self-consciously after only one beer, as he put his hands on his head, flexing his arms and abs as he rolled his hips, then moved smoothly from side to side. This was a side to him I'd never seen before, and good God, was it hot. He came closer, spreading my legs and putting one knee on the chair between them. Trailing one finger down my neck to the "V" of my sweater, he dipped it briefly into my cleavage before he tilted the chair back lowered the chair down to the floor with me in it, moving to the heavy beat of the music the entire time.

I didn't recognize the song, but I didn't think I'd ever forget it.

Following me down, he crawled up my body and dry-fucked my mouth without touching me before rolling me out of the chair onto my stomach. His fingers tangled in my hair and pulled my head up as he rolled his hips into my ass. I felt him, hard as a rock, before he rolled me over again and lifted me up off the floor with him as he stood, my legs and arms wrapped around him. "Is this what you do back here?" I asked him, the fire of my jealousy still burning through me.

"Do you really want to know?"

No. I didn't think I did.

He carried me over to one of the booths and sat me on the table. Unable to help myself, I touched his bare chest, but he danced away, leaving me wanting.

For the next few minutes, he teased me without mercy, until the only thing I could think of was getting him out of those pants.

The song switched, and something slow and sultry came over the speakers. Killian walked toward me, each step on beat, the bulge in his jeans giving him away, but still, he was completely in control. "What do you want, Lizzy? Why are you here?"

That was the question, wasn't it? I didn't respond. I had no answer. All I knew was some kind of morbid curiosity had brought me here, and a feeling of possession I didn't know existed had kept me from leaving.

"Is this what you want, then?" Oh, so slowly, he unzipped his pants.

I wet my lips when I saw the wide head of his cock, dripping drops of cum.

"Tell me, *Acushla*. Tell me what you want."

I clenched my teeth together. I did want him, it was true. I wanted him more than anyone I'd ever met before. But I'd be damned if I was going to play his power game.

Still just out of arm's reach, he opened his jeans a little more, pushing them halfway down off his narrow hips until his sex was free. I kept my hands clenched around the edge of the table I sat on, but I couldn't keep my eyes off of him.

"I'll tell you what I want, then." He took himself in one hand, running up and down his length with a hiss of pleasure. "I want your mouth on me." He took a step closer. And another. "I want to feel those perfect lips wrapped around my cock, your tongue tasting me." He stopped in front of me. "I want to come in your mouth."

He was so close, all I had to do was bend my head.

One hand wrapped in my hair. The other held his cock out to me like an offering. "Suck me," he demanded.

Although his hand was firm on the back of my head, he didn't force me. Instead, he waited for me to make up my mind.

Lowering my head, I took him in my mouth. He tasted slightly salty and all male, and I loved it.

"Ah, Christ. Yes, Lizzy." Killian moaned my name, keeping his hand in my hair and the other wrapped around the base of his cock as I flicked my tongue over the head and then sucked it into my mouth.

I released the table from my grip and grabbed his hips, pulling him in closer so I could take him deeper into my mouth, the sounds he made urging me on as I sucked him off. Soon, both of his hands were in my hair as he tried to direct my movements, but I was having none of that. He did not have the power here.

I did.

Taking him deep, I scraped my teeth along his length as I pulled away again. His hips jerked forward and he cried out.

I sucked him hard a few times, finding his balls with one hand and using the other to follow my mouth up and down his shaft.

I was suddenly flipped around and bent over the table, my cheek against the wood. Cool air hit my bare ass and my feet were kicked apart as far as they would go with my pants around my ankles. Killian's weight pressed me down as he bent over me and growled in my ear, "If you don't want this, tell me now."

When I could only answer with something between a whimper and a moan, his weight was gone and his hands were on me, spreading me wide. Wet heat licked me from my clit to my ass and I sucked in a breath.

"So sweet," he murmured.

Then his tongue was back, licking, teasing, flicking that perfect spot where all of my nerve endings came together and sent waves of pleasure shooting through me until my womb felt heavy and achy.

I was about to come when he slapped me hard on the ass, then ran his tongue all the way up again as he rubbed the sore spot he'd just created, spreading the heat. He did it again on the other side. And again. And again. Until I was squirming on the table, my breath coming in pants, my ass burning and my pussy wet. No one had ever spanked me before, and it was fucking hot as hell.

Something sharp scraped along the inside of my thigh. Instinctively, I spread my legs wider, giving him more room. There were two sharp stings, and I sucked in a surprised breath. Then the heat of his mouth as he began to suck, fucking me with his fingers at the same time he rubbed his thumb on my clit.

There was pleasure in his bite, something I didn't expect. With every pull on my vein, pure lust shot from that spot straight to my core, hitting me over and over until my legs were shaking and my orgasm hovered right there on the edge. I cried out, begging him to finish.

His mouth was gone from my thigh and I felt the head of his cock pushing at my entrance. His thumb pressed against my ass as he slid inside of me, filling me, hitting that ache so deep inside. It penetrated me just a little, and I pressed my hips back, enjoying the slight pain mixed with the pleasure. "Killian, please..."

Grabbing my hips he held me steady as he fucked me hard. I didn't feel the edge of the table digging into my hipbones. I didn't feel anything except him inside of me, his thumb teasing my ass. His weight on me as he bent over, driving deeper, reaching around my hip to find my clit.

"Drink from me, *Acushla*," he moaned in my ear.

What? "No," I panted just as wave after wave of raw, hot pleasure rolled through me, centering in my core, until with a sharp rise it crested, my body jerking against the table as my orgasm crashed through me.

Killian pushed my hair away from the back of my neck and bit me, sinking his fangs deep as I felt him swell inside of me right before he pushed impossibly deeper and came with a yell against my skin. He didn't release his hold on my neck as he slid lazily in and out of my body until we were both breathing normally again. Only then did he lick at the wound, then pulled out and did the same to my thigh, dropping soft kisses on my ass cheeks before he helped me stand up straight.

He handed me a clean hand towel from a pile behind the booth. I didn't dare ask what *those* were there for. I cleaned myself up and put my clothes back in order, then searched for a place to put the towel.

Killian took it from me, his eyes never leaving me as he used it on himself.

"I need to go," I told him.

"Go where?"

"Home." There was so many things buzzing around inside of me, I didn't know where to start. Or what to think.

"I want you to come back to the house."

"That's not my home."

"Neither is a cheap hotel room."

I laughed. "It's not cheap."

Tossing the towel on the tabletop I'd just vacated he studied me as he fastened his jeans. I couldn't read the expression on his face.

"So, you're just going to keep running away? You're going to run away from me, just like you run away from everything else in your life."

My anger was back. "I'm not running from you."

"Yes," he said. "You are."

I glanced over at him. I wanted to ask him why he was here. And if he planned on going back out onto that stage. I wanted to know what he was thinking. I wanted to know what it meant that I'd let him bite me, and if it changed anything. But I did none of those things.

Checking my clothes one more time, I paused, but I could think of nothing to say. So, I walked out of the room. My thoughts and my emotions were in chaos. I didn't know why I'd come here. What I'd hoped to prove.

He didn't follow me as I retrieved my coat from the chair near the bar and left the club.

22

KILLIAN

Four nights had gone by since Lizzy walked out of this club. Four long, agonizing nights of not knowing where she was or what she was doing or who she might be with.

It was enough to drive me insane.

I craved her blood. Her body. The way I felt when her eyes were on me. I ached for her touch. To smell her sweet scent. To see the way she moved beneath me when I was inside of her. Even just to hear her voice. To sit across the table from her and talk.

I knew, once she accepted this thing between us, we would have all of the time in the world together. We'd have forever. And yet I couldn't help but feel we would never have enough and I didn't want to waste one minute of it. I wanted her near me now. I didn't want to wait anymore.

But I'd kept my vow and I'd given her the space she'd asked for, even after she'd come here seeking me out. Jamal was right. Forcing her to be glued to my side would only make her hate me. And I didn't want that.

So, I spent every night either at the club or back at the house with Kenya. When I wasn't with her, Jamal was. He was there right now, actually, because we could both see the boost she'd gotten from Lizzy's blood was wearing off even though she swore she'd be okay alone for a few hours. But I didn't want to risk it after seeing her fall into such a rapid decline that one night. So we took turns staying at the house with her as we had from the beginning. I think Jamal actually liked it. If he was with Kenya, it meant he wouldn't have to see me.

"Killian," Dae stuck his head into the office where I was supposed to be going over the club's numbers. "You have company."

My head snapped up at the exact same moment he made his announcement. I knew exactly who it was. I rubbed my face. "Let her in."

"I'm already here," Judy Moss announced as she squeezed past Dae and came into the office. "You can go," she told him. "This conversation is between Killian and I."

I saw Dae-Jung's jaw clench with the casual dismissal and stood up to catch his attention. "It's all right," I told him. "Go on back out to our customers and keep them entertained."

"Just yell if you need us," he told me, completely ignoring the affronted look the High Priestess of the Moss witch coven gave him.

"Aye, I'll do that." Once he'd gone, I walked over and closed the door, shutting out some of the noise. "What can I do for you, Judy?"

Walking over to my desk, she took off her coat—a frumpy blue thing that made her look as harmless as any grandmother and did not fool me in the least—and laid it over a chair. "You can tell me where my niece is," she demanded.

"Well, now, that I don't know," I told her honestly. "I haven't seen Lizzy in quite some time."

The look she gave me was skeptical.

"I'm telling you the truth."

"Funny," she said after a moment. "But I really think you are."

"Glad we got that straightened out," I told her. "Now if there's nothing else I can do for you..."

"Why are you hunting Lizzy?"

"Hunting?" I laughed at that. "I'm not doing any such thing."

"You went to see her at her at Ancient Magicks. More than once. Why?"

"I think you already know that."

"Yes, she told me you asked her to help one of your friends."

I felt her magic touching me, testing me, and a released a heavy sigh and went back behind the desk, taking a seat in the black, leather chair and indicating for her to do the same. The wooden barrier between us would make no difference at all if it came down to it. But at least now I had access to the panic button near my right knee. A quick push was all it would take to bring every vampire in here running to my aid.

Once she was seated across from me, I said, "I would offer you something to drink..."

"I'm fine, thank you," she told me. "Now, tell me what game you're playing with my niece."

Anger filled me, swift and hard. "It's no game, and you know that."

"Don't you bare your fangs at me, vampire. It's rude."

"Don't act like you don't have any idea of what I'm talking about," I countered. "I wouldn't have had to go to Lizzy at all if it wasn't for your coven and *your* games. You went after one of my own. I think that makes any agreement we had about your safety null and void." I tilted my head to the side as I studied her. "I'm surprised you had the balls to show up here like this. Alone. Outnumbered."

Slowly, she sat back in her seat and linked her fingers over her rounded stomach, but her blue eyes were cold as ice. "What are you talking about?"

"I'm talking about what you, or one of your witches, did to Kenya."

"Kenya?" Her careful expression cracked, replaced by one of genuine concern. "What's happened to Kenya?"

"Don't act like you don't know."

Judy leaned forward, her blue eyes gleaming nearly white as they pierced mine. "Killian, I swear to you, we did nothing to Kenya. If something has happened to her, it was not me or any of my witches who brought it about."

My instincts were telling me she was sincere. Could she be telling the truth?

"Go ahead," she told me. "Dig around in my head if it'll make you feel better."

Without pause, I took her up on her offer and quickly discovered my instincts had been right. "This isn't possible."

If it wasn't the local witch coven, then who the hell had done this?

"She was struck down by a spell. Jamal saw it happen with his own eyes and I, myself, can feel the magic that cursed her every time I'm around her."

"It wasn't us, Killian." She threw her hands in the air. "For the goddess's sake, why would we go after Kenya? She's a sweet girl, for a vampire. I actually like her. If I wanted to cause any one of you misery, it would be you. Or perhaps Elias," she added as an afterthought. "He's too cocky for his own good."

"That's been our question as well."

"Why didn't you come to me right away?"

Disbelief twisted my features. "So you could do the same to me?"

She sat back again. "I see your point."

"Shite!" I leaned back in my chair and studied the priestess. She was telling the truth. Either it wasn't her witches, or someone had gone behind her back. "Is it possible you just didn't know?"

She lifted one eyebrow, her thumbs rubbing one over the other. "Are you asking me if one of my family went behind my back?"

"Aye. That's what I'm asking."

To my surprise, she didn't immediately respond. "No," she said after a pause. "None of them would risk being banished from the coven."

She was probably right. "If it wasn't any of you, then who was it?"

Judy shook her head slightly. "I don't know, but I don't like it."

My anger was swiftly cooled by an icy layer of hopelessness. If the witches hadn't put the curse on Kenya, then it was very possible they wouldn't be able to heal her.

"Will you come see her?" I asked. "Kenya?" Much as I tried, I couldn't completely disguise the pang of desperation in my tone.

Immediately, Judy shook her head as she got to her feet and grabbed her coat. "No. I'm sorry. We can't interfere."

"What the hell do you mean? She's *dying*, Judy." I didn't bother to tell her that only the blood I'd forced from her niece had kept her alive this long.

Still, my words were enough to bring her up short. When she turned back toward me, I could see true empathy in her blue eyes. "I'm very sorry for that. I am. I liked her."

I rose to my feet. "Don't you dare talk about her like she's already dead. She's not gone. We still have a chance to save her if you'd just *help* me."

But again, she shook her head, her lips pursed together. "I can't. We can't. And please, do not try to get Lizzy to help you. If I'd known this is what you were asking of her I would've forbidden her to speak to you anymore." She paused. "I still might do that." She looked up at me. "It's for her own good, Killian. And ours. I'm sorry, but we can't get involved. And she would be no help to you. Lizzy is a witch, yes. But she's completely unaware of her magic."

I tried to keep the smirk off my face, I truly did. But I was angry at her refusal. Angry she would do nothing at all to help one of us. And I wanted to hurt her the only way I could. "You can't keep Lizzy away from me, priestess."

Satisfaction filled me as her eyes filled with alarm. "She cannot help you, Killian. Cannot help Kenya. What else could you possibly want with her?"

"Why don't you ask her yourself?"

"Because I don't know where she is, you bastard. Apparently, there was a fire at her apartment she never told me about and her assistant tells me she hasn't been to the store all week."

"Maybe it's not me she's hiding from."

I didn't know why I was antagonizing her like this. Angering a witch was dangerous, as Kenya could well attest to. But I couldn't seem to help myself.

"But when I see her again," which I would, very soon, "I'll tell her you're looking for her."

Magic curled around me, raising the hair on the back of my neck as she came around the desk to stand directly in front of me, each step slow and precise, until she was so close she had to crank her head back to stare up at me from her meager height.

It took everything I had to hold my ground and not back away.

"Do not play with me, vampire. Or what Kenya is going through will seem merciful in comparison to what I do to you." Shifting her coat to one arm, she stuck her finger in my face. "Stay away from my niece. I'm ordering you. Or our nice little arrangement we have going on here will be finished."

"That's not happening, Judy. Lizzy is *mine*."

The outer layers of my skin began to burn.

"She is NOT yours. You have no claim to her."

I smiled. "Oh, aye, but I do. I'm sorry to be the one to tell you this, but we've recently discovered Lizzy is my mate. Given to me by the fates, you see. And you've been around long enough to know that there is no way in hell I'll be staying away from her. And I truly believe she feels the same about me." Or, at least, she would. Lizzy already craved my body. Soon, she would crave my blood. And then my soul. "So, if you truly care about your niece, you'll take a step back and stop trying to burn me alive with your magic. She'd never forgive you."

Judy stared at me for a long moment. "That's impossible."

I leaned down into her face and bared my fangs. "Ask her yourself." I cocked my head. "When you find her, that is."

I felt her feeling out the truth of my words, and I allowed her to do it. A moment later, the fire left my skin, leaving it feeling warm and raw but unharmed to the eye.

"Then it will be you who'll need to protect my Lizzy," she ordered. "At least for now. I don't know who or what we're dealing with here, and she cannot do it herself. Not yet."

I acknowledged her demand with a nod of acquiesce.

Never taking her eyes from my face, she backed away from me, then turned and walked out of the room, slamming the door behind her.

I couldn't let myself relax until I felt the weight of her aura leave the building. Then, I slowly lowered myself back to my chair, the adrenaline draining from my blood.

I put my elbows on the desk and rubbed my jaw with one hand. The only reason I'd gotten out of that meeting unscathed was because I'd told her Lizzy was my mate. Otherwise, there was no way Judy would have let me speak to her like that. If there was one thing the witches demanded, it was respect. And they had every right to. A witch's magic was the only real threat to us, other than the sun.

Well, and perhaps a dragon's fire. However, I had yet to ever meet one.

Taking my cell from my pocket, I called Jamal. "I need to find Lizzy," I told him when he answered. "No. No. It's not what you think. Don't fight me on this, Jamal. I just had a visit from her aunt. Yes, at the club." Briefly, I told him what the high priestess had relayed to me. "If you care about Lizzy as you claim, you'll tell me where the fuck she is." I didn't need to write down the address. It was burned into my brain as soon as he told me. "Thank you," I told him. "I'll be there to help you with Kenya as soon as I can."

Ten minutes later, I knocked on the door of the room number Jamal had given me. I knew Lizzy was inside. I could smell her. Her shampoo. Her blood. Her little dog. Her scent grew stronger as she got closer to the door and the thirst hit me hard and fast. I took a few deep breaths, calming my greedy nature.

There was a pause as she looked through the peephole, and then I heard the slide of the lock, overly loud to my sensitive ears. When she opened the door, I nearly lost my breath from the sheer beauty of her.

Christ. How could I have forgotten?

"Hi," she said. She didn't seem upset that I was there.

"I gave you some space," I told her.

A smile played around her lips. "I noticed."

"I'm done doing that."

She stared up at me for long moments, and then she stepped back, opening the door wider. "Okay."

I heard her heart speed up as I walked past her and into the room. It was one of the nicer rooms in the city, with a sitting area set apart from the bed.

"How long did you plan to stay here?" I asked as I looked around.

The closet door was open, and it was filled with clothes. New, I gathered, from the tags still hanging from half of them. The desk was set up with her laptop and a cell phone was charging beside it. It irritated me that there was a way I could have at least had some contact with her and yet she'd never bothered to let me know.

"I don't know. Until I decided whether or not I was going to stay in the city."

Once again, ice cold fear filled my soul. It caught my breath and sped up my heart until the beat of mine matched hers. But it wasn't the end of my own life I was afraid of, it was the possibility I would never see her again. I couldn't let that happen. I *would not* let that happen.

"What?" Worry crossed her face, but only briefly, before her eyes hardened and her jaw set into a stubborn line.

"Killian, you can't force me to stay with you. I know you think I'm your fated mate, or whatever, but I don't know what the hell that means. Not really. And I've got my own life to think about. Things that don't involve you and your weird vampire needs."

"So you would leave me? Is that it? Just disappear from my life without even telling me?"

"Killian, I barely even know you."

Oh, Acushla. That's where you're wrong. "Yes, you do, Lizzy, if you would let yourself. If you'd open yourself up to it."

"Open myself up to what exactly?"

"The inevitable," I told her. "You were created for me. There's no escaping that. If you tried to leave me, I'd follow you to the ends of the earth and beyond." The truth hit me hard as soon as I said it. "You *belong* with *me*."

Wiggles chose that moment to wake up and dig his way out of the nest of blankets he'd been sleeping on. When he spotted me there, he waddled over to greet me as fast as his arthritic legs would go. Tongue hanging out of his mouth, he pawed at my leg.

I took a breath, calming myself, and squatted down to pet him. "Hey, boy." At least someone was happy to see me. With one last good rub I stood up again.

Lizzy was watching her dog as he wandered off to check his food bowl by the dresser. Reaching into her head, I tried to decipher what she was thinking from the chaotic web of her thoughts. I didn't like what I found. "Why do you insist on fighting it?" I asked her.

"Because I have to," she told me. "I can't lose myself again like I did in New York. And I feel like if I gave in to whatever this is between us, you would"—her eyes wandered around the room as she reached for the words—"consume me completely."

The seven feet of carpet between her and I felt like a void I'd never be able to cross. Unable to stand the feeling a minute longer, I quickly closed the distance between us.

She startled, inhaling sharply when I suddenly appeared in front of her, but didn't try to move away. Her hair was loose, falling over her shoulders to tease her breasts. I took a few of the soft strands between my fingers, brushing the backs of my knuckles across the curve of her breast, enjoying the contrast of texture between her hair and her blue cotton shirt. Lifting the strands to my nose, I inhaled the scent of coconuts and flowers. She smelled like the sea, her skin warmed from the sun. Something I'd almost forgotten in all my years of darkness.

Blood lust roared through me and I reeled where I stood for a second, then touched my tongue to the tips of my fangs, trying to relieve the sudden ache there. But it only made the thirst worse.

Lizzy's eyes traveled over me, taking in the changes in my appearance and mood, but there was no fear within her and for that I was grateful. If she'd run from me then it would've broken me. She raised her hand to my face, her expression curious, and I felt her fingers trace the lines around my eyes and mouth.

Capturing her hand in mine, I turned my head and pressed a soft kiss to the center of her palm. "I've missed you so much, *Acushla*."

23

LIZZY

My pulse picked up as Killian ran the tip of his nose over the heel of my hand. There, at my pulse point, he inhaled deeply, taking in my scent before pressing his lips against the inside of my wrist. I felt that kiss all the way to the ache between my legs.

I hadn't realized how much I'd missed him until he appeared at my door. For most of the past week, after the night at The Purple Fang, I'd hidden away in this hotel room, only leaving it to work at the shop, take Wiggles for his walks, or to pick up food as I tried to sort out my feelings about everything. Mike had taken over closing the store for me, working extra hours so I could be back here by dark.

I really owed him a raise.

As I'd chowed down on takeout and binge watched whatever I could find on the television, I'd tried to come to some type of acceptance about everything that had happened and how I felt about it. But by the end of the week, I was as confused as ever. However, the entire time, I'd felt like I was waiting for...something.

Or, someone.

But now Killian was here. I didn't know how he found out where I was—if Jamal had finally told him or if he'd hunted me down on his own—and I didn't care. I was just glad he did. Because I realized now what it was I'd been waiting for.

I'd been waiting for him.

"I've missed you, too," I admitted.

He placed our joined hands over his heart, unfolding my fingers until my palm was flat on his hard chest. His heart was racing, the beats strong. "Do you feel what you do to me?"

I could only nod.

His eyes traveled over my face like he was trying to memorize my features. "Don't run from me anymore, Acushla."

"I can't promise you that," I told him honestly. "My life is so up in the air right now, and I honestly don't know where it's going to end up. This," I paused, searching for the words that would make him understand. "My coming back to this city, I'd always planned for it to be a temporary thing until I decided what I wanted to do next. Where I wanted to go. I never really meant to stay here, Killian."

"This is where you belong, Lizzy. With me."

I wish things were as clear to me as they were to him. I'd come back to my home hoping I could reconnect with my family, but running a voodoo store in the middle of the French Quarter wasn't my idea of a life. Finding out the only living relative I remembered was in charge of some kind of a witch coven was just another thing I wasn't willing or ready to accept.

And this...*thing* with Killian. My feelings for him were strong. Much too strong for the length of time I'd known him for. It was strange. And overwhelming. And too much.

Killian stared at me like he could see straight through to my soul. "I'm your family now, Lizzy."

"You're a vampire, Killian." I couldn't believe I was even saying that word out loud. "You're something I read about in horror novels or watched in movies. Something that shouldn't even exist."

"But I do exist, *Acushla*. And I have for a long time. Waiting for you."

Before I could say anymore, he dipped his head and took my lips with his, pulling me into his body with only our trapped hands providing any kind of barrier between us. His kiss wasn't timid. No. He claimed my mouth just like he claimed my body and possibly my heart. Because he was right.

I knew practically nothing about him, and yet, at the same time, I'd felt like I'd known him forever. Like we'd lived many other lives together and had only just now found each other again. It was exciting. And frightening.

He cupped my face for a moment as his other hand slid up my back before they both slid into my hair, holding me still while he ravished my mouth with his lips and tongue and teeth. I tasted blood as one fang cut into my bottom lip and Killian moaned deep in his throat, sucking my lip into his mouth and running his tongue along the wound. The stinging stopped, and then he was kissing me again until I was gasping for air and my breasts felt full and heavy. Until the ache to have him between my legs was almost painful. A sound escaped me, something between a whimper and a moan, begging him to ease that ache.

Breaking off the kiss, he tipped my head back, running his tongue along the artery in my throat before whispering in my ear. "Are you wet for me, *Acushla?*"

God, yes.

He smiled a self-satisfied smile. Had I said that out loud? I didn't know and I didn't care. My hands gripped his lean waist as my entire body strained toward him, trying to get closer.

"Say you'll stay with me," he ordered.

"That's not fair," I told him.

"You're right. It's not. And I don't give a shite. You're mine, Lizzy. I just need you to admit the truth to yourself."

As he dropped wet kisses along my jaw, my throat, and back to my lips, I slid my hands beneath his shirt and up over his tight abs to his chest. My fingertips brushed over his nipples, eliciting another moan before I slid them around his ribcage and dug my nails into his back. It was a gesture that perfectly described how I felt, both desperate and resentful of my need for him. I felt his hard length against my stomach and went for the fastening of his jeans.

A few seconds later he was free, thick and hard, filling my palm. Running my thumb over the wide head, I felt drops of moisture leaking from the tip before I tightened my grip and ran it up and down his length as he'd done that night at the club.

My stomach flipped as the world rushed around me, and then suddenly I was on my back with one of Killian's hands beneath my head and the other beneath my hip, the weight of his body pressing me into the floor. His fangs grazed the side of my throat, scraping along the sensitive skin.

"Do it," I told him.

His fingers tightened in my hair, pulling my head to the side. My pulse picked up and I heard him groan just before I felt two sharp stings. But the pain was minuscule compared to the pleasure that streaked through my body when he drew on my vein and his hips rocked against mine. Drawing my knees up to better position his sex between my legs, I hung on to him as the pleasure spiraled out of control, my body tensing as I teetered on the edge of an orgasm.

He withdrew his fangs from my neck only long enough to order, "Come for me, *Acushla*," before he reared back and struck again, harder this time, his fangs sinking deeper as his hips thrust against mine, hitting that perfect spot even with my clothes still between us.

I did as he commanded, riding the pleasure centered low in my belly until with a sharp, almost painful crest, it broke over the edge, shooting out from my core, so intense I couldn't stop my body from convulsing in his arms with each wave, his name a keening cry on my lips.

As I fought to catch my breath, he pulled my shirt and yoga pants off, and I'd never been so glad that I wore nothing underneath. His eyes never left me as he removed his own shirt, then stood to kick off his shoes and jeans. He gripped his sex as he kneeled over me, his eyes so intense they left a trail of heat everywhere they wandered. I'd never had a man look at me like that, with such longing, such possession, and with a sense of wonder, like he didn't quite believe I was there.

His upper lip pulled back, exposing his fangs as his gaze dropped between my legs. With a feeling of power I'd never had before, I let my knees fall open, exposing myself to him without shame.

With a hiss that raised every hair on my body, Killian's powerful body dropped to his hands and knees. He reached for me, spreading my thighs as he lowered himself to the floor. My hips jerked when his warm, wet tongue touched me, tasting what he'd done to me. He teased me until I felt the pleasure rising again and my hips began to rock against his mouth, needing more, before he settled in, his arms wrapped around my legs, holding me to him.

Just as I was about to come again, he surged over me, sliding inside with one smooth thrust. I cried out as he filled me, his mouth crashing down on mine for a deep, fast kiss before he broke away and began to move. At first, he held his weight off of me, his elbows on either side of my head. But it wasn't long before he slid one arm beneath me, thrusting deep and hard, over and over, his breaths ragged in my ear until I trembled against him, crying out as pleasure exploded inside of me. With a low growl, Killian pulled me so close until I didn't know where I ended and he began, increasing his thrusts as he sank his fangs into the muscle between my neck and shoulder.

I held on tight. There was nothing else I could do. I was his for the taking and that's exactly what he did. Took my body, my blood, my mind and my soul, until there was nothing else but him and me.

With a roar he pushed deep, his body tensing and releasing above me as he found his own pleasure.

Exhausted, I laid beneath him as he healed my wounds, still inside of me. "Is that what it's always like?" I asked him.

Lifting his head, he stared down at me. There was something in his eyes I hadn't seen before. The fire wasn't gone, but it was definitely tamped down. He seemed almost at peace. "That's what it's always like with you," he told me, brushing my hair back from my face. "Are you all right?"

I smiled. I couldn't help it. "I'm hungry."

He flashed his fangs. "You need to drink."

"I have vodka in that little fridge over there."

"I meant, from me," he said. He watched me closely, taking in my reaction.

"Why would I want to do that?"

"Because with my blood, you would never age. Never get sick. Never die a natural death. You would be with me forever."

Oh. "I don't know that I'm ready to do that, Killian."

With a sigh, he rolled onto his back, pulling me with him until I was sprawled across his chest. Crossing my arms over his chest, I rested my chin on my forearm. "Plus, I don't think I'd like the taste."

His hands tightened on my hips. "It can give you immortality, Lizzy. It would stop you from aging anymore..."

"So, you're saying I'm old?"

He smiled. "A right old hag."

I laughed.

His eyes traveled over my face. Gently, he brushed my hair back. "You're beautiful."

My smile faded. "So are you."

Wiggles chose that moment to get up from his nap spot and come over to lick Killian's face. I grinned as he wrinkled his nose, but accepted the love from my dog gracefully before he suddenly sat up, bringing me with him. "Come with me," he said.

I looped my arms around his neck. "Where?"

Shadows darkened his eyes. "I need to check on Kenya."

Oh, my God. I'd nearly forgotten about her.

"She'd like to see you," he told me. "To apologize for taking what wasn't hers to take."

"You kind of forced me on her," I reminded him.

He made a disgruntled noise. "I think you'd like her." Then he smacked me on the ass and lifted me off of him, standing me on my feet as though I weighed little more than the pillow from the bed.

"I need a minute," I told him. Picking up my clothes, I went into the bathroom to clean up. I didn't want to go with him to the swamp. Didn't want to "like" the vampire who would've killed me if Killian hadn't stopped her. And I had no doubt she would have. I wanted to stay here with Wiggles.

"Wiggles can come, too," Killian called from the other room.

Why did he always know exactly what I was thinking?

When I came out, Killian was dressed—all except his sweater, which was lying across the bed—and standing by the window, looking out at the city below. "I love this city," he confessed. "I always have. Despite the fact it's full of witches." He grinned at me over his shoulder, and my heart skipped in my chest.

"How long have you been here?" I asked as I joined him by the window.

"Since before you were born, off and on."

"I would think vampires would stick to places that had less sunlight, like in Twilight."

He gave me a bemused look.

"Oh, come on. You can't tell me you've never heard of those books. They even made them into movies."

"They're pieces of shite movies," he stated.

"I don't know. I liked them. Of course, I don't know how well they'd stand the test of time…"

"Lizzy."

I tore my eyes away from the city lights and looked up at him.

Killian was staring down at me intently. It took a long time for him to talk. "I'm about to lose one of my very best friends," he told me. I could hear in his voice what it cost him to say it out loud. "Are you sure there's absolutely nothing you can do to help her?"

I shook my head. "I'm so sorry, Killian. I can't. The only thing I've ever managed to do is destroy things, not save them. And I think if I had any sort of healing powers, I would've discovered them when my mom died. I didn't always like her, and she was completely weirded out by me most of the time, but she was my mom and I loved her. She was sick for a long time." I crossed my arms and looked back over the city.

"There was nothing I could do. There was nothing anyone could do."

In retrospect, I wished I'd called my aunt sooner than I had. If I'd known what she really was, maybe she or one of my cousins could've done something to help my mother.

An idea suddenly appeared in my head. "Have you approached my aunt about this?"

"Actually, I have. She came to see me tonight at the club."

"She did?" I was surprised. "Is that a normal thing for her?"

He gave a derisive laugh and picked up a lock of my hair, rubbing it between his fingers. "No. As a matter of fact, the witches normally stay off of Bourbon Street." At my look of confusion, he dropped my hair and gave a little shrug. "They stay on their side and we stay on ours. We only ever cross those lines when something happens that's a threat to all of us." His mouth twisted into an ugly line. "Except for this time. This time, I was told by Judy the witches would not get involved."

"But, I thought it was a spell that made Kenya sick?"

"It was," he told me. "Just apparently not from any of them. At least, not that she knows of. And she seems convinced none of them would do anything like that without her knowing about it."

"If it wasn't my aunt or any of the others, then who did this to Kenya?"

"That's what we need to find out," he said. "But I don't think it will be possible before I lose her." His eyes caught mine, and his were dark with loss. "I have no idea where to start even."

That idea I had began to take on more shape. "Maybe I can help in a different way." Walking over to the closet, I pulled out my shoes and coat and put them on. Then grabbed the leash for Wiggles.

"Where are we going?" Killian asked as he shrugged into his sweater.

"To see my aunt."

"I'm not allowed in that part of town," he said as he held the door open for us.

"You are if you're with me."

24

KILLIAN

The back of my neck tingled as I pulled up to Judy Moss's home in the Garden District. This time, I pulled right into her drive alongside the house. As I got out of the car and walked around to assist Lizzy, I heard the slam of a screen door.

"I let you off easy the first time, Killian. But this is twice now you've come around here. You know our deal."

Dammit. She *did* know I'd been here.

Lizzy looked up at me, a question in her eyes.

"I was looking for you," I told her. "I just wanted to make sure you were okay."

"Leave him alone, Aunt Jude," Lizzy told her as she took my hand and allowed me to help her out of the car. "He's here with us."

Opening the back door, I lifted Wiggles to the ground so he wouldn't hurt himself jumping out.

The high priestess stood on her back porch wearing a loose, blue robe with a flowered night gown beneath it and fluffy slippers. It would be funny if not for the dense cloud of magic lingering in the air. I lifted my hands in front of me in a gesture of peace.

"I mean you no harm, Judy."

Her eyes shifted back and forth between the Lizzy and I. "I don't like this."

"There's nothing you can do about it," I responded.

Lizzy looked up at me sharply.

"She knows about us," I told her.

Before she could say anything about my sharing with her family, Judy said, "We'll see about that. But for now, you might as well come in before someone sees you."

As we walked into her kitchen, I glanced around, somewhat unbelieving I was in the home of the high priestess. Whenever we would meet before it would always be on neutral ground, and always only when absolutely necessary. And now, here we were, twice in one night. Once in my territory and once in hers.

Her house was small, but neat and homey. "Tell me what you want and then get the hell out of my home," she told me.

"Aunt Judy!"

"You," she told Lizzy, "can stay."

I raised a hand. "I would like it noted that you were treated with much more respect when you invaded my club."

"Hmph."

That fact didn't appear to sway her in the least. I watched Wiggles greet an old, gray cat. It stared at me with its owlish eyes for a moment before it hissed and went to curl its body around Judy's legs.

I had the urge to hiss back, but managed to control myself. Leaning against the counter closest to the door, I crossed my arms and ankles and waited. Lizzy wouldn't tell me what she'd dragged me over here for, but if there was any chance at all it would help Kenya, I would do whatever I needed to do.

Lizzy pulled out a chair and sat at the small kitchen table, waiting until her aunt did the same before she started talking. "Aunt Jude, we need your help."

Immediately, Judy shook her head. "We can't get involved Lizzy, I already told Killian this earlier."

"And I relayed that information," I told her. "But she seems to think otherwise."

Judy pegged me with her blue eyes. "I find it hard to believe you didn't put her up to this."

"No, Aunt Jude, he didn't." When she had her aunt's attention again, she continued, "This was my idea. Killian told me what you said to him at the club earlier."

"Then why did you bring him here?" Her tone was casual, but I could sense the anger beneath it, and it was all I could do not to step between them to protect my mate.

Threatening Judy in her home would not bode well for me and my vampires. And I doubted she would hurt her own niece. The high priestess was many things, but she sincerely cared about her family.

"I made Killian bring me here because I wanted to ask you, myself, if there was any one of you who could help Kenya."

Judy immediately shook her head.

"Aunt Jude...please." Lizzy paused. "I take it from Killian's earlier comment you know what's happened between us."

"I do," her aunt told her. "But that doesn't mean I have to accept it."

I gave a derisive laugh. "It doesn't matter if you accept it or not. Lizzy is *mine*. And nothing can change that now."

"There *is* one thing," she told me.

Yes. She was right. There was one thing. "I don't know if killing me in front of your niece will help you win her affections."

"Oh, my God. Stop it!" Lizzy slammed her hands on the table, rattling the rooster shaped salt and pepper shakers in the middle. Interestingly enough, they didn't stop rattling for quite a time. Not until Lizzy had taken some deep breaths and calmed herself down.

Judy made no comment, but I did notice her eyes flick down to the shakers and then back at her niece. She frowned in thought.

"Aunt Jude, you can't kill Killian until I can make a decision about how I feel about him and this whole"—she waved her hands in the air—"fated thing." She dropped her arms back down to the table, then immediately raised one again and pointed a finger at Judy. "But right now I can say that he's right, I would not forgive you if you harmed him."

Her aunt leaned back in her chair, tapping the fingers of one hand on the table as she took her measure for long moments. "I'll try to control myself. But only if you agree to visit your family more often."

The casual request fooled no one. Judy was making Lizzy a deal: She wouldn't kill me, and in return, Lizzy had to agree to join her in her coven.

"Can we please discuss our family issues another time?" Lizzy asked her.

"Actually, I think this is the perfect time," Judy told her. "You want our help? Fine. But in return, I want you to come back into this family the way you always should have been here."

"Why are you doing this?" Lizzy asked her. "You think forcing me into something I don't want is the way to go here?"

"It seems to have worked for him."

I'd been silent long enough. "I have as much control over what happened between myself and Lizzy as you do, and you know it. Don't try to guilt trip her over something neither one of us had any choice about."

"And how, exactly, did you find out my Lizzy was your 'mate'?" Shifting in her chair, she laced her fingers together on the table top. "'That requires you tasting her blood, am I right?"

"You are," I told her. But that's all I would give her. I was treading on very dangerous ground here. I should have kept my damn mouth shut. If she found out what I had done...

"It was completely by accident," Lizzy told her. "And that's all you need to know."

Judy's mouth tightened and she looked away.

Lizzy sighed. "Look," Reaching across the table, she covered her aunt's hands with her own. "I love you, Aunt Jude. You're the only family I have left. Or, at least, the only family I remember," she corrected. "I understand you all don't get along with Killian and his vampires, but I always thought you were a better person than to just sit by and let an innocent person—"

"She's a vampire," her aunt said. "Not a person."

I'd heard enough. "You know what?" I told Lizzy. "I appreciate what you're trying to do here, *Acushla*. Truly, I do. But I think it's time we go."

After a moment, Lizzy nodded and stood up from the table. "Come on, boy." She waved for Wiggles to join us.

We were walking out the door when Judy said, "Fine. I'll call the coven together tomorrow night. But I'm not promising we'll be able to help her."

Lizzy and I exchanged a look, and she gave me a small smile. "Understood," I told her aunt.

"Where is Kenya? Your house in the Quarter has been empty."

"I can take you to her. Just let me know where to meet you all."

"Lizzy, I'll text you tomorrow."

"Oh, yeah. About that..." Lizzy gave her aunt her new phone number. "Thank you," she told her sincerely.

"I'm only doing this for you," her aunt told her. "And Lizzy," she stopped us again before we could leave. "Please think about getting to know your family better. I know you've made it this far in your life without our help, but there's no reason not to have it for the years we have left."

Lizzy only nodded, and then took Wiggles out to the car.

"Vampire."

Ah, the moment I'd been waiting for.

"If you hurt one little hair on my niece's head—"

"You know damn well I would never do that, Judy. I couldn't, even if I wanted to. Your niece has never been safer than she is with me."

"I'm holding you to that."

I gave her a nod. "Understood."

The next night, Lizzy and I led a small parade of cars out to the swamp. I was putting a lot of trust in the witches by showing them where we were. If things went bad between us, it would destroy the fragile trust we'd managed to build over the years.

After we left the high priestess's home the night before, I'd dropped Lizzy and Wiggles back at the hotel and then stopped by the club and informed the others what was happening tonight. Although they didn't like it, I'd made them agree to stay at the club. Even Jamal. He'd tried to convince me to let someone else take my place, but there's no way in hell I was about to hide out at The Purple Fang and let one of my vampires put their life on the line. I know that was the way some master vampires worked, but it wasn't how I worked.

Shite, but I was nervous.

As though she sensed my unease, Lizzy reached over and took my hand. It was the first time she'd ever done such a thing, and it touched me more than I could say. Bringing our linked hands to my face, I inhaled her scent and kissed the pulse in her wrist, letting the proof of her life force calm me.

"It'll be okay, Killian."

"I wish I had your confidence, *Acushla.*"

She was quiet a moment. "I guess it's hard for me to picture my aunt as some great and powerful witch."

I'd told her some stories after I'd gotten back to the hotel the night before. We'd talked for many hours, only stopping when Lizzy could no longer keep her eyes open. Pulling the drapes closed over the big window by the bed, we slept on the couch in the sitting room, just in case. I'd held her in my arms the rest of the night and half the day, and I'd never felt more at peace.

"Appearances can be deceiving. Once you see her in action, you'll never look at her the same again." I glanced up in the rearview mirror, watching the string of headlights turn behind me onto the narrow road that would lead to the house where Kenya lay alone. Helpless.

"I won't let anyone hurt her."

I gave her a tight smile. I had to believe the witches would live up to their word. I'd never known them to do otherwise. "What if they can't help her?"

Though I felt Lizzy's eyes on me, I wouldn't look at her, afraid to see the truth in her eyes. And she didn't respond.

A few minutes later, we pulled up to the house. I drove up into the yard to give the other two cars room to park, then waited on the front porch for the group to join us.

"Nice digs," the red-haired witch commented, sarcasm dripping from her tone.

"It's only temporary," I told her. "Please, come in." Holding the door open, I ushered them all into the house. "This way."

Kenya was in bed, her eyes alert but bright with fever. They grew wide when the five witches crowded into the room behind Lizzy and me.

I approached the bed and felt her forehead. She was burning up.

She gave Lizzy a tired smile. "I'm so sorry about that night..."

But Lizzy shook her head, cutting her off. "We'll talk about it another time." Then she gave her a smile. "But it's very nice to officially meet you. I'm Lizzy."

Kenya's return smile was tired. "Kenya."

Judy walked around to the far side of the bed and I pulled Lizzy out of the way to stand beside me as the other witches made a circle around the Kenya. They were eerily silent as they studied her. Though I'd never made it back to the swamp last night, I'd called Kenya and explained to her what was going to happen tonight.

Kenya's feverish eyes found the high priestess. "Hey," she told her.

"Hi, Kenya."

"Killian told me it wasn't any of you who did this to me."

Judy glanced around the group and then shook her head. "No, hon. It wasn't. And I'm so sorry."

"I appreciate you coming here," Kenya told her. "I know it's a big risk you're taking, and I want you to know you will forever have my loyalty." She looked over at me. "Well, after Killian, of course."

Judy smiled. "Of course. But Kenya, you need to know, we'll do what we can, but that's *all* we can do."

"I have faith in you," she told her. Then she closed her eyes. "Magic away, please. I'm very tired of feeling human again."

Judy laughed a bit at that. "Lizzy, would you join us, please?"

Lizzy startled. "Me? Aunt Judy, I don't have your powers."

"You do," she informed her. "Somewhere in there. Isn't that right, Killian?" Judy's blue eyes met mine.

"Aye," I said.

Lizzy frowned up at me. "How do you know?"

"I can feel it," I told her. "I knew it the night we met as soon as I walked into your store."

"Honey." Her aunt laid her hand on Kenya's arm. "You have magic inside of you, and every little bit will help us find out what's going on with Kenya here. We need your help. You don't have to do anything, just join hands with Alice and concentrate on Kenya. Alice will channel whatever's inside of you."

"Oh. Um. Okay." I watched as Lizzy stepped up beside Alice. The innocent-looking witch smiled as she took Lizzy's hand. "This won't hurt," she told her.

I stepped back out of the way as they all linked hands and bowed their heads. Judy pressed her free hand against Kenya's shoulder and began to chant, the others joining in. Time seemed to stop as I watched them, their magic thickening the air and crawling along my skin, but I refused to leave Lizzy and Kenya.

After what seemed like hours but was probably only minutes, they all stopped as one. My eyes darted from one to the next, trying to read their expressions.

It was Judy who spoke. "I don't know this magic," she told me. Looking around the circle, she questioned the other witches with her eyes, then shook her head. "I'm so sorry, Killian, Kenya."

Kenya's eyes opened and she looked up at Lizzy's aunt. As understanding dawned, they became frantic. "What are you saying, Judy?" She looked at the others, her voice rising in fear. "What are you saying?"

Lizzy reached for her hand, then looked over her shoulder for me.

I started to step forward when the male spoke up.

"I think I can help her."

All eyes turned to him.

"Alex," the little one whispered. She shook her head.

"I can help her," he told her. "This magic, I know it."

"What are you saying, Alex?" Judy asked him.

He looked down at Kenya, meeting her eyes. To my knowledge, they'd never really met before other than to see each other in the rare times when vampires and witches met to discuss the terms or something or another. And yet something passed between them in that moment. Something true.

Something I didn't like.

I frowned. But now was not the time or the place for confrontations.

"I know this magic," Alex told her, his eyes never leaving Kenya. "I recognize it. I think I can help her." He turned to me. "I need a sacrifice. An animal. Mammal, preferable. Can you handle that for me?"

I smiled. "I'll be right back."

Fifteen minutes later, I was helping the male witch, Alex, pull out the guts of a rabbit. The rest of the witches watched with mixed emotions on their faces as he dumped the carcass over Kenya's stomach, then pressed his hands into the smelly mess.

"Alex, what in the hell are you doing?" Judy asked him.

"Healing her," he responded. He glanced at her over his shoulder. "I'll explain later, but please trust me. I *can* heal her."

Judy shook her head. "I don't like this. You're messing with things that should be left alone."

"It's the only way," he said. "Would you rather see her die?"

Kenya reached for me and I took her hand. "Please, Judy." I met her stare with my own. "Please. I'm begging you."

Lizzy spoke up. "Aunt Jude, you promised."

The high priestess looked at us, then the others, before she sighed. "I don't like this."

Sensing his win, Alex told her, "I'll need your help."

Once again, the witches formed a circle around the bed. This time, Judy laid a hand on Alex's back as he bent over Kenya, his fingers buried in the dead rabbit.

They linked hands, and Kenya closed her eyes.

I don't know what happened in that room that night, but whatever it was, it was evil.

Once the witches were linked together again, including my Lizzy, Alex began to chant strange words, ancient words. The others stayed quiet. Heads down, holding hands, their power channeled one to the other until I felt it tingle my palm where I held Kenya's hand.

The magic Alex brought forth was not something I ever wanted to experience this up close and personal again.

As he chanted, his body began to vibrate from the force of what he was calling forth. His hands on Kenya's stomach, he channeled it into her until she shook on the bed like something possessed, her back arching into his hands until I feared her spine would break. His eyes still closed, he pressed against whatever force was inside of her.

Bolts of light streaked with blood from the rabbit shot up through his fingers, so bright I could barely watch. They coiled around each other, beautiful and ugly at the same time. I bared my fangs, hissing at the menace I felt within this spell.

Alex's voice rose, grew more insistent, more powerful, until suddenly, he lifted one hand and grabbed hold of the writhing lights. Twisting around, he threw it at the window. It smashed through the glass as though it were made of solid steel.

The room went dark, and the witches collapsed as one around the bed.

Releasing Kenya's hand, I pulled Lizzy up and into my arms, frantically pushing her hair back so I could see her face. "Lizzy? Lizzy, talk to me."

Her eyes fluttered open. "What the hell was that?"

I hugged her to me.

"Killian?"

Kenya's eyes were open.

Giving Lizzy a quick kiss, I set her down, sitting her on the bed as I bent over Kenya. "How do you feel?" I asked her.

"Tired, but...good. Hungry." I didn't miss the way her eyes darted over to the male before focusing on me.

"We need to check her again." Judy made her way back over to Kenya and laid her hand on her shoulder. Closing her eyes, she became completely still.

Again, I felt the fingers of her magic crawling along my skin, not as heavy this time.

After a few seconds, she opened her eyes. "I don't see anything," she told Kenya. "It's gone."

I helped Kenya sit up. Her eyes filled with tears as she told the high priestess, "Thank you."

"Thank him," she told her with a nod at Alex. "He's the one who healed you, not me."

"But you let him do it, and I'll forever be grateful."

"I'm glad I could help," Alex told her.

I watched as his eyes traveled over her face before he quickly stepped back and looked up at me. "Can I go wash my hands?"

"Bathroom is down the hall," I told him. Humans were so squeamish about blood.

Judy pointed her finger at me. "Not a word of this to anyone outside of those of us who were here. I don't know what this was, or who cast it, but if the fact that we were here threatens any member of my family I will be coming after you, Killian Rice."

"I wouldn't do that," I told her.

"Make sure you don't," she told me. Looking around to see the others were all on their feet and well, she said, "All right. Let's get out of here."

"I'll see you out," I said.

"I'll stay here with Kenya," Lizzy told me.

When I returned after washing my own hands in the kitchen sink, Lizzy was alone in the bedroom and I heard the shower running. "Is she okay in there by herself?" I asked her.

"I think so." She smiled. "Her strength seems to be coming back by leaps and bounds."

I ran my eyes over her, relieved to see her own appeared to be coming back as well. "I'll never be able to thank you enough," I told her.

She frowned. "I didn't do anything. Not really."

"They would never have come here if it wasn't for you," I told her. And it was the truth. She no longer owed me for her life. Or for Wiggles life. She'd given me Kenya back. But more than that, she'd made *me* alive again.

Her debt to me was paid in full.

25

LIZZY

ONE MONTH LATER.

I woke up as the shutters rose over the windows. With a moan of contentment, I rolled over, searching for Killian. Instead, I found a small piece of paper on the bed.

Sitting up, I switched on the lamp. There was a local address written in Killian's neat handwriting. I turned it over to see if something was written on the back, but there was only the address.

I heard Killian's voice coming from the kitchen and decided to hop into the shower. As I let the hot water soothe my aching muscles, I hoped I'd be able to get back to sleep at a halfway decent hour. I needed to get back into the shop tomorrow. The holidays were coming up fast and I had things to do. Plus, I just wanted to check in with Mike and see how business had been while I'd been taking time off to settle in with my vampire.

Dressed in loose stretchy pants with a comfy light blue top and my wet hair hanging down my back, I found Killian talking to Jamal and Elias around the kitchen island. He smiled when he saw me, but it didn't quite reach his eyes.

"What is this?" I asked him, laying the paper with the address on the counter. "I assume it was for me since you left it on the bed."

"You assumed right," he told me. He hesitated, and then said, "I called an old friend of mine today. You have an audition the day after tomorrow with Broadway across America. It's only an audition, you still have to prove you're worthy of the part. I know it's not New York," he rushed on. "But you'd still be on stage. And this way you'd get to travel." He nodded down at the paper. "That's where your audition is. You have to be there tomorrow at 8am sharp. I assume you can be ready by then."

I stood speechless, not quite comprehending what he'd just told me.

Killian studied me closely, waiting for my reaction.

"I don't understand," I finally said. "You're trying to get rid of me?"

"Would you both give us a minute?" he asked Elias and Jamal.

They both looked more than happy to leave. "Sure thing," Elias said with a smile in my direction as he grabbed Jamal and dragged him upstairs.

Taking my hand, Killian took me over to the table and sat me down, then pulled his own chair around to sit in front of me, our knees touching. I set the paper down on the table and stared at the address written on it. An audition? I was so out of practice. Was this even something I wanted?

"What about you?" I asked aloud.

"This isn't about me. It's about you. This is what you've always wanted, isn't it?"

I met his eyes. "But, why?" I asked him. "Why now?"

He smiled, but his eyes were filled with sorrow. "That's easy, *Acushla*. I'm giving you what you've always wanted. Your freedom."

"But what about you?" A wave of possessiveness heated my blood. "I don't want you to be with anyone else," I admitted in a rush. Then quickly moved on, ignoring the smile that played around his lips. "You'll need to feed." And strangely enough, I would miss the intimacy of it.

"I'm a vampire of a certain age." His eyes danced with humor. "I'll be well enough while you're gone as long as I don't wander in front of a large truck, or an angry witch." He sobered. "And maybe you'll stop by and see me when you pass through New Orleans."

I searched his face for some sign that this was just a game, but he was completely serious. "You're letting me go. Just like that."

He brushed my cheek with the back of his knuckles. "I am."

Sitting back in my chair, I waited for it to hit me. The feelings of relief. Of joy. But there was nothing. Only a strange sense of disbelief and numbness.

Killian suddenly pushed his chair back and stood. "I need to go to the club tonight."

Something sour and ugly rushed through me at the thought of him there, even if he wasn't going to feed from another. I didn't want him in that club, dancing to make other people lust for him.

He gave me an amused look. "I need to work behind the bar tonight, and maybe tomorrow, so the others can feed and Kenya can take a little time off. She's been working every night since she got well."

Oh. "Are you coming back here? After, I mean?"

There was a tortured look in his eyes as he shook his head. "I think it would be best if I didn't. It would give you some time."

Time for what? To decide? To prepare?

To mourn?

Only, it hit me suddenly that there was no decision to make. These last few weeks had been fun, but blood bond or not, I didn't belong here with him. And a second chance to live my dream had just been handed to me. I'd be an idiot not to at least try. "What if I don't make the cut?"

"You will, Lizzy. Of that I have no doubt." Taking my head between his palms, he leaned down and pressed his lips to my wet hair. I reached for him in turn, but he was gone before my fingers touched his shirt, the back door swinging shut behind him.

"Are you okay?"

I blinked hard to clear away the tears in my eyes before I turned to face Jamal. "Yeah, I'm fine." I picked up the piece of paper. "I just don't understand why he would do this."

"Don't you, though, Liz?" When I just looked at him blankly, he said, "He's doing for you what he's never done for me. He's giving you your freedom."

Yeah, I guess he was right. And I shouldn't waste this opportunity because I had a feeling it was the only one I was going to get to have my life back. And like Killian said, I could always come by when I was in town and see him.

Jamal wandered over to me and laid his large hand on the top of my wet head. "I'll miss you, though. So, make sure you hit me up whenever you're in the area, because you know damn well Killian won't tell me."

"I will," I promised.

"Cool." He cleared his throat. "I gotta get to the club, too. The ladies aren't gonna wait all night." With a flash of his white teeth, he strode out the back door and I was alone once again.

Wiggles came waddling out to the kitchen from wherever he'd been sleeping and started slurping noisily from his water bowl. Wiping my eyes, I got up from the table to get him his dinner and let him outside.

While I waited for him to get done, I was overwhelmed by what this would mean. Not just that I would finally realize my dream, but what I'd be leaving behind.

Other than a quick phone call to thank her for all she had done, I hadn't spoken to my aunt since that night at the swamp. If I was going to be leaving, I owed her a visit. She was my family, as was the rest of the coven. And even though I wasn't ready to explore what magic I may or may not possess myself, I'd seen what it could do, and I knew she meant well.

Grabbing my coat and Wiggles' leash, I locked up the house and went to see my aunt.

"I just stopped by to tell you that I'm leaving," I told her once I was ensconced in her kitchen with a hot cup of tea between my palms.

She sat down across from me at the table. "Leaving? Lizzy, you just got here."

"I know. But I have an audition with a talent scout from Broadway Across America." I tried to make her understand. "I can't pass this up, Aunt Jude. Being on stage has been my dream for as long as I can remember."

Lines of worry creased her face. "Lizzy, you can't just up and leave like this. You just can't."

I sighed. "Aunt Jude—"

"He won't just let you go."

"You're talking about Killian."

"Yes! Lizzy...didn't he tell you? Don't you understand? You're his now, honey." Her mouth twisted in disgust, much as she tried to hide it. "You belong to a vampire."

A few weeks ago, those words would have made me bristle in anger. But not now. Now they only gave me a rush of warmth. "Killian is the one who got me the audition," I told her with a sense of satisfaction. He wasn't the epitome of pure evil she seemed to think he was.

"What?"

"He got me the addition," I repeated. "Apparently, he called in a favor to someone he knows."

"Hmph, I bet."

I gave her a look and she sighed.

"So, he got you a part. Just like that."

"No." I shook my head. "He got me the chance. I have to try out just like anyone else."

She took a sip of her tea, eying me over the rim of her cup. "You seem pretty sure you're going to get it."

"I have to," I told her. "I don't think I'll get another shot after this." I reached across the table and covered her hand with mine. "Don't you get it, Aunt Jude? He's letting me go."

She shook her head. "There has to be a catch."

I rolled my eyes. "There's no catch."

"But he'll die without you." A sudden gleam lit up her blue eyes. "Or is that your plan?"

"No!" Yanking my hand from hers, I sat back in my chair. "How could you think I would do something like that?"

"Holy crap." Her teacup clattered on the table as she suddenly set it down. "You actually care about him."

I looked down at my hands, twisted together on the table. She was right. I did care about Killian. Of course, I did.

"Yes, well, even so, I have to say I'm not comfortable with this, Lizzy. And what about you?"

"What about me?" I asked her.

"Honey, by some miracle, you've made it this far in your life without hurting anybody with your magic. But that's not gonna last. The older you get, the more powerful you will be."

I tried to blow off what she was saying, but she gripped my wrist tight, forcing me to look at her.

"You have magic inside of you, Lizzy. We all feel it. I can feel it roiling around in there right now. It's powerful, honey. And if you don't know how to contain and control that power, things can get really bad really fast. You could hurt someone. You could hurt yourself." She released my arm, rubbing her temple. "I wish you would stay here with us."

"I'm sorry, Aunt Jude, but I can't. Broadway has always been my dream, and I'm going for it. It's not New York, but it's as close as I'm ever going to get. Besides," I tried for a smile, but didn't quite make it. "I'll be back to visit whenever I can."

My aunt searched my face. "You belong here."

I shook my head. "I'm not a witch. And I never will be."

"But that's where you're wrong," Aunt Judy said. "You *are* a witch. And you always will be."

I didn't try to argue with her, knowing it would be pointless.

"What about the store?" she asked.

"I'm going to see if Mike wants to take over for me while I'm gone. I don't want to sell it," I assured her. "It's been in the family for a long time."

"Maybe I'll have one of the girls help him out. That is, if you'd like." She raised her eyebrows in question and I nodded. "And that way, we'll have access to the back room. If you agree."

Pulling the spare key to the store from my pocket, I slid it across the table to her. "That's okay with me," I told her.

"Are you sure there's nothing I can do to change your mind?"

"Nothing at all," I told her gently.

Her smile was sad. "Well, you're a grown woman. I suppose you can make your own decisions."

I snorted. "Thanks."

"But you know where I am," she told me. "Please, *please* don't hesitate to call me if anything at all happens. I don't care where you are. Or what time it is. You call. We will come to you."

"I will. I promise." Standing up, I took my cup to the sink and then reached down and gave her a hug.

"I'm sorry about everything," I told her. "I really am."

"Oh, I know you are, honey. And I am, too. We're family, Lizzy. I'll always be here for you."

"Same here," I told her. After all, this woman and her coven were all I had other than Killian. And honestly, I didn't want to live my life alone. It was nice to know someone would always be there.

"When you get all this showbiz stuff out of your system," she said. "You come back to me." Grabbing my hand, she stood up. "Promise me that you'll come back to me."

"I promise," I told her with another hug. She squeezed me back with more strength than a woman her age should have. Gathering up my things, I got ready to head to the door.

"And don't forget, call if anything strange happens. Anything you can't control. If you notice an ant doing what you tell it to do, you call me."

"I will."

The day after the audition, at the shop with Mike, I found out I'd gotten the part. "Hey Mike!" I called into the back room.

A few seconds later he came walking out from behind the curtain with his hands full of scented candles. "Yeah?"

"How would you like to be promoted to manager of the store?"

26

KENYA

It was almost surreal to be back at The Purple Fang.

I finished adding in the night's totals, backed up the file, and shut down the computer. It had been a little slower than usual tonight, but I was kind of glad. I hadn't mentioned it to the guys, but I still wasn't feeling quite back to normal after my little jaunt to the threshold of death's door.

I shut off the computer, turned off the lights, locked the office door, and went out into the club. It was quiet. The guys had already gone home. Checking my watch, I only then realized how late it was. Another hour and my skin would feel that prickling sensation it always did with the upcoming sunrise.

Retrieving my coat from behind the bar, I shoved my arms into the sleeves and shrugged it on, pulling my hair out from underneath the collar. With one last look around, I turned off all of the lights except one behind the bar, got my bag—large enough to hold my laptop—and walked to the front door.

Once again, my mind strayed to the night the witches saved me. I didn't remember much. Just a bunch of faces looking down at me, a lot of chanting, and the pain of somebody trying to rip out my insides. It still surprised me that I walked away from that night completely intact. Yet, every once in a while, I lifted my shirt in front of a mirror to make sure that was, indeed, true.

I didn't remember who all had been there other than Killian.

And one other.

The one who had reached inside of me and pulled the spell from my ailing body, his magic as dark as my rotting insides.

Locking the door behind me, I dropped the keys in my bag and looked up.

As though I'd conjured him up from within my mind, he stood across the street, leaning casually against a light post. Dressed in jeans and boots and a fitted pine-green jacket, he seemed completely out of place amongst the broken glass, discarded cups, and other trash that always littered Bourbon Street at the end of a Saturday night.

When he saw me there, he straightened to his full height—a good foot taller than me. Although he appeared to be alone, I smelled no fear as his eyes caught mine.

Tentatively, he lifted one hand in greeting. Quickly, I searched up and down the street, making sure no one had seen him there. But the street was empty.

I waved him over and unlocked the door to the club again to bring him inside, standing back as he jogged across the street and slipped inside.

"What are you doing here, Alex?" I asked him. The words came out a little harsher than I wanted. But if anyone found out he was here alone, without the high priestesses knowledge...

"I just wanted to check on you. See how you were doing."

"Oh." Hiding my surprise, I set my bag down on the nearest tabletop. I wanted my movements to be unhampered, just in case I had to fight. Witches and vampires kept our distance from each other, and for good reason, except for the few and far between times when we had to bang out new rules in order to reside within the same city in peace. So, him being here like this, it wasn't normal.

Plus, there was something dangerous about this one. More so than the others.

"I'm feeling okay," I told him. "I think."

"That's good. You look good."

I'd just fed a few hours before, but I didn't mention that fact. It was a touchy subject. "Alex, you shouldn't be here."

His eyes, dark as pitch, roamed over my face as one side of his mouth lifted in something of a smirk. "It's all right," was all he said.

I shook my head. "No. No, it's not 'all right'. Not at all. You're not supposed to be in this part of town without permission."

"Are you going to do something about it?"

The challenge in his voice, though slight, was hard to miss. "No," I told him. Not because I was frightened of him, although I was, but because he had saved my life. And I seriously doubted he would go through all of that trouble just to come here now and finish me off.

Unless he had been the one to cast the spell over me. And only healed me because the rest of his coven had been there as witnesses.

But why would he have done that? Killian and Lizzy told me no one had known the magic inside of me or how to heal it until Alex had stepped up. He could just as easily have pretended not to know and no one would've been the wiser.

"I can see everything you're thinking flash across your pretty face," he said. Stepping closer, he took a curl of my hair between his fingers, feeling the texture as he searched my expression. "I'm not here to hurt you, Kenya. I just wanted to make sure I'd removed it all."

"How did you know?" I asked him.

One dark eyebrow rose, but he didn't answer my inquiry. Instead, he released my hair and held his palm over my chest without touching me.

"May I?"

I hesitated, not sure what he was asking.

"I just want to check that it's all gone," he told me. "That's all."

With a quick nod, I gave him permission.

He pressed his hand against my chest, right between my breasts above my heart.

The moment he touched me, I sucked in a quick breath. His touch was like fire, branding my skin through the material of my shirt and bra as his fingers splayed wide. My heart began to pound, not from fear, but from something else entirely.

He had been looking at his hand, but now his eyes flashed up to mine, and I saw the same fire I felt reflected there before he dropped them again.

Slowly, I felt a tingly warmth warm my ribcage, spreading from his palm. It crept through my body, traveling to the furthest reaches of my fingertips and toes before it slowly withdrew back to his hand over my heart.

As soon as he removed his hand, I took a step back, breathing in some much needed oxygen. I had to clear my throat twice before I was able to speak.

"Well?" I asked him.

He was frowning slightly, and I began to worry until he spoke and I realized that look had nothing to do with what he was about to say. "I think you're okay. But I need to tell you something, Kenya. And I need you to listen to me."

"Tell me what?"

He pressed his lips together, drawing my attention to his mouth. I'd never noticed before how perfect his lips were.

"This magic that was inside of you, Judy was right when she said it was like nothing we'd ever dealt with before."

"What does that mean?"

"It means...I don't really know. But it's dark. And it's evil. And whoever cast that spell on you won't be happy to know that you lived through it. So I'm asking you, please, be careful. I don't like you being alone like this at night."

There was a light in his eyes. Possessive. Intense. It made the hair rise up on the back of my neck and sent chills down my arms.

I tried to smile to break the tension and failed miserably. "I'll be fine," I told him. After all, I was a vampire. I had senses above and beyond the normal human. Even a witch. "But if it makes you feel better, I'll ask one of the guys to hang back with me when I'm closing."

"It would," he said carefully, although somehow, I had the feeling my answer didn't satisfy him at all.

He stared at me for so long I had to suppress the urge to make a face. Or tell a joke. Or do some other awkward thing my nerdy self resorted to whenever I didn't know what else to do. But then he touched my face, trailing his fingertips along my jaw before he stopped and ran his thumb over my bottom lip.

"Please heed what I told you."

I nodded.

With one last, longing look. He was gone.

27

KILLIAN

I found out Lizzy had gotten the part when my friend called me to thank me for sending her. Apparently, she was perfect for the role, and he'd been searching for weeks for the right person to play it. Rehearsals were starting that week in Austin, and he'd already helped her make arrangements for her and her dog to move out there. She was on her way. He didn't know what I was, or what Lizzy meant to me, and after exchanging a few pleasantries, I ended the call.

Agony flared inside of me. The pain raw. Uncontrollable. Turning around, I smashed my fist through the piece of shite wall in the living room of the swamp house. But it wasn't enough. Screaming the hurt inside of me to the heavens, I vented my pain on this house where I'd been staying since I told her about the audition. Even after I'd torn apart the kitchen, ripping the appliances out and throwing them through the walls to splash into the swamp, it wasn't enough. Sunlight streamed into the house, so I moved to a different room, chucking out the old furniture. If it wasn't still daylight, I would've torn the place down around me.

When I could do no more without burning myself alive, I stood in the center of the hall, breathing hard. But not from exertion, no. I could rip this house apart. Tear out trees. Run for days and hardly feel it at all.

But because I had no other way to release the pain inside of me.

What had I done?

Ripping off my sweater, I threw it to the floor. I was suffocating, my blood burning like fire in my veins, my heart like a bomb in my chest, every beat more painful than the last until I wanted to rip it out. If I thought it would make any difference, I would do it, and give to Lizzy. It was hers, anyway.

The tips of my fingers dug into the center of my chest as I fell to my knees on the hard wood, my head falling forward as the weight of defeat pressed me down.

What the *fuck* had I done?

She had left me. My *Acushla*. My pulse. The reason my heart beat within my chest. I'd given her the choice, and she'd taken it. She didn't want to be with me. Didn't want any part of this life. No part of the immortality I could offer her. The protection. The loyalty. The love.

She wasn't mine. She never was.

Rain began to fall, echoing off the tin roof above me. The wind kicked up, blowing in gusts through the holes I'd made in the walls, wetting the shite floors. If it hit me at all, I didn't know. I was there, but I was gone, drowning in the loss of my mate. How did anyone survive this? How could I go for days, months, without seeing her? Without smelling her clean skin or the sweet scent of her blood? How could I go about my days knowing she was out there in the world on her own without me there to protect her? Without watching the way she walked across a room? Or feeling the soft strands of her hair sliding across my palms, my bare chest?

The thought of another watching her, talking to her, wanting her as I did was enough to make me completely mad.

But I couldn't force her to stay with me. I'd tried that before, first with Jamal, and then with the others. They didn't hate me as Jamal did, for unlike him, I'd given them the choice to become vampires, but they still weren't *mine*. Not really. I was their creator. The master of their coven. At times their friend and at other times nothing but a pain in their asses. They stayed with me because I made them what they were and they owed me that loyalty, but that was all.

I was constantly alone in a house full of people. And I could deal with that.

Finding Lizzy, however, had been something entirely different.

Her, I loved enough to let go.

I don't know how long I stayed there as I was, kneeling on the floor. I'd retracted inside of myself, living in the few memories I had of my mate. Her smile. The sounds she made when I was inside of her. I would give anything to hear her moan in passion, or even to have her ranting at me in anger. It was infinitely better than this reality.

"Killian?"

She sounded so real. Like she was right there in front of me.

"Killian? What are you doing?"

A heavy blanket was thrown over my shoulders, dragging me from the comfort of my mind. I blinked open my eyes. "Lizzy?" My voice was raspy, like I hadn't used it in a very long time, or had screamed it away. Breathing in deep, I inhaled her scent. Immediately, my fangs shot down, aching to sink into her soft flesh. It made me woozy and I swayed on my heels.

"I've been waiting for you to come home," she said. "Kenya told me she hadn't seen you in days and they were all starting to get worried. She was going to come out here to see if you were here but I told her I'd come. I thought I'd find you licking your wounds, not destroying the place."

She was teasing me. She was here and she was teasing me.

With a shaking hand, I reached for her. *"Acushla."*

And then she was on her knees in front of me. Her smile blinding me. "I'm here."

A low growl rose from the depths of my pain. I was afraid to move. Afraid she would disappear.

Lizzy smiled even harder when she heard it.

Questions, so many fucking questions, flew through my mind. But I couldn't grasp one enough to ask it. Lizzy was here. She had come back to me.

And this time, I wasn't letting her go.

I was suddenly on my feet pulling her up from the floor and into my arms. A second later, my fangs sank deep into her throat. Her blood flooded my mouth, coating my dry throat. I hadn't realized how starved I was until she was there in front of me.

She moaned as I drew on her vein, tilting her head away to give me more room and I released her vein only to strike again, deeper this time. I wanted to talk to her, to find out why she was here and how long she planned to stay, but my vampire instincts had taken over completely.

MINE.

This witch was mine. And she wasn't leaving me again.

My body came alive as her blood filled me. I turned to press her into the wall but the wall wasn't there. With a snarl I rushed to the back bedroom. I hadn't made it there, yet, and the bed Kenya had occupied for so many weeks was still there, but it stunk like a sickroom and I couldn't take Lizzy there. My eyes shot around the room, desperately searching for a place, until finally I released her vein and licked the wound closed. The musk of her desire rose around me, driving me mad as her soft lips pressed against my throat.

"Yes, Killian," she breathed. "I need you so much."

With my hand wrapped in her hair I pulled her face to mine and kissed her mindlessly, tongues and teeth clashing. In my haste, I nipped her lip, drawing blood, and I fell to my knees with Lizzy on my lap. Desperately, I pushed my hips up into her core, but it wasn't enough. I needed to feel her wet heat on my cock.

She was yanking on my shirt. I broke off the kiss to help her get it off. Her hands were all over my shoulders and chest as I tugged her coat and shirt off. Her bra fell in pieces on the floor and then her beautiful bare breasts were exposed, the nipples hard. She arched her back, begging silently for my touch. I took her into my mouth, teasing one hard nub with my tongue and then the other. I was so hungry for her I was about to come in my jeans.

Rising up on my knees, I set her down and tugged at the fastening of my pants with one hand while I pushed hers down with the other. She helped me, kicking off her shoes and managing to get one leg off before I was pulling her back on my lap.

Lizzy held herself up, denying me as my fingers dug into her soft hips. "Lizzy," I growled. "I need to be inside of you."

"I know," she whispered as her hand wrapped around my cock.

I almost lost it. Even though she'd said she would come back, I honestly thought I'd never feel her touching me again. I had planned to sit in the hallway of this ruined shack of a house and do nothing until I starved to death.

But now she was here. Her hands were on me and she was sliding me inside of her, her body tightening around me, hot and wet and so, so, sweet.

"Oh, God! Killian," she moaned.

As I guided her with my hands, I couldn't take my eyes off of this perfect woman of mine. My mate. My lover.

My friend.

She threw her head back, arching her back until her long hair brushed my knees, allowing me to sink deeper inside of her. With a hiss, I bared my fangs, then sank them into her breast.

Lizzy cried out, rolling her hips faster, but it wasn't enough.

Holding her still so I wouldn't lose my bite, I curled my body and increased my pace, going deeper, harder, until she was crying out my name, her hands on the back of my head, holding my mouth to her breast.

I growled low as I felt my cock swell to the point of pain. Releasing her breast, I held her tight in my arms as I chased the pleasure she promised me, one arm around her back and the other under her rounded ass.

"Bite me," she moaned. "Please, Killian."

Lizzy exposed her throat. Unable to deny her anything, I did as she asked, hanging on to my control for dear life. I drank, every cell in my body coming alive, charged with her blood until I felt like I was indefinable. A god. Something not of this world. Something that couldn't be contained in this skin. I drank until I felt her entire body tighten, and I growled my encouragement, the little sounds she made right before she was about to come like music in my ears.

I bit deeper and she cried out as her body tightened almost painfully on my cock. With a roar of pleasure, my own orgasm crashed through me.

We sat there for a long time as I rocked my hips against her, not wanting to be apart from her again. I moaned as I removed my fangs from her throat and licked her wound, but I didn't release her from my arms. I couldn't.

"What are you doing here?" I finally asked her.

Her head was heavy on my shoulder. She sighed. "I missed you," she whispered.

"What about your part? You're supposed to be in Austin."

"I didn't like Austin."

My heart beat heavy in my chest. "Why?"

She lifted her head and met my eyes. "Because you weren't there."

I think it stopped beating altogether. I definitely stopped breathing. Only her sudden look of concern made me remember to start again. "I think I lied to you."

The concern in her eyes turned to fear. "About what?"

"I don't think I *can* live without you, Lizzy. Actually, I know I can't. Because I think I'm falling madly in love with you. And when you were gone..." I trailed off, unable to put into words the hell I'd gone through. "I can't do this again." I wanted to tell her more. To tell her what she meant to me, but I didn't have the words.

She smiled. "Does that mean you're going to start being nice to me and stop trying to dominate me all the time?"

"Probably not," I told her honestly.

Her smile grew. "Good. Because that's my favorite part about you."

"You have favorite parts?"

"I do."

"What are the others?" I asked, a part of me still starving for her reassurance.

"I'll tell you in time. Because from what I understand, from what Kenya was telling me while I waited for you, we'll have tons of it."

Though she was right in front of me, though her wet warmth still hugged my cock, I was afraid to believe. "Aye," I finally managed to get out. "If you'll have me, Lizzy."

The smile slipped from her face, and I squeezed her hips, terrified she was about to change her mind. "I will have you, Killian. I've wanted nothing but you since the first night you walked into my shop." She frowned. "I was worried it was you making me feel the way I did. Your vampire mojo, or whatever. And so, even though it was the hardest thing I've ever done in my life, I left you." She met my eyes again. "I didn't plan to come back."

"I know."

She took that in. "Why didn't you tell me?"

I tried to smile, but I couldn't. "Tell you how I would die without your blood?"

"Yes. That. Why didn't you tell me?"

"You said you would come back," I told her. "And I wanted to give you a choice."

"I didn't even make it to Austin," she confessed. "The farther away I got, the more miserable I became. And I know now it wasn't because you were putting the thoughts and feelings inside of me, because you were nowhere around."

"No, I was here. Waiting for you."

"What would you have done if I hadn't come back?"

I tried to smile. "Probably sat there in the hall until I died of thirst or the house fell down around me and I burned to death in the sun."

Her eyebrows lifted. "Wow, you vampires are serious about this whole mating thing."

"Apparently."

Her arms slid around my neck. "I guess it's a good thing I'm not going anywhere."

"No, *Acushla*. Never again. I don't think I could do that again." I flashed my fangs. "You are *mine*."

She shivered in my arms, but her eyes were happy as they looked into mine. "I think I'm falling in love with you, too."

"I don't deserve you," I confessed.

"I know. But you have me." She paused. "And Wiggles, of course."

"You'll need to drink from me, Lizzy."

Her eyes met mine.

I waited, listening to the steady beat of her heart. I didn't want to rush her, but I wanted her with me forever. And only my blood could ensure that would happen, could seal the bond between us.

Bringing my wrist to my mouth, I bit deep. I held it up for her, and waited.

She eyed the blood warily, then leaned in and flicked her tongue over the wound I'd made, tasting me. Her eyes closed and she moaned. When she opened them again, her eyes were hungry, locking in my wrist.

A low hiss escaped me when she pressed her mouth to the bite and sucked. Sharing my immortal blood with my mate was completely different than creating vampires. It was erotic, pleasure shooting through me with every pull on my vein, possessive to a degree I'd never felt before. She drank for a long time, and I didn't stop her, even though my cock grew hard inside of her and my own thirst returned. I would give her whatever she wanted, whatever she needed, whatever she desired.

Lizzy was *mine*.

But I was also hers.

Thank you so much for reading Killian and Lizzy's story! I hope you enjoyed going back into the world of the Deathless Night series. I know I did. <3 And I can't wait for you to read the next book in the series...

Secret of the Vampire

Bad boys were never Kenya's thing, unless they existed within the pages of a book. Until Alex Moss came to her rescue like some sort of avenging angel...

And if you haven't read the original Deathless Night Series, Book 1, **A Vampire Bewitched**, is currently FREE. Happy Reading!

ABOUT THE AUTHOR

L.E. Wilson writes romance starring intense alpha males and the women who are fearless enough to love them just as they are. In her novels you'll find smoking hot scenes, a touch of suspense, some humor, a bit of gore, and multifaceted characters, all working together to combine her lifelong obsession with the paranormal and her love of romance.

Her writing career came about the usual way: on a dare from her loving husband. Little did she know just one casual suggestion would open a box of worms (or words as the case may be) that would forever change her life.

On a Personal Note:

"I love to hear from my readers! Contact me anytime at le@lewilsonauthor.com."